Praise for Subimal Mis

"When I read him for the first time, I saw that his stories rebelled against dominant literary conventions. His stories were anti-stories, a violent mix of fragmentary narratives and essays, even statistics, juxtaposed together to deliver a shocking statement."
—Amitava Kumar

"Misra leaps and alights from branch to bough in a cosmic garden of characters. . . . These two anti-novels are an invitation to engage with discomfort, through purposeful silence, jump cuts and ferocious prose."—Percy Bharucha, *Hindustan Times*

"Misra's stories are not seductive; their power lies in their subversion. They look straight into the dark heart of the middle class and use an array of startling techniques to undercut the pretensions and hypocrisies by which we live."—Jerry Pinto

"The book is a Guernica of sorts in printed letters and words—stark, chaotic, gut-wrenching, and confounding in its immensity of interpretations."—Nabina Das, *Dhaka Tribune*

"Misra's anti-novels are as much a reinvention of the novel, that has been congealed and commodified into a methodised, stationary, inert 'cultural object', as a critique of the bhadrolok, the bourgeoisie, whose totalitarian impulses have alienated and antagonised the rest in Bengal."
—Rohit Chakraborty, *Open Magazine*

"What was Subimal Misra thinking? Why can his stories catch your attention despite them not having a linear plot, a simple thing to tell? Who knows? They're worth reading and, if your imagination works, you could hear his laughter at the very end."—Luis A Gómez, *National Herald India*

THIS COULD HAVE BECOME RAMAYAN CHAMAR'S TALE TWO ANTI-NOVELS

TRANSLATED FROM THE BENGALI
BY V. RAMASWAMY

SUBIMAL MISRA

OPEN LETTER
LITERARY TRANSLATIONS FROM THE UNIVERSITY OF ROCHESTER

First edition, 2020

Library of Congress Cataloging-in-Publication Data: Available.
ISBN-13: 978-1-948830-15-7 / ISBN-10: 1-948830-15-9

This project is supported in part by an award from the New York State Council on the Arts with the support of Governor Andrew M. Cuomo and the New York State Legislature

Printed on acid-free paper in the United States of America.

Cover Design: Anne Jordan and Mitch Goldstein
Interior Design: Anthony Blake

Open Letter is the University of Rochester's nonprofit, literary translation press:
Dewey Hall 1-219, Box 278968, Rochester, NY 14627

www.openletterbooks.org

Contents

THIS COULD HAVE BECOME RAMAYAN CHAMAR'S TALE

TWO ANTI-NOVELS

Introduction

Subimal Misra was born in 1943—the year the monstrous
structural violence of late-colonial Bengal came to its
grisly apex, with the annihilation of more than one million inhabitants in that single year alone. In the district
where Misra was born, whole villages were being wiped
out by starvation, trenches and waterways were heaped
with bodies, and wild animals tore flesh from human
bone—sometimes while the starvation victim was still
hoarsely gasping for breath. Now, we know that memory
begins to index our experiences only at a somewhat later
stage of development, after three or four years of age. But
sensory awakening—accompanied by acute curiosity—
happens almost immediately. Who is to say how these raw
and unfiltered perceptions, even at the very first stage of
sensory awakening, imprint themselves on our later lives?

In 1946—during which time several million more
had been ground to death by famine in Bengal—Kolkata
exploded in cataclysmic violence that sent reverberations
deep into that same countryside, and also set the course
for the vivisection of Bengal. It is likely that Subimal Misra
did index into memory some context of these events,
including the dismemberment of Bengal in 1947, and those
memories were stamped on to his character. Much later

in life, because of his fierce and unrelenting critique of social and political structures—which only ever continue to annihilate the bodies of the poor in Bengal—he adopted a sort of nom de guerre: "Bagher Bachcha" (Child of a Tiger). But how does one identify the tiger that gave birth to Subimal Misra? It could even have been Blake's tiger . . .

In the 1950s, particularly in rural Bengal, dislocation, insolvency, hunger, and hopelessness remained endemic. The promise of a new India did *not* extend to the Bengal countryside. Destitution, a violent social order, and the politics of naked ("democratic") brutality defined the historical landscape. Since at least the famine, flight to Calcutta (a bleak and often unforgiving journey) had remained a desperate and primary survival strategy for many. Throughout the 1950s, continuing Hindu-Muslim violence in East Pakistan led to waves of refugees coming to Calcutta; the city ever buckling, ever accommodating, ever wheeling out of control and teetering on the verge of collapse. And from within West Bengal as well, waves of daily workers, also surviving on the barest margins of existence, were coughed in and out of the city every day—along the very same routes that famine victims had traveled to die on the city's streets a decade earlier. How does a society, no less an individual, digest such a historical present? Misra's literary visions, over several decades of relentless *seeing*, give us some idea.

Subimal Misra himself traveled to Calcutta sometime in the early 1960s, to pursue an MA degree at the university, and to escape the bitterness of property disputes within his family at the time of his father's death. By that time, he was already writing, and assumedly, already exploding with the visions and indignation that have fueled his iconoclastic, uncompromising, and prolific writing career ever since. As a teenager in the mofussil, he had started a village "wall magazine." While nothing is known of these early writings, one has to imagine that something of the incendiary nature of his later work saw its inception as organized graffiti, which is appropriate enough. Throughout Misra's writing career, his work has remained a kind of anarchic protest slashed across the walls of power. In 1969, he published his first critically acclaimed story, "Haran Majhi's Widow's Corpse or the Golden Gandhi Statue," in which the beaten and stinking body of a boatman's widow floats down the Ganga into the city of Calcutta, eventually disrupting a ceremony to inaugurate a golden statue of Gandhi sent from America. It is essentially an allegory, conveying a distinct message that whatever forces may be aligned to annihilate the marginal citizens of Bengal, the trace of their existence will remain, and matters. At the same time, Subimal Misra was also already writing much more experimental, unstructured, and inventive prose, as evident from stories like the apocalyptic-surrealist "Radioactive Waste," written in 1970 and first published in 1972. Around the same time, Misra was offered a job as a lecturer at a small-town college and returned to district-life briefly, before Calcutta lured him back again. He was offered, and took up, a position as a schoolmaster in a school in Ahiritola, near the red-light district of Sonagachi, in north Calcutta. Students at the school were children of the urban poor, including children of sex workers in the neighborhood. Like other teachers at the school, Misra helped students complete their enrolment forms, filling in fathers' names, etc. He also began self-publishing his writing at his own expense, as well as placing select stories in reputable little magazines with small and somewhat rarefied intellectual audiences. Some recognition of his ferocity of style and purity of purpose began to circulate on the margins of the literary world in Calcutta. Meanwhile, his writings continued to push at the boundaries of narrative device, and also the boundaries of middle-class, bourgeois mores, structured toward the maintenance of a pernicious and predatory sociopolitical order that ensures both the destruction and erasure of lives lived at the margins of bare existence. In almost all his writings, the figure of the downtrodden and debased pierces through the framework of a minutely described structural violence, like an insistent open sore that no bandage can hope to cover or heal. It is in that insistent reemergence—in that indestructibility and stubborn resistance to ultimate annihilation—that Subimal Misra's most incisive critique of power can be found.

At the same time that Misra was reaching his full powers as a revolutionary writer, the political landscape of Bengal was going through further paroxysms of violence, fragmentation, economic dislocation, and change. The intransigent poverty of the countryside, coupled with the appropriation of Left political activism by bourgeois elements of society, as well as ideological divisions internationally, led to a split in the united Communist Party of India in 1964. By this time, the Communist Party had very deep roots in Bengal. Famine in the 1940s had resulted in a mass contact campaign (more movement than campaign) that saw committed Communist Party workers penetrate deep into the ravaged countryside. Mass contact during famine was not merely a matter of famine relief or ideological commitment. Instead, communism in Bengal took a deeply cultural turn, and the Communist Party took a dominant role in representing and *processing* the catastrophe that was unfolding. By 1944, there was an outpouring of visual art, drama, music, and literature aimed at making meaning—and cause—out of famine, much of it directly affiliated with the Party. Over the next several years, tens of millions teetered on the verge of annihilation, while millions more died of hunger, exposure, and epidemic disease. By late 1946, the party was entrenched deeply enough in rural Bengal to direct an armed uprising of tenant farmers (the Tebhaga movement) which was met with police and military violence—by both the colonial *and* the postcolonial State.

The mass industrialization of Calcutta in the early 1940s, in the name of war against Japan—and at the expense of the rice economy of Bengal—also made labor action in the late 1940s and early 1950s an effective threat to the established order. After the 1964 split, the Communist Party of India (Marxist), or CPI(M), turned the temperature up, both in industrial Calcutta and in the still-reeling districts of a truncated Bengal. They were again met with mass arrest and state violence. Then, in 1967, a peasant uprising erupted at Naxalbari in northern West Bengal. The CPI(M)'s enmeshment in this new armed struggle deeply radicalized (as well as polarized) the party. Violence spread to urban Bengal. By the early 1970s, student activists were being gunned down by policemen in the lanes of Calcutta, and Maoist action against the state escalated. By 1977, ideological division, Emergency, compromise, state repression, and fragmentation had channeled the still-volatile, but now scattered, political energies into the election of a Left Front coalition government in

West Bengal. Radicalism was the victim, even while abject destitution in the Bengal countryside and peri-urban Calcutta only continued to brutally dehumanize and degrade the lives of tens of millions. The Left Front government engaged in land reform and selective devolution of power, but compromise had broken the back of militant urgency and humane purpose.

During this entire period, Subimal Misra was writing and publishing prolifically: searing social critique, caustic political commentary, and unrelenting exposés of injustice, violence, greed, sexual predation, hedonism, and moral collapse. He experimented with print art, cut-up methods, surrealism, reportage, found poetry, filmic device, thematic rupture—and so much more. Throughout the political storms raging around him, Subimal Misra's *writing* remained his politics, and that remained anarchic, eclectic, and blistering. He would not be part of any party. But the disillusion of radical leftism haunts his work toward the late 1970s, in a distinctive manner that a reader has to assume is personal. It is at this phase of his career, and in this historical context, that the two texts here ("anti-novels," as the author himself calls them) were created. *This Could Have Become Ramayan Chamar's Tale* was begun in 1977, and first published in Bengali in 1982. *When Color Is a Warning Sign* was first published in 1984, the same year Indira Gandhi was assassinated by her Sikh bodyguard. These two texts represent Misra at his most fierce, creative, and intellectually committed.

Ramayan Chamar is a Bihari Dalit, from a caste that historically has been associated with processing animal hides. Ramayan Chamar himself is a tea-plantation worker in north Bengal, starved into political and moral righteousness by a production system akin to slavery. In the text that carries Ramayan Chamar's name, a few broken bits of his story ricochet through the din of hypocrisy, moral failure, state violence, unreconstructed feudalism, governmental corruption, elite indifference, environmental precariousness, sexual violence, and political hooliganism. His voice echoes thinly through the text as a kind of haunting of idealistic promise unrealized: "We mete out the punishment that the law is unable to deliver. We let the ruling class know that they do not have impunity." Ramayan Chamar is killed off early in the text, after organizing against the tea plantation owner and being executed by the police for the same. The story that could have been his, is dead with him. In the narrative void left by Ramayan Chamar's incidental (and insignificant) murder crowd the craven venalities of heartless babus, the jarring explosions of country bombs, reports of vote rigging, bribery, judicial intimidation, governmental malfeasance, and (almost mutely) the despairing voices of the powerless. What Ramayan Chamar's tale might have been is impossible to delineate. The reader is instead left with a sense of grief at his absence, in the bas-relief of which resides the shadow of reverence for political and human potential (denied).

The literary devices deployed in *Ramayan Chamar*, like the "plot" structure, are experimental. Scissors rend paragraphs, transcripts of taped interviews are included, film scripts are blocked out in unidentified dialogue, and the writer steps forward, out of the text, to comment briefly on the cacophony that abounds—as well as the conditions of *societal* censorship that he is wrestling with—before slipping back behind the authorial curtain. There are voices of maidservants, college boys, babus and bibis—the lords and ladies of Bengali society, upper-caste, upper-class elites—folk singers, and ghost voters. One has to assume that some of these fragments are actual quotes that Misra had notated in his daily rounds. He also includes diary entries and poetry, reportage and fantasy. Even Jean-Paul Sartre makes an appearance. Yet, however chaotic the text might appear, the studied skills of an extraordinarily disciplined writer at the height of creative expression result in a coherent impact on the focused reader (who is also brought forward in the text as a participating "character").

In *When Color is a Warning Sign*, Misra widens the lens still further. Narrative is even more attenuated, and the din that silences conscience and any voice of justice is globalized. Ramayan Chamar, as noted in this second text, is still dead. The red of congealing blood turns black, and the rosiness of the Left endeavor follows suit. Axiomatic declarations and a multifocal discourse on the brutality of margins and centers holds the place of liquidated potential. The story of the lovers, Subrata and Manjula, is just one chip of glass in a kaleidoscopic exposition. Even as corruption deepens in the still-starving Bengal, the Pope appears at a "gold-ornamented religious ceremony in famine-afflicted Poland," and the Israeli occupation of Palestine becomes catastrophic with the support of American weaponry. There are excursuses on Hitchcock's films, Matisse's paintings, the artistic conceit of Rodin, and the proliferation of handguns in America. Meanwhile, a half-starved youth approaches the writer in desperation, hoping for some employment. The writer dismisses him from the room and from his mind, justifying his indifference in relation to his own "myriad responsibilities and problems." The moral vacuum is complete, and even the writer himself is guilty of ruthless self-absorption. Greasy chicken gravy dribbles down the jowls of mindless MLAs even as "imminent famine in the country and the crop failure for two successive years" is reported. No doubt there is another Ramayan Chamar somewhere in this second anti-novel, but his voice has been entirely erased. In a narrative panel construction that pairs reportage on the reception of a Godard film in Calcutta, and a discourse on Marxism that we are led to assume represents Misra's own voice, there is an admission of "support [for] the communists in those cases where there is a convergence with our anarchist writing."

In several texts over the years, Subimal Misra has warned off the faint-hearted reader in no uncertain terms. His explosive and iconoclastic writings demand too much from armchair social critics or drawing-room literati. Throughout his writing career, Misra has reinforced this prohibition by a fierce defense of his works against commodification. He has been known to sell his self-published texts at the Calcutta Book Fair with only a "suggested" price, and also to leave blank pages in various works for written responses from dedicated readers. In this way, he has preserved his intellectual integrity as well as his authorial freedom. Both have won him a dedicated and enthusiastic following in intellectually engaged reading circles in Calcutta (and elsewhere). In truth, it might very well be that Subimal Misra has consistently written ahead of his time—as is always true of writers as deeply immersed in the present as he has been. But given the continuing deepening of inhumanity, poverty, authoritarianism, and violence that define our present political moment—in Bengal, in India, and globally—it may very well be the case that the time is ripe for a widening of the audience—locally, nationally, and internationally. The conventions of thought and creative expression that have shaped (and continue to shape) our response to the social and political world we inhabit, have not served us well. Creative expression that explodes the boundaries of failing convention, in this day and age, is a form of liberation in and of itself; and a liberation of the *mind* may at present be the most important political necessity of all.

—*Janam Mukherjee*

The Anti-Novel: A Manifesto

Subimal versus Subimal, continuously, just continuously

He considers his creation to be more powerful than himself, separate from his own existence, confronting him, like another rival. Work is agony for him, he identifies strength with mercilessness and creative work seems to be a fatal yet definitely futile exercise. It's his own work that stands in opposition to him, against him—something over which he has no control.

—Karl Marx's words, in my own way.

It's a harsh and yet an ultimate truth that, however great various efforts have been, the possibility of failure too exists just as much within them. And it's also an ultimate truth that there is no ultimate truth, there cannot be. Everything is only apparent, dialectical. In a society in which only things possess value, man too has become another one among countless things, and apparently he is the one that is, relatively speaking, the most easily procurable and the most despicable. This is the so-called bourgeois humanism which overwhelms all our thinking and which we brag about—and has been strongly criticized in my anti-novels (and stories too) from various viewpoints, in different contexts—but it has only failed terribly. Yet I must say once again, it excludes man himself in the name of humanity, sometimes directly and sometimes indirectly.

This is the ultimate elucidation of the antiestablishment mentality, which is not really backed by any "isms" currently on offer; it also hurls questions at whatever has been recognized so far as great art and literature and at all the other aesthetics surrounding us. Yes, questions are raised in every regard, difficult, harsh, a harshness pervaded by questions, nothing is settled unless place and time are bound, nothing is true, everything is relative—that's the direction truth heads toward. We are dependent beings living in an era when even the most fundamental expression of beauty has come to be true, and if taken properly, this statement too is relative. What is the subject? We see that writing begins to occupy a kind of place where sometimes, by some method, the act of writing itself becomes the real subject, shabda (the Word) is then not merely brahma (the Creator), but brahmanda (Creation) itself, not merely God but the entire Universe. It resides in a kind of unfettered narration. And through that, it becomes the supreme literature of protest. Protest is opposed to any kind of stagnancy, protest is opposed to every kind of inhumanity donning the mask of humanity. Finally, it does not remain a novel, there's no smooth story-form with a beginning and an end, no so-called character construction. It is neither history nor diary, not an essay either, nor research—and yet everything—cuttings, newspapers, campaigns, news, pamphlets, proclamations, a glowing true story—an admixture in collage, montage, and new form—and in the traditional viewpoint, an uncorrected form of writing—extremely fragmented, obviously in an apparent way—which does not reach any conclusion, in the sense in which the term "conclusion" is understood.

Here the reader is not ignored either, the reader too is a comrade in arms with the writer in the creative act, sometimes the writer and reader merge into one. There is no longer any difference between "them" and "me," perhaps it is not even necessary. The distance between place and time is gradually wiped away. Real incidents and imagination do not go hand in hand, rather they are completely intertwined, they cannot be separated. Sexuality is transgressed in a kind of opaque torpor, somewhat like another *Hiroshima Mon Amour*. And so naturally, complexity becomes a feature in its construction, all the commas on the verge of exclusion . . . Hadn't Apollinaire done that long ago, various passages entering into the same sentence, incomplete subjects from before suddenly returning without prior preparation, the insertion, while dwelling on one thing, of a long digression on something else, consciously sometimes, bearing in mind the helplessness of the reader as well? Yes, the reader too has to participate in the creative act. It is definitely not a story, and not really an incident either. Again, where necessary, inwardly, everything, everything is raw material then— the way raw material is, the way it is used. The original grassroots form emerges in the language, raw, which this techno-progress-professing civilized society does not permit at all times, sometimes new word constructions too take place. Thinking is apprehended from its source. Not an explanation of emotion and feeling, rather their union emerges in fragments. In short, in the midst of resorting to the material, seeking questions going beyond the material, searching, keeping oneself and one's act of writing occupied in this search. In this context, the established forms of realism also arise. Even if reality—which for me is a situation of conflict between the past and the future—is not merely a fixed moment of unchanging present, there is an endeavor to try to capture that in my anti-novels, in some places. Just that.

In this way, gradually, everyone from Cervantes to Dostoyevsky is left behind, Joyce-Proust-Borges and Kafka-Camus most definitely, for that matter Beckett of *Malone Dies*, Michel Butor of *La Modification*, Robbe-Grillet of *La Maison de Rendez-vous*, Burroughs of *Naked Lunch* and Kurt Vonnegut Jr. of *Slaughterhouse-Five*. Also discarded are Bengal's writers Manik Bandopadhyay, Satinath Bhaduri, Jagadish Gupta, Dhurjatiprasad Mukhopadhyay, Kamalkumar Majumdar, Syed Waliullah, and Amiyabhushan Majumdar—whom, at least, even if partially, at one time, Subimal used to acknowledge, could acknowledge, used to be content acknowledging. So, who remains then? Other than the arrogant Subimal? Subimal then stands in opposition to Subimal, against all his writings until now. He gradually keeps discarding himself. He himself raises questions regarding his own position. All his work stands in opposition to him, all this is not for himself, for he is not in control of all this.

Addendum

Most of the writers in our country, or for that matter abroad as well, lay emphasis on so-called reality. Some on "normalcy" as well. The basic foundation of popular literature is more or less built upon the stilts of such reality. In the early phase of writing by some of these writers from the traditional stream, a stamp of intellectual maturity could be observed. But subsequently it did not develop further. They portray characters, they write stories of personal relationships, some of them leave out events too, it is the exploration of character that is their prime concern. The same old blah-blah, which had already reached a dead end several decades ago. For some, portraying the background is the real task, with the characters appearing to have been pasted with gum on to that; sometimes it is extremely lengthy—which was the ideal of novelists of the nineteenth century. We have already received *War and Peace*, *Buddenbrooks*, *Pather Panchali*, or *Todai Charitmanas*. What is to be gained by preparing another copy of all these? None of them seemed to realize that the very highest stage of description of events, portrayal of character, or explanation of mind had been crossed long ago in *Anna Karenina* or *The Brothers Karamazov*, or in *The Puppet's Tale* in recent times. Again, in the view of some camps, the perspective on society does the main job, and based on that thinking they construct characters, with talk of "socialist reality" on their lips. Notwithstanding an abundance of pedantic writing, the experts were unable to show this thing called "socialist reality" separately from so-called reality, they could not correctly explain this sorry state. (Perhaps Maxim Gorky, while speaking about "critical realism," was responsible for putting into currency its polar opposite, the term "socialist realism." Even if that includes the socialist world and the writer's commitment to workers, let's say, nonetheless, its use in the practical sphere is, at least until now, not as clear as it should be.) In this regard, in another context, Arnold Hauser's or Lucien Goldmann's Marxist explanations and analyses could not satisfy us adequately either. And there is another band whose tendency is to create psychological novels. They don't care about reality and suchlike, there are some young writers like that too. In their writing, they want to lay emphasis on form, in their view the subject does not change, only the form changes over time. I consider my writing, whatever little there is, a few stories and novels, to be different from all these forebears, and I say this without any arrogance whatsoever. When any stationary or moving thing is presented directly, in many cases its actual visage cannot be captured, but if bits and pieces of myriad incidents, characters, diaries, reportage, comments—if all these, everything in accordance with the time, from different viewpoints, can be projected, are sought to be shown, then it could well be the introduction of a different kind of endeavor. Actually, the real objective is to be able to reach the truth, an immutable route-circumambulation, most difficult, which literature has been trying to do for two-and-a-half thousand years (or is it three thousand?) but has been successful only in very few instances. Obviously, one cannot but admit that all such thinking has arisen as an outcome of decadence, and together with that it is also true that much new thinking—as well as the possibility of the opening up of avenues for ways of expression—is also manifested in this very fashion, it manifests class struggle, and going further, even the possibility of revolution. In this way, our demolitions are able to transcend meaninglessness, they attain a larger dimension. Revolutionary presentation too becomes inevitable for what is revolutionary. Personally speaking, I try my best to come face-to-face with truth, employing all my anti-convention forms, which are dialectical, which present a different point of view, and density, of the audacity of standing in the opposite corner, face-to-face with myself. Yes, face-to-face with myself, in no uncertain terms. When will you ever show the courage to be able to efface yourself, will you be able to do that, Subimal? This long journey—riddled with contradictions—and going beyond it: when? There is no end to man continuously creating himself, there has never been, Subimal. Because— when a medium as powerful as literature begins to speak in a single mold and tune, then what can make one more despondent than that, can there be anything?

Further Addendum

All this talk of mine will appear, or may appear, to some people to be merely advocacy in favor of form-centricity. In our so-called progressive criticism, on the one side are placed all those literary creations which are clearly straightforward, real incidents or established on proximate visualization, and on the other side are placed all those creative works that did not follow the ordinary rules of reality. After qualitative examination, the first, which speak in one's favor, are considered progressive, and the other side is labeled as reactionary, practicing the literary art of decadence. The oversimplification that this formula involves is a big fissure in the stream of Marxist criticism, and its gaping maw only widens. In the literary arts, the evolutionary viewpoint does not always remain in our sight. We forget that the different schools of thought in currency at different times, despite their dialectical limitations, attain the mantle of the historical and artistic truth of the time. Sometimes, those parts of all these "decadent creations" are granted recognition when they are related purely to realism and are located at a comfortable distance from all the acts of anti-realism. Actually, the non-dialectical viewpoint is apparent within the use of realism as a measure of qualitative ascent. However, as an example one can say that the witches drawn by Goya are more real than many of the so-called realist works of art, El Greco's realization is more visible to our eyes than Constable's, Shakespeare's common folk are more alive than the masses portrayed in the postrevolutionary social reality formulae, Don Quixote and his companions are much more real, Tolstoy's characters are also just as alive. Notwithstanding all the clamor regarding social realism, never could those portrayals reach anywhere close to these. Moving away from the so-called traditional arrangement, Mayakovsky demolished poetry mercilessly, but his form was just as potent in bearing the reality of revolution, something that was not seen often in the flowing stream of poetry. Brecht presented another imaginary world, in a different form, which unmasked the bourgeois social system, with an imagination that was much sharper than the dull reality of the popular stream. Mayakovsky or Brecht used all their demolitions and experiments as one of the weapons of class struggle, and if we forget this fact and cry hoarse about their form-consciousness—which is the case with our popular Marxist criticism—then we will simply jumble up everything. Because all these are not the cause of decadence, not at all, rather they are its outcome, a movement through historical progression.

—*Subimal Misra*

THIS
COULD
HAVE
BECOME
RAMAYAN
CHAMAR'S
TALE

The last 2-3 years' newspapers, letters, writing, interview extracts, reportage . . . whatever I thought whenever I thought, all of this, everything, was used, fiercely, with broken type, and me too

"I don't-want don't-want don't-want, dear
this measured out love of yours."

Bedana Dasi (Bengali singer, 1905)

Here's Ramayan Chamar's tale

Much about the character remained unknown to me, and as I continued to read, with all of you, I became enthusiastic, yet I kept waiting. But nothing occurred according to rules, just the bare body and the perspiring face—even the dialogue got continuously jumbled up on the tongue, becoming loose and inert. It's one in the morning now, the rotis have become dry and hard. The lights in the house next door were turned off long ago. The social context, the *frame*, suddenly becomes an adversary, a palimpsest, of him, the Character—and right then, a major part, which at the time of writing was unclear even to me, gradually emerged from the shadows. I was compelled to provide explanations: the promises, the ethic of never denying humanity—but I don't refer merely to the Telangana or Tebhaga movements. Consequently, the wooden planks of the hanging-bridge catch fire, the chemicals for country-bombs illicitly bought from Allahabad at 40 rupees a kilo get sold for 400 rupees a kilo in the Line No. 3 basti, a slum by the rail tracks, in Jorabagan. Perhaps it's because of this that he, Ramayan Chamar, had laughingly revealed to me: "Only if you wet all the seeds with water—do you follow?—only if you wet all the seeds with water . . ."

Dam, check-dam

Until now, man has not been able to make
a firearm

Dam, check-dam

Until now, man has not been able to make
a firearm
that fires bullets only in a single
direction
and avoids
other directions

Back in the village, we never had to buy food, only salt
and kerosene were purchased. I used to visit Calcutta
every now and then. I never knew what deprivation was.
I liked Sarju, who lived next door, she was as pretty as
a fairy, but I didn't get married. The song, "With every
wish, I swing in bliss," had just started becoming popular
then—Kanan Devi's song, Sarju sang it beautifully. The
wages for rolling bidi cigarettes were six annas in those
days, one got by well. Father died in 1950. I had begun
to savor babudom. Frilled sleeves, cross-collared punjabis,
and a fine-hemmed Sengupta dhuti.

Panu Mullick, Pannalal, was a militant laborer of the Howrah Bidi Workers' Union at one time, whom I first came to know even before I started wearing trousers— a soft, red-checked cotton towel slung over his shoulder, puffing a bidi, and walking briskly to the field of clumps across the railroad tracks to do his business, the crisp morning sunlight in every direction, the kind of light in which the Robi Thakurs sat by the window and wrote poetry. Every part of Pannalal was alive, his teeth, mouth, hair, genitals, all of it, and the yellowish brains in his head too. I hadn't asked whether he had heard the name of Ramayan Chamar. Later I saw he had become that, wanted to become that. As I listened to him, I correctly surmised that by pinching handfuls of meat he was warming the meat—making it really warm.

"Which party were you in?"

"There were no leftists at that time, so it was to the Congress party that I paid subscription. There was a meeting once in Goila, in Barisal, I saw Netaji there. I had also seen Gandhiji in a public meeting at Madaripur. I did love Gandhiji. Who doesn't love him? People had given over a lot of gold ornaments to him for the nation's cause. He set up twenty-six cloth mills across the country with that money. Is that true, babu?"

"Had the partition taken place?"

"Yes. Once my refugee card was issued, I got seventy-five rupees for the land and five hundred rupees for the homestead from the government. Later the government gave another five hundred rupees for a small workshop."

"Which party do you like?"

"Why—the communists. There's no party other than them that thinks about us. I had been with the bidi workers' movement. Surya, Nani, and I—we used to collect donations. Harihar babu was the president. After him, it was Bishwanath babu. And after him, all of us together made Bimal babu president. I was the main organizer. Now Bimal babu is a minister—and I'm a pauper. Do you see?"

"Do you know that the National Security Act has been passed?"

"To hell with national security—the black law has been passed."

"Do you receive pension?"

"Pension? Earlier I used to get twenty-five rupees, now I get thirty rupees. Can you get two hundred grams of flattened rice a day for that amount? Where am I to get the money from?"

"But you can go to the party office now, can't you?"

"Nobody gives a damn if we go now, babu. It's Haran Sadhukhan and company who are there now. As soon as they begin to smell of political stature, all of them become veritable Hanumans—do you get that, Hanumans, all of them, ardent devotees, monkey-gods worshipping the holy Lord Rama . . ."

Muscling his way in, Ramayan Chamar nods his head animatedly: "Whatever else I might be, at least I'm not Panu Mullick. Descendants of slaves, they are all slaves— each and every one of them. Sure, there's no mark on their throats, but the vote-casting mark on the thumb remains. The mark of impermanent ink."

Moonlight gleams on the railroad tracks. On the railway overbridge in Tikiapara, two groups of hoodlums fight for control over the locality, people from one platform cannot cross over to the other platform. The battle steadily spreads beyond the rail yard toward the Line No. 3 basti. Guns and bombs, from nine at night to seven in the morning. Our dream: a united and prosperous India.

BEWARE OF DANGER

An importunate request to the people at large, that without, first of all, solving the riddle elaborated below, no one can read the novel. Otherwise, there exists the calamitous possibility of inviting divine retribution. A progressive youth, a resident of Berhampore in Murshidabad district, flagrantly disregarded the riddle and began reading the tale studiously. Consequently, in the evening, when he was going home on his bicycle after attending an important party meeting, two country-bombs landed on his head and right there he attained dissolution into the five elements. About the bombs that were directed to finish him off, all that the police could say was that there was no evidence in their possession about who had thrown them. An independent gentleman, a clerk from the Kasba locality who always avoided every kind of party politics, who was forever reciting shlokas as if he were showing off his claws and fangs, exhibited laughing disregard for the said riddle and ran his eyes over the story. That afternoon, for not being able to give the donation demanded for the puja ritual, he was thrashed under the papaya tree he himself had planted. He was admitted to the hospital half-dead. Evidently he had received this punishment for going against God—why else was no one arrested for the incident? Considering the gravity of the situation, there is only one instruction to the fraternity of readers: Beware of danger!

THE RIDDLE

A monkey goes and attaches himself to the very end of a suspended rope. The rope hangs from a frictionless, stand-alone pulley. At the other end of the rope swings a bunch of full-sized martaman bananas. The monkey now begins to climb the rope. Can you say when there will be no distance between the bunch of bananas and the monkey?

The scavengers poke the oven   ash blows out on to them

The flames and the thick smoke

The smell of burning corpses in the air

Go about enraging

9:00 in the morning

The idea of Ramayan was coming into my head, bit by bit, then. As it happened, at the Rashbihari crossing, I ran into the editor[1] of a weekly that had a print run of about

---

1 The weekly had a salaried editor. His name was not printed,

fifteen thousand. He wore a yellow punjabi.[2] He asked: "What happened . . . Where's the story?" A nice means to shut you up isn't it? His wife stood to his right, craning her neck, staring—a lot of dirt around the cuffs of my pajamas. Two girls, chatting, passed by. They were headed for Dhakuria Lake: "Do you know how many editions there have been of *Chowringhee*?" The high heels of one of them slipped upon stepping on cow-dung, the other held her and arrested her fall: "What the hell! Look where you're going!"[3]

---

but it was he who looked after the weekly. He had the freedom to publish short stories, poems, and memoirs. But he was strictly forbidden from publishing anything untoward and the permission of the official editor had to always be obtained. Any deviation would mean losing the job at once. The poor boy had to censor even his own writing before publication. People said that once he almost lost his job after publishing a different kind of story. The story had a nurse as a character—who, outside her profession, went about doing nefarious deeds. The editor was seething with rage. "Hey, why do you publish such stories, putting nurses in such bad light— what if nurses stop reading our paper? You are not to publish any stories that attack anyone's profession. Do you understand? Our business will suffer. Never forget—our paper is not a place for all these experiments of yours. Only articles that everyone can read and understand must be solicited and obtained, which will increase sales when published. In order to sell, you can definitely stuff in a bit of sex—the writing will appear modernist—but never politics. Of course, I don't consider the politics of non-violence to be politics. That's acceptable." After saying that, the proprietor-editor began reciting the Name, using a string of prayer beads. This habit was a hereditary one.

2 The yellow punjabi was a favorite of his, he loved to wear it. What's it that yellow signifies—I won't lie, this fat editor had made many mediocre writers famous, it was because they were ungrateful that . . .

3 That day was the day of the West Bengal assembly elections in 1977, the day the Left Front got a huge number of votes. Rabin Ghosh, Ajoy Dey, and Kalyan Bandyopadhyay were witness to the

The writer . . . punjabi-pajama bought at a discount sale
. . . a special price for Gandhiji's birthday, it had cost Rs
38.75, I remember, after the thirty percent rebate. A pair
of secondhand binoculars in hand, he had gotten from
somewhere . . . a shoe-polish box hanging around his neck
. . . he stands on the left, the left of everyone.

In order to survive in the capitalist system, artists, and
litterateurs have to be amicable sometimes and sometimes
they need to wrestle . . . he stands on the left, the left of
everyone . . . I do not want my writing to be converted
into capital, or be capable of being digested by the intestines of middle-class babus. I want to make my writing
into a weapon against this repression-based civilization.

Just as the speech is coming to an end, Phantom comes
rushing out of the pages of Indrajal comics, his fists ready
for action, he pushes and fells his foe. The police too find

---

entire incident. On that day, they were chatting and drinking tea in
Amritayan restaurant at nine in the morning. Rabi-da had served
them tea. The editor, with his wife, had finished voting early, and
had just arrived and sat down here, the voting ink visible on his
fingernail, impermanent, he couldn't wipe it off. He said he had
a terrible headache, and it was this writer who brought him an
aspirin, walking quite some way to do so. He had missed his tea.
Whatever it may be, after all he was a senior writer . . . Class
enemies are our enemies, we don't have any personal enemies . . . if
they haven't forgotten, let it be . . . But thereafter, it was probably
a year later, reminding him about having asked for the article that
day—who was it whose story the editor had asked for and then
not published?—Rabin had broken into loud laughter, in this very
restaurant . . . Rabi-da had become worried, our dear old Rabi-da,
the eternal waiter of Amritayan. Yes, our adda site was still intact
then, the metro rail had not yet demolished our tea-shop.

a bucket full of bomb-making chemicals. Just then, mingling among the people, he begins to polish shoes; every now and then, he looks through binoculars to see whether the heels are cracked or not, and how much. The bomb-making business reaches right up to the village.

A penknife in hand, the man comes face-to-face with a band of half-wild, half-urban animals.[4]

He will be awakened again after eleven, twenty-two, or thirty-three years.

12:45 in the afternoon

That day, at around a quarter to one in the afternoon, a truck carrying scrap iron overturned and fell off the Howrah bridge, killing six laborers. Four people kicked the bucket at the accident site itself, and two were admitted to the hospital. At that time, on that day, the democratic voting-festival in West Bengal was underway with gusto. The leftists were getting six out of ten votes. Telephoning Lalbazar to ascertain the names and particulars of the men who were crushed to death, the busy police officer had reacted testily:

"It is not my duty to find out about all these coolies and laborers, I have other very important work to do—don't you know, today is election day—phone the hospital!" The

---

4 The line is written remembering poet Sukamal Roychoudhary, who had committed suicide in harakiri fashion, with a bread knife . . . A year or so after his death, a little magazine brought out a special issue on him. Although invited to contribute to the issue, I couldn't write anything . . . the time was spent just thinking about what I could write . . . it was too late . . . perhaps that's why the line, this line . . .

sweet aroma of his 555 cigarette wafted even through the phone, a very pleasant aroma.

One of the distinctive features of capitalist art and literature is to push contemporaneity as far away as possible, and to make it seem as if all that is written is permanent—an eternal truth for all time that they alone have discovered, suitable for all classes of people.[5]

5:40 in the evening

Walking along, he reached the Ganga riverbank that evening. Many boats were crowded together at the riverbank. The scene suddenly appeared in his sight. A small coal-stove on the floorboards of a boat. Rice boiling-bubbling in a clay pot. The lid on the pot rattling. He saw it from afar. The aroma of cooking reached his nose—rice being cooked. Sitting on the prow, the boatman, clad in a checked lungi, puffed on a hookah. Another person sat

---

5 Someone had reminded me, "Hadn't you written a story about our urinal on Rashbihari Avenue . . . in which an unemployed youth cleverly sets up a private urinal, and charges people to allow them to piss and so he makes a lot of money, and then, even after spotting his girlfriend going in there, he does not put away his money-box and step outside, the perverted mentality of it . . ." ("No, the story was not like that at all, brother.") The venue being in Rashbihari, at the crossing, beside the road, where the Tollygunge-bound trams come and stop now, there really was a urinal then, the only public urinal of this locality. Dirty, malodorous, it was even more unsanitary than a dry latrine. I don't remember exactly when it was demolished, it was probably around 1973 or '74. Laughing, Ajoy says, "Your Gandhi statue on Park Street and your urinal at Rashbihari are both gone now—what do you say to that?"

near the awning, her ghomta drawn over her head. A deep-red sari. A pair of artistic earrings gleaming. Glass bangles on her wrist. The glow of the red Alta on her feet. Putting down the hookah, the boatman advanced with small steps: "Wife, won't you get up?" In answer to the soft-voiced query, her haughty reply was heard: "I won't."

He didn't stand there for long. On the way back, the strap of his slipper tore. Someone had stepped on it from behind.

7:10 in the evening

That same evening, he went to a relative's house, meaning, to the house of a distantly-related uncle in the Shyambazar locality, Mohun Bagan Row. The uncle had recently retired from a bank and his blood pressure had suddenly shot up. Although he had long planned to visit this uncle, he hadn't gotten around to doing so. He bought a packet of lozenges from the street corner for the children, and as he went to give it to the five-year-old girl of the house, he heard: "But I don't eat anything other than Cadburys." On the television in the house right then, a terrific action scene from a Hindi film. Everyone was watching, rapt.

12:15 at night

[DIARY EXTRACT]

The servant wears plastic slippers. He discerns that the sound of this footwear is different from that of leather shoes, quite different.

I say, does the soul ever have something like difficulty breathing? That guy, Bergman, how superbly, in his film *Winter Light,* he utters—"God's silence." That was in the year 1961. The communist party had not yet split then.

To the side of the path in front of Nanibala's house, a reddish cow is tethered. Every now and then, she shakes her horns, chews grass, licks the calf, and sometimes she wants to raise her head and gaze at the road with woeful eyes. Our dream, a united and prosperous India.

This was all he had been able to write that day, the day of the elections. A day's writing.

Gorment folk

Full of shame and hatred, Parulbala did not even turn to look in the direction of the accused's cell. In reply to the judge's repeated questioning, she somehow managed to say that, yes, four people had raped her, but none of those accused. The sessions judge was stunned to hear this. He looked once in the direction of thirteen-year-old Parulbala, then in the direction of the public prosecutor, and finally in the direction of the witnesses. Parulbala's mother was among the witnesses, as were her father and brothers. All of them had testified that the accused were without blame, as if they only wished for their release.

The case had been filed three years ago, the charge was of rape. The incident had taken place in a jute field in Barasat. The rapists numbered four. Four of them, one after another . . . all night long. Parulbala stood in the witness stand, her face hostile. She somehow dealt with the judge's questions, saying yes and no. Tears flowed from her eyes.

The judge said to the public prosecutor: "Can you tell me what's going on?" The lawyer informed him in whispers: "These rogues are all seasoned criminals. The victim and her family have been threatened with death if they speak the truth. They have sealed their lips in fear." Hearing the reply, the judge scratched his balding pate helplessly: "What's the value of the court if a sense of security can't be instilled among ordinary citizens? The court can understand who the real offenders are, they can also be seen in front of our eyes, but they can't be punished! The role of the law is becoming akin to that of a mute spectator. This can't be tolerated!"

He exclaimed out aloud:

"Although we are a free nation, the hand of law is terribly weak.

He can see the offenders,

and yet he cannot apprehend them.

It only creates more fear and anxiety in the minds of the witnesses.

It's my misfortune that

although I know

that the heinous crime of destroying this young girl's chastity has been committed

the accused have to be let go . . .

Shall I bite off my thumb in rage?"

In his summing up, he unequivocally pointed to the

failure of the government and the framers of the law for being unable to provide any assistance. The powers that be in this sovereign republic had to think immediately about how justice could be obtained so that citizens could feel secure. Or else, a day would come, and it would come soon—the structure had already begun to teeter—when throughout the country, such rogues, sheltered by the political head-honchos, the dadas, *redacted*

Abdul Momin stepped down from the high court building. Obstinate as a pig. He constantly clenched and unclenched his hands. He owned three bighas and seven kathas of land in all. Five years ago, the nephew of an influential leader forcibly registered himself as a sharecropper on Momin's land. In an age when supporting evidence and witnesses could be had simply by feeding them a bellyful of meat and rice, obviously, it did not take very long to become a sharecropper on the property of the owner of three bighas and seven kathas of land. Momin said: "The whole fucking world is fraudulent. The police station does nothing. Just the opposite actually, it was the police who had filed the complaint of disturbing the peace. The matter went to court but there was no evidence as such. The magistrate understood and castigated the officer-in-charge for filing a false case. But nothing came of that either. I knew nothing would happen, the judges and magistrates belong to the same class as these shoe-wearing bhadralok. I had already mortgaged the plow and bullocks, so now I mortgaged my homestead and went to the high court. It was the first time in my life that I saw the high court. The national flag flutters on top of the tall steeple. We got a decree here too, but the fucking local police act as if they've seen nothing even after reading the court order, as if they've heard nothing even after hearing everything. They've been kept well-fed and happy. Got money too. Someone gave me the idea, so I wrote a letter to the leader of the ruling party, Namboodripad. He forwarded my appeal to the chief minister of West Bengal. The chief minister sent it to the secretary. The secretary sent it to the village council. The head of the village council wrote, his pen rustling over the sheet of paper: 'I am the elected head of the village council, a resident of Habibpur, under Gogacha police station. With my own eyes, I have seen Abdul Momin and his brothers install a shallow tube-well and farm the land with their own hands. Some local influential persons, with the help of criminals, wish to force him off his land. Sadly, I belong to the party behind the matter.' Folding this certificate carefully and thrusting it in my hand, he said: 'Mominbhai, I know everything, I understand everything—but what can I do?—it's very clear who the opponents are, antisocials—you have to save your one's life first, don't you?—I have a wife and a family.'"

"I lived near the Dum Dum airport. I've never seen my father in my life, Mother's simply Mother—what other name can a mother have. Yes, I had a brother, he was tiny, didn't get much to eat, fought with dogs for food from the garbage pile. One day, he was bitten on his face, his nose and face swelled up bad and he died after three days. My name's Malati. I've heard my father's name was Shambhu Mondal." Malati was first put into Barrackpore Sub Jail on April 19, 1974. Last April, she completed six years of life in jail. The registration No. is 7541 of 1974.

Malati does not know

why

for the last six years

she lies

in prison

without trial.

Here's the summary of the case as recorded in the court of the sub-divisional judicial magistrate of Barrackpore: On April 2, 1974, between 9:20 and 9:45 in the morning, the accused was seen eating from discarded packets lying on the floor of the lounge in Dum Dum airport, and consequently, she, Malati, was tarnishing the image of the Republic of India. Hence Dum Dum police charged her under Section 290 of the Indian Penal Code and brought her to court for disposal of justice. Her mother worked in babu-homes in the city. She left in the morning and returned late at night. She then made a few rotis and gave these to me and my brother to eat, with salt and chilies. On some days, she brought back rice and vegetables packed in a plate. We used to eat that.

The whole day I roamed the airport, searching for food. The police caught me one day. I had effaced the image of the great Indian nation. They took me to the police station. And then one day to the court. Eventually to jail. It's there in the court papers. On September 24, 1974, in the court of the Barrackpore SDJM, after hearing everything, the order was passed that Malati be presented in court again when instructed. Thereafter, for five years no one remembered Malati. She had entered jail at the age of twelve. In the language of the court, she was an accused under trial. For five years, the honorable court completely erased any memory of her.

Malati also gradually forgot everything. Whether in police lockup or in jail—at least one got something to eat there. She once said her mother's childhood home was in Gomdipara, near Dum Dum. The police did not think it necessary to try to locate it. Malati said: "Mother, father or brother—I have nobody now. During the last six years, no one ever came to visit me, no one at all." In the last year, she had to go to the Barrackpore court thirty times. The jail superintendent said: "I came across the name out of the blue one day as I scanned through the register. Malati had not been brought to trial. She was rotting in jail without trial for five years. I immediately wrote a letter to the court. On receiving my letter, the judge himself wrote a letter to the state government. The judge's note remained stuck inside some file in the Writers' Building. Everybody forgot about Malati once again. I wrote once again to the judge. He wrote another letter to the government. 'May the honorable government be so kind as to arrange for the proper rehabilitation of this girl, in a proper environment.'

That order has so far crossed only three tables in Writers' Building."

Malati wanted to learn some skill, tailoring or any kind of work, so that she could fend for herself. "Can't the gorment help me a little?" Yes, she knows the name of the prime minister of India. She had also heard that this was a great woman. Casting her eyes down on her toes, biting the nails of her left hand, she said: "I really want to have a family, a handsome husband . . . I want to eat well twice a day—rice with sweet tamarind chutney."

Today, after such a long time, she does not remember that six years ago she had gone to forage for food thrown away by babus in the airport lounge, an offence for which she lost six years of her childhood in jail. In a jail in independent India. Without trial.

Unseen, Ramayan Chamar

We mete out the punishment that the law is unable to deliver. We let the ruling class know that they do not have impunity.

In the course of writing, the newspapers begin to fill up with reports about the Deoli carnage, and the Malatis, in routine fashion, following custom, keep becoming mere stories. The incidents keep coming, one after another— Deoli, Belcha, Pimpri, Medak . . . Two high-caste thakurs shot and took out *only* twenty-four Dalits, all at the same time and all from one family. Only twenty-four people, including women and children. A few years earlier, in Tamil Nadu, in exactly the same fashion, *only* forty-two persons had been burnt to death, they were Dalits too. Do you remember Medak in Andhra Pradesh? Our one and only woman prime minister had been elected to parliament from there. The newspapers reported that a young woman from the Dalit community had been made to parade naked in a village there. It took a lot to get this news in the papers—the journalists wrote about all that. In their view: The government was busy trying to deny the incident in the most unbelievable way. Oppression of Dalits on the pretext of being associated with the Naxalite movement was not something new in this country. Mulish bureaucrats smile blissfully and twirl their moustaches. The government is apathetic. It is necessary to reflect upon whether it would be appropriate, or safe, to attach the word "purposefully" here. My light goes off. Everyone knew He would come again, yes, that's right, may the realization of His deliverance be speedy. Oh, compassionate Guruji, what's the method for the twenty one thousand six hundred recitations of the Name?

The watchman has lit the lantern

Affluence has a special odor. He discerns the smell. Different from the smell of deprivation and poverty. A special fishy odor. His arrival in the city for the first time from the village.

The city sprawls in front of him. Streets. One street wending its way to another street. That street, in turn, leading to yet another. Each one with a different name, and of a different length.

A wall of wild wind keeps growing higher in front of his eyes. The wild wind rubs itself against the inside of his head.

The city spreads north, south, east, and west. There is a circular urinal in the center of the city. It is as if the city has grown around it. Amid the stench of ammonia that burns the eyes, he discovers that pimp and gentleman, professor and idiot, babu and beggar, are all one here

We, the poor people, offspring of the disfavored queen's womb—the cuntry's become independent while we're left to forage cow-dung . . .

He keeps the line ready to be uttered by Ramayan Chamar, and then he sees that, by doing this, his last refuge, the base of the tree, has already been appropriated.

Muralidhar Singh fled home when the bomb attacks began. He was a worker in the Alexander Jute Mill and a member of the CITU-affiliated union. "I'm holed up somehow with wife and children in the mill's warehouse. I'm even unable to go to the union office in the No. 3 Line for fear of bombs. Knives will be pulled out the moment I'm seen. Each day, the situation becomes more dire with the politics of taking over a locality. Mister—right in front of my eyes, the country has become a den for satta games, gambling, illicit liquor, whores, and thuggish mastaans."

He adds: "I see the police walking arm-in-arm with the very people who are accused."

The leader's manner of speaking was like something from a cartoon film

He climbs onto the dais and keeps delivering his speech

The dead people keep getting heavier

The watchman has lit the lantern

A hut of thatch over earthen walls that's our home
sleeping, sitting, cooking and eating, goats, chickens, and ducks,
all beneath this single shade
when native sahibs come rest in the dak bungalow
on hunting trips
we get to eat their leftovers and bones.

our life goes on through joys and sorrows
like a bullock cart
every now and then the babus come with women
to have fun
as they get drunk on liquor
they shed their clothes
they cavort naked
in front of us
right in front of our little children
the intoxicated bibi straddles the naked babu
they don't even think we're human
hey—are servants and watchmen human?
just slip a ten-rupee note
and everyone bows their heads and *salaams*
Phuli, frightened, takes the children
and runs away
seeing the sexual frolicking of the big sahib
the one-and-a-half year old kid sucks noisily
at the teat
and gapes, wide-eyed, in alarm
the wife scurries around in concealment
she doesn't even want to come to grind masala actually, as they're lowly folk
they've still retained a bit of shame and decency
the watchman has lit the lantern
while the meat cooks he kneads flour into dough
his two muscular arms move up and down
all ten fingers seize the watery flour, and that babu-white flour paste
slips so easily through the crevices between his fingers . . .

A market for sex-love-perversion has been created in the country, and it's happening very rapidly, posters come up of Smita Patil in the film *Chakra*, the scene of her bathing at a street-side tap . . . Whenever the subject of sex arises, to say it's bad—all these broad-stroke, gross criticisms—given that which takes place flagrantly all day, the mentality of avoiding all that and escaping it is idiotic, but if a perspective of social conflict does not emerge from all this—if that is not elaborated upon—it's nothing but a ploy to make money off the business of cheerful matters. When sexual titillation is the only objective—a rape scene: if it remains just a rape scene, if it's not saturated with the economic backwardness and the conflict-ridden process behind the rape—if upon reading it, hatred toward the social system does not arise in the readers' minds, if it does not make one aware of the terrifying nature of the capitalist scheme of things—the fundamental thing is the point of view, from which angle it's being shown . . . just as the writer who denies reality is dead, similarly, the writer who merely writes about reality is also just as dead, and for the same reason I say, for the river-crossing scene, couldn't it have been done without using all this colored cellophane—it seems terribly childish.

Those who used to go around waving red flags and enraging the bulls in the arena have moved the bull away in another direction.

Predawn breeze at the river, then.

How unbearable it is to watch a Satyajit Ray film nowadays. Whereas there was a time when one thought they were so rich. I hang my head back, then I sit with my chin resting on the seat in front. I turn to the right, I scratch my wrist, I inhale, I exhale, deeply—the two hours just don't seem to pass. In color: a camel, with Soumitra Chatterjee and Jatayu on its back, keeps walking across the gray desert.

It's you who ought to shoot first
It won't do to wait for the other
side to act

The seed of socialism
within the bounds of the Constitution

The net-buoy moves a little bit, but neither rui nor katla take the bait. These are the antics of the mrigal carp. Mrigal are like that, shrewd as hell. They circle around the bait, peck at it sometimes, and sometimes swim by with a light slap of the tail, but they never swallow the bait.

Visible on the left, a few feet away from the buoy, a kingfisher dives into the water with a splash. It picks up a small fish and flies away again.

And just beneath that incident, news stories suddenly begin appearing. A group of students from Delhi's St. Stephen's College took off their clothes and began singing and dancing, fully naked, in front of the dorm of the well-known women's college, Miranda House. The female students did not feel ashamed or embarrassed at all by this, rather they enjoyed it, began singing along and, drumming the window panes in rhythm, they kept egging on the dancers; a progressive group of female students did not want to be outdone by male students under any circumstances. Amid loud applause, they too removed their clothes and undergarments and joined the dance party. The singing and dancing reached a crescendo. Things descended to the extent of   *redacted*

Following the report that was submitted after making enquiries at police stations in north Bengal, Ramayan Chamar's family chronicle, history, curriculum vitae, and so on are known by now and so we—all of us—already know it.

Maidservant

. . . . .How much money the babus have— bundles and bundles of notes . . . .

Saheb Ali Mondal

"My daughter is eight years old. She goes to the train tracks every day to forage for coal. Tell me, what can I do? I'm poor, we can't survive unless we do these things. Even after taking care of a family of six, there are two more mouths to feed. Around evening on Saturday, she was returning home, walking along the tracks. Suddenly a few people sprang up from the shadows of a clump of bushes and caught hold of her. They dragged her to the thicket nearby. At eight at night, searching for her near the thicket—I saw my daughter lying on the ground near the illicit liquor den. Without any clothes. No sound coming from her."

God of life

On the day of the fire ceremony, Yama, the Lord of Death, descended to earth and wrote the fresh-faced youth's destiny on his forehead. Whatever he wrote became sacred precept, no one could avoid or undo that script. On the highborn boy's forehead, he wrote: House and car, you'll be a doctor-engineer if you wish, a seat shall be reserved for you in a reputed English-medium school, you will always benefit from your mother's family—judge, barrister, minister, MLA, you don't have to worry about anyone. On the forehead of the lowborn boy, he wrote: You'll starve to death, won't have land or property, won't have work, lacking any "source," you won't be able to enter anywhere unless you pay the requisite fee, under the table—

On my forehead, he decreed I would be a fool—

All this—everything—is the fruit of past lives. No one can efface that. Brahminicide in the earlier life finally returned as feticide. You'll be a mlechha, a barbarian, in this life. You'll join the band of heretics. You'll eat cow. Finally, you will have to become a communist. You won't even have money to buy two kochuris in the evening. There'll come a time when even smoking a Charminar cigarette will seem a luxury, you'll puff bidis.

Officer-in-charge

"We know there are illicit liquor and prostitution rackets here. But tell me, what can we do? Every time we carry out a raid, we are unable to catch anyone. Besides, this is a *troubled area*. We have many issues to deal with here. The force is not available at all times, so we cannot send for them as soon as we get a tip."

Ramayan's village-woman

A sattu-wallah sits under the shirish tree, sattu basket and shiny washed brass plates arranged in a little bit of cleaned-up space. A group of rickshaw-wallahs crowds around him. Cars now move along all four sides of the large, open space of the Maidan

Arithmetic and development

"We serve the entire land. We always abide by God's commandments. If we are told that a green-colored revolution is happening in the country, we prepare our reports accordingly. We quickly prepare graphs and charts. Even if the production of rice does not increase in the fields, it rises in our graphs. Even if the crop dies and rots in drought and rain, we can show record-making production. Only hoarders say we can't see anything. If you wish, we can prove just now that prices in our country are falling dramatically. Tell me the per capita income you want and I'll send you the report within three days. The entire progress of the nation, every kind of progress—gushes forth from our pens."

Aloka

"I couldn't get a job even after a lot of effort. Finally, I was called for an interview in an advertising company. Sitting in a swivel chair on the other side of a massive desk, the boss said: 'The work is not the main thing, it's the personality that's the real thing.' After saying a few things more, he leaned forward a bit and inquired: 'Your figure is splendid—would you like to be a model?' Being of simple mind, I said: 'Why not?' Then he said, 'In that case, open your blouse—I need to get a proper view of your bust line.'"

Felling the foe by smashing his balls, meaning, castration of the bull

In the cluster of four villages, it was only in the Choud-hury household that there was a gun. An ancient musket. After paying the annual fee and renewing the license at the district headquarters, the gun was taken to the shrine of Vishalakshmi and a puja ritual was performed, with vermilion and bel leaves applied with devotion. In times of difficulty, the Choudhurys lent money to needy folk against their possessions. They took ceremonial utensils, silver necklaces, and brass pitchers as collateral. When people had nothing to give in lien, the Choudhurys began taking their land. Money was lent at an interest of ten paise per rupee every day. If the interest was not paid, they took away the cow. Debtors had to work gratis in their fields in exchange. The debtor's wife, even if she was pregnant, came and boiled and dried the paddy in their courtyard, she also pounded and husked it. Wiped the floors. Come night, the husband watched over the house until dawn, with the help of a kerosene lamp. And also a five-battery searchlight. Robbers were rife in the countryside.

Is it dawn yet, boy
Yes, stay awake
Exert your body, do the work, mister, plant for harvest, the day shall come
                    Yes, yes, the day shall come

So the day shall come
Joint exultation and dancing
Yes, yes, the day shall come
So the day shall come
Operation Barga's started
The land now belongs to the one who ploughs
A gorment of the poor
[Of course, he does not know what exactly "gorment"
means]
The day shall come
Yes, yes, yes
So the day shall come
But brother
Don't try to take the law into your own hands

Year after year the budget session in the assembly takes
place
prices of things rise
the salaries of babus in jobs rise
and as for their kind of people
for three-fourths of the cuntry's people
only their cries of distress rise

Chorus

Whatever you do brother   just see

that you don't try to take the law into your own hands

Ramayan Chamar

But our democracy is like a brassiere's elastic—
One can expand or contract it at will.

Diary

It's raining at the pond   the first rain of this monsoon
water accumulates on the pathways
water accumulates over water   water
Now he discerns the difference between fresh and old water

Mediyabari police post, where Ramayan will be kept in custody

Encircled by the shadows of sal trees, there are no living quarters in this police post. Bungalow-type structures
on all sides, with elevated verandas. Tin roofs. A table is
laid in the veranda, a sub-inspector, who is the officer-in-
charge, sits there. The lockup is at the back. Metal cots
on one side—for the constables. The OC's family doesn't
live here, their quarters are in the police station in the
district headquarters. He's here on patrol duty. Lunch is
over by afternoon. The OC, Makhan babu, sits on the
table in the veranda, smoking a cigarette, signing important files. Mishra-ji, a sergeant, stands beside him. There
is some kind of salacious talk about the breasts and buttocks of the Adivasi girl walking by on the road. He twirls
his moustache and laughs aloud. In the lockup room, an
imprisoned cow-thief and a Naxalite youth. Birju, the
sweeper, lies on a string cot, knees drawn, his legs shaking.

Diary

It was two at night on College Street—he runs fast along
Mahatma Gandhi Road, sprinting further ahead, he turns
at full speed and enters the lane at Mechua market. Crossing the narrow strip of Bidhan Sarani, he staggers past

the boundary walls of the university. A police picket had come up near the circular tank after the head of the statue of Vidyasagar had been knocked off for a second time. What are you doing here—so late at night? What do you think you're doing? . . . The road curves toward Harkata Lane. Opposite the Medical College, just across the road, a bakul tree. Astonishingly, he's been in this neighborhood for twenty-five years, and yet, never observed this in daylight. Daylight, they say—but is it that? He is thrilled at this midnight discovery on the way to Harkata Lane. He bends down and picks up some flowers strewn on the road. A half-moon hangs over Bowbazar . . . the continuing darkness that Bhikhu and Panchi collected from their mother's womb, hid inside the body, arrived on earth with . . . does anyone collect and bring these things from the mother's womb, Manik babu, or is it incorrect . . . somewhere . . .

Tape

"But the Naxalites spew venom at your writing . . ."

"Yes, a lot of CPI(M)-folk too."

"Don't you get it? You're completely isolated."

"I don't think so . . ."

"You write for the people, but the people don't understand it . . ."

"It's not exactly that . . . they're not allowed to understand . . . they're frightened away by it being called difficult at the very outset . . . this is a planned process . . . the reader is not allowed to think . . . if one thinks too much, if they fathom the relation between exploiter and exploited—as in their own situation—then . . ."

"Whatever you may say, you're a failure . . ."
"No, I don't believe that's true . . ."

Diary

The woman has a Sicilian kind of nose. A lot of diamond jewelry hangs around her neck, like it hangs around the virgins' necks when jatra theater companies enact historical dramas. Blue eyes, a lot of makeup around them. It's difficult to say what she really looks like under all the embellishment.

Neighbor

"When will I read your story? There's a huge problem hanging over my head now. It's our ground-floor tenant. He's in the party, he has contacts in the Writers' Building. I've been trying to get him evicted for the last ten years or so. Do you know, even now the rent for the three rooms is just eighty-five rupees? Just think about the situation . . . The matter has gone to court. The water supply was stopped, later they found a way around that by themselves. I've tried talking to a lawyer time and again, but there's nothing to be done. He's told me, get the dadas of the neighborhood on your side first. And then set goondas on him. Nothing will happen through legal means. You're writing stories about lowly chamars and so on, why don't you write about me, it's such an important and real problem . . ."

Kuldip Nayar

"Each member of parliament has to spend five to eight

hundred thousand rupees on the elections, there's no hope of winning with less than that. A major part of the money is mobilized by industrialists and businessmen. Later, by utilizing their candidates, they recover the money, together with interest. Every big industrialist has five to ten obedient Members of Parliament. There's no need to talk about Members of the Legistlative Asemblies."

Diary

Pay attention to Ramayan's statement: "But our democracy is like the elastic on a woman's brassiere, one can expand or contract it at will." The debate can begin from here, what's generally called a political debate. It does not end with imputing a measured name, after going here and there you finally have to return to the same place: the relativity of liberation. And is this why Ritwik Ghatak said before he died: "I am confused . . ." Or did I say something wrong? Rather, one could also say that just the seeing, only that, was not confined like this, here. I feel like looking at Pablo Neruda's *Memories* once again now. Specifically, the part about Stalin. And not wanting to go around itself means choosing something or the other, meaning, in simple terms, a pit. Which is actually about fixing the level. Barricades are laid across lane after lane.

Police report

A youth was injured in a bomb explosion in Line No. 3. The local people think the youth was an extremist—that he was careless while making the bomb. He lay in the field all night long. He was still alive. He divulged something, and so, around dawn, five or seven people came and hacked him to death.

Ramayan's patrimony
[This extract from the diary was supposed to be used as an introduction]

I see the boy returning every day by the 9:33 local train to Canning. A key—in lieu of the ritual piece of iron—hangs around his neck from a cord made of rags. He wears a half-dhuti made of single cloth. A month's unwashed dirt on him. Dry hair that has never seen oil. Falling all over his face. An earthen begging bowl in hand, some loose change in it. Seeing him, one would surmise from the ritual garb that his mother or father had died a few days ago. He goes around begging. Not ordinary begging, but for parental funerary duties. I see him every day, I've been seeing him for one and a half years—"How long have you been mourning your parents, boy?" He didn't get alarmed, not the slightest bit. "Tell me, what can I do, the babus don't want to give alms for nothing. I thought about it a lot and chose this way of begging. Please, give me one of your cigarettes." "You smoke?" "Why, shouldn't I? Can't we have tastes and desires?" "What do you do with the money, boy? Do you bring it home or . . . all these tastes and desires . . . ?" "Why wouldn't I bring it home? . . . My dad took another woman and went away. I live with Mother. With Mother and my little brother and sister." "What does your mother do?" "Mother's not well now, she has a bad disease. She's in bed all day long. That's why I've chosen this line. When Mother was well, she used to come to sell toddy in the street in Calcutta." "Do you drink toddy too?" "Yes, of course I do, we all do. The youngest one, my brother, is eight months old now . . . Mother has no milk . . . so when he cries too much, Mother gives him toddy. He calms down when he drinks toddy. Why, is drinking toddy bad, babu? So many sons of bhadraloks, all of them gulp down glass after glass . . . Mother says all the bhadraloks have only foul things in their mind."

"And your mother's illness?"

"You want to know what her illness is, babu? It's a very shameful thing. Mother was returning home from Calcutta by the last train, after selling toddy. It was a night in the month of December. There was no one in the vendors' compartment. Finding an opportunity, two home guards and their pals raped my mother. Mother told me everything, she wept her heart out on my shoulder. She told me a lot that day. She said it's the rule of the big folk, no one cares about the poor. The police and everyone else are there only for the suited-booted bhadraloks and moneyed big folk. Give money and turn the case around, there's no one to protest. Let me grow up a bit, let me get strong . . . Mother's told me it's I who have to take revenge."

Bipinchandra Pal

"There's no straw on their roofs, no clothes on their hips, no rice in their stomachs—but even such poor and helpless people could go at any time to the East India Company's police stations and file their complaints against the mighty and powerful zamindar's oppression, and if they had evidence and witnesses, they could bring the zamindar to the court of the English and make him stand in the defendant's cage."

Diary

Ramayan is the beloved creation of my pen, my inheritance. As I write, I can see that it has become an obsession. I'm unable to discard a single scenario. I also read about other things, and so, in a scattered way, I managed to read something about Munshi Premchand. In my own way. In a somewhat inconsistent manner. A question arises, why didn't Premchand meet Rabindranath Tagore despite numerous invitations of various kinds? Was he avoiding it, or was it the pretext of not having time? Or something else, something different? Something else, something intense. I already knew then that Premchand had uttered the word "effeminate" regarding Bengali novels; about dwelling of Shantiniketan—"flower vase," a floral decoration. Of course, nothing is revealed by all this, logically speaking. For that matter, not even the piece of information that Munshi-ji used to hang a picture of Khudiram in his room. After that, I re-read *Kafan* through the night. Two in the morning, sleepless, by candlelight, as there was a power outage. The relationship takes on more faces, questions keep springing up in Ramayan Chamar's tale, all slippery and inconsistent. And so the night was spent in this manner, the smell of the burning wick emanating from the melting candle. Even the squirrel had assisted in bridge-building, and that's why it received Lord Rama's blessings. What did Rabindranath receive—he got the people's unwavering love, didn't he? The man had terrific gall, in that era, so it was suicide that he chose.

Pir Ali's song comes wafting in from far away
[This extract is to be sung by two persons, the writer
and Ramayan]

"You can shoot and kill me, but you can't make me surrender. I fight for the exploited, I protect the honor of
women. This land shall one day belong to the one who
plows it. Even if you people kill me, this is going to happen. Behind me are many more like me, lining up. They
shall come—they will come—they will keep coming."

Panu Mullick: "But what do the people say?"
Bimal babu: "Let it pass, you can't retain your dignity if
you listen to what each and every one says at all times . . .
we can think about the people at the time of elections."

At first, an entire chapter is deleted. Next to be deleted is
the important section where the writer becomes mired in
his real-life writing crisis.

In the following pages, one will find quite a few bits
from the history taught by the colonial sahibs, which has
been copied without quotation marks.

The subject matter, arranged according to its loftiness,
is lowered and the shot is taken—this use of the camera is
a low-angle shot. The villain must be given prominence,
he has to be shown like the hero, there's no problem—use
a low-angle shot. In Indian films, the villain is an eternal
truth. And at some point, he has to go and rape the heroine. Later, he will also engage in judo and karate with the
hero. In such scenes, in order to show the heroine as being
extremely helpless, frightened and terrified, shoot the
scene from high above. You'll see tears come to the eyes

of the audience. And at that moment, in order to show the villain's oppression, shoot the scene from down low—in the distance and from a corner—you'll see that the flow of tears will be uncontrollable.

Everyone's branded
[Casting new light on the Gandhi assassination]

Three people, and sometimes four or five people, they have headphones over their ears and they keep talking. A strange and ghostly atmosphere, like an El Greco picture; the nation burns in the moonlight and corpses emerge from their resting places, breaking the earth; zombies roam around in all directions, standing at the back, green in color; snip-snip-snip-snip, the scissors cut away—all the papers are cut, the papers, all the papers.

This section can never be completed without the readers' active penetration. The readers themselves enter into the writing, they ask questions, the questions become entangled until finally the writer and reader become one. The sentences marked out by them for query lend another dimension to the writing, can do so, for that matter it can even be that, suddenly, according to one's mental capability, our regularly employed sense of understanding is altered. The main thing is the reader's active participation, or else the writing only manifests futility.

Unseen, the announcer

Sunlight moves from the upper floor to the floor below, and it keeps descending like that, as if some invisible sweeper were descending along the stairs, from the top to the bottom, cleaning the succession of steps.

: Goats will be sacrificed here, in this arena, in God's name, isn't it—
: Yes, actually that zombie—that walking corpse—
: That's our nation's Janak
: Tell me, tell me, please tell me the name—what happened, why is your head lowered—tell me, the name is being asked for

The corpse lies covered in white cloth—it does not say its own name.
The writer's slippers left outside, gray with mud.

: Now I can understand, I can understand that you are one of the murderers
: Some people can use the power of their will over the dead—draw them out of the grave, and get them to do things
: I get that—I get it that you're one of the murderers
: And were also the killer of Archimedes long ago
: Yes, went to kill Kingsford, but two innocent lives were lost
: All of it, everything, and in this manner—whatever is our pride and whatever is shameful
: We were educated but have no taste . . . right, master, isn't that so
: *Nothing begins and nothing ends*
: Does the program consist only of all this?

: No, the program takes form gradually. Over many days, in the very process of going beyond bounds—
: What happens after this?
: Nothing at all, nothing in particular, however, for the protection of the elected members of the legislative assembly, more and more policemen have to be posted all around
: And our polity—I mean, what's to become of democracy?
: What does Ramayan-da say about this?
: I don't know, but there's one thing he often says—if, like Lord Rama, the ghost of upholding truth possesses you, then you'll have to go and weep in the forest and someone will come and run off with your beautiful wife
: Master! Look! Civilization's tail has caught fire
: Really, a terribly heartrending enticement
: Look here, I am what I am
: Actually there was no purpose for all this, for all these things.
It was completely burnt, wasn't it, everything had to be prepared anew
: Master, look, see the whole place is redolent with the odor of illicit liquor,
wavy images are flooding the screen

A dark green Ambassador follows them
keeping a few feet behind.

: The incident took place in public, on the road, at noon, among lots of people, didn't it?
: That was just the commencement, I don't have anything more to say in this regard
: You say it wasn't planned?

: Look here, if I have to say it, then I'll say it was not the associations and assemblies of ten or twenty educated, middle-class folk, but pulling the whole country into the movement that was his achievement

: Yes, drawing the masses into the struggle and keeping them far away from the struggle of toiling people

: Do you know, if someone scalps tickets standing more than ten yards away from the cinema hall, he can't be legally apprehended?

: But the pair of dragons drawn on the flag—with alluring eyes, staring intently at your face

: I've understood everything, but who'll play the role of Brutus?

: The zombie can play both roles simultaneously. Has done so many times

: There's been a terrible mistake in this regard, Ramayanda has not been asked about anything at all

: The police found lots of papers inside the folio

: Sure they found them, the independence of the colonies was sold at quite a good price

: And the intellectuals were then—

: They'll stand in front of the mirror and comb over their hair so that their progressively expanding baldness is covered

: [pokes him in the stomach, laughs quietly] And what was inside the lockers of the Swiss banks, pal?

: Master, whether you believe me or not, they used to call this the golden coffin

: Rubbish

: In that case, let it be me who sings the ditty, in the way they say it, in tune

: Say it

: A for abuse
B for black-marketing
C for cunning
D for dishonesty
: Actually it was supposed to be this way, exactly like this
: Believe me, master, everything went away into the files of the Ministry of Foreign Affairs
: And all these relations—it's called matrimony or something—the husband-wife sleeping together business
: If you say obscene things, the censor will catch you—yes

Far away, the sound of the clock striking 2 A.M. can be heard. The zombie stirs.

: They have prepared codified ideologies to be employed for specific purposes
: There has not been any proper discussion with Ramayanda
: But is there any notion that has not become old by now?
: Yes, it's a fixed pillar, above which is a circular dome, a circular one
: *Nothing begins and nothing ends*
: But all these streams are very useful, at least at present, at this time
: Look! The zombie is waking up—its hands and feet and head are moving—its eyes are flashing—beware [screaming] the zombie is waking up—beware—everyone beware
: Damn! It's green in color
: A few thousand times in its lifetime, a few million times
: What's the role of the zombie?
: It should never be prompted loudly or audibly—the ghostly atmosphere gets destroyed by that

: If Ramayan-da were here, he'd say this is no ghost story
: But what's the role of the zombie?
: It has no consciousness of its own, if one doesn't speak loudly it can't hear
: *The day Mother India arose from the deep blue ocean*— the zombie shall sing this song as it's about to enter, and all of us will sing the chorus
: Good heavens! That song on the lips of the zombie— people won't understand, they'll get enraged and throw stones out of patriotic rage
: I have a nice part memorized, master, it's very exciting, people will flock to hear, it can be put into the zombie's voice—[reciting]

> *Oh you wicked one, what gall you have*
> *Go, brother Dushasana, fetch Draupadi*
> *Let's see what Bhima, the son of Pandu, can do*

: But that's Duryodhana's dialogue
: It will match the zombie's voice, master, and everyone will just love it, no one will be interested in knowing the relevance
: But what if Ramayan-da says something?
: You and your Ramayan-da all the time—it's because you pay him so much attention that he lords over you now
: Of course, master, whatever all of us decide together
: Nowadays revolutionaries no longer use cleavers
: But yes, at that time, in the days of revolution, what a song Sachin babu had sung—*Ooooh dear friend, knoooow that this spring month was fruitless*
: But love's imperishable, master, in every age the love story of India

: But a resemblance is indestructible
: Only a single wall in between
: Yes, beneath the arch, in the distance, and within a corner

In the electric light, one can see a person driving nails into notches in the stone.
Brow furrowed, the zombie observes the activity.

: Look, see how the screen sways in the breeze
: It happens like this and this is what is called "nationalist mentality"
: Within a cordon, confined within a geographical limit, right?
: Alexander's battle against Porus begins—I expect to be treated like a king by a king
: But Ramayan-da does not talk so vaguely
: The precise matter is that even if nationalism was not there, love for the nation did exist
: That's what we have been made to understand, right?
: Carry on, sir—carry on—Akbar versus Rana Pratap . . . Siraj versus the English company . . . Aurangzeb versus Shivaji—a festival of Shivaji festival
: But weren't Shivaji's Marathas marauders?
: I'm burping, I ate too much—the chicken was brilliantly cooked
: [in a loud voice] Come let us become united through struggle—and what's the rest of the expression? I'm terribly forgetful
: The people have to be made aware of the goal of complete democracy
: No, no, that comes in the end—where's the prompter

: I have matches—this dynamite's bad—nothing ignites with one stroke nowadays
: A thousand lives bound together in a single thread—does the song come here?
: It is through the struggle against ignorance that one stays aware
: Yes, yes, that part
: Instead, why not have this song, master, it'll be grand, no one's going to see whether it matches the part, [singing]

I didn't come to this world   to laugh and play
We have to serve   the mother alone

: Ramayan-da has a role here—wonderful dialogues [speaks in overdramatized jatra style], don't you recognize your mother? She's everyone's mother, the ruffian's mother, the black-marketeer's mother, the goonda's mother, the gentleman's mother, the villain's mother . . . this sattu-wallah who sits under the shirish tree, sattu basket and shiny washed brass plates arranged in a little bit of cleaned-up space, around whom is a crowd of rickshaw-wallahs, under the noon sun . . . she's his mother too, and then again, also J. J. Birla's mother
: But you didn't mention the names Naxalbari and Srikakulam in the song
: Careful, counter-revolutionary thoughts are arising
: Can't these names be inserted in the middle of the song, master? That will solve all problems
: We have to face the frenzy of the intoxicated masses
: Yes, burnt bedding, broken suitcase, smashed hinge
: The disavowal of liberation too
: You could say this is only an imposed limit

: It's the second stage now

: Those who are in their thirties, they won't understand any of this. Everyone's a paint-factory worker now, changing their colors

: At a meeting of party supporters the other day . . .

: Everyone had to shout and scream

: Yes, the zombie too

: And this red coat?

: If I have to explain everything, then I'll have to laugh like a nincompoop

: But where will the protest agitation be inserted? It's an ever-changing situation

: But actually becoming stiff-necked

: I suppose this is what's proverbially called spilling the broth on one's own lap

: We did not search at first in that direction, there was no need for that

: How was it reported to you?

: The exact words were—"Please put on your coat quickly, we're waiting outside"

: In the middle, the trickling stream flows along—that ditty wasn't taught

: But it's taught to everybody

: There are various things that have not been said, it would be unbecoming to raise a public outcry about them

: The kind of conduct that should be expected of responsible citizens—that lesson too

: Everything was taught by rote, no one mentioned anything about understanding

: Despite that, the murder was premeditated—it was premeditated eventually

: It has to be, there's only the one subject matter

: Nonviolent cruelty

: No, the two aren't the same, master, cruelty may be all right, but violence is not acceptable, it's against the Constitution

: The zombie doesn't have any sense of its own—it's simply a mobile corpse—it was made to do it

: In the end is the scene with Ramayan-da engaged in a sword fight with this very zombie, right? To the sound of drumbeats—a marching song

: I don't exactly know the ending

: But master, the writer says that Ramayan-da himself doesn't know that his death is not to be at the hands of the zombie but at the hands of his own people

: Oh, I don't know much—it's all ganja-smokers' conjectures—come on, give me a cigarette

: We don't have matches, master

: All of us know that revolt is a prelude to revolution . . .

: What happened to your matches?

: They're damp, master, they don't light

: So in that case, you had only so much to say to Gandhi-ji

: Yes, I can only finish him off in the way I finished him off

: I've heard a few hundred thousand dollars were given to get this done

: But the incident depends upon whom you voted for at the time of the elections

: Since when have the words "false voter," "ghost voter," and so on been in circulation in our democracy, master?

: So the thing happened in just that way

: Of course, the reactionaries are not at all self-indulgent dream-lovers, like we concluded

: It's because the bullet was fired from two feet away that people are now talking about suicide
: *Nothing begins and nothing ends*
: But what exactly happened?
: Ramayan-da says that under specific conditions, even as society is sought to be advanced toward people's liberation, yet so many incidents

> Someone in a long green coat, who looks at them suspiciously, crosses from the left to the right. A faded rough wall in the background. A poster made on a newspaper page, about the politics of annihilation, is pasted on it.

: It could also be that the man who was killed ran toward the bullet
: In that case, it could also be that all of you are in the party for your own agendas—getting ten thousand people together so that ten people can do as they please
: It is a proven truth that the person who wished-to-be-killed had a pet bird at the time . . . yellow-green
: Yes, everything returns to the rules of history—the bird is only a bird, even the pistol, which was aimed at the enemy, turned on himself

> The poster made by hand on a newspaper page becomes clear now: *Until now, man has not been able to make a firarm that fires bullets only in a single direction and avoids other directions.* The incorrect spelling of firearm will definitely remain here.

: A silencer was fitted
: That's why I say, there's no basis for what the party has done
: Is that why it was not possible to get the people's trust?
: The zombie then rose up from the grave—the country was plunged in green terror
: That's for sure, love for the nation is a splendid thing, crisp and delicious
: And that's what is a barrier
: I don't think so
: And trustworthiness
: A very bold gamble—and then it wouldn't have been possible to carry on these crafty ploys
: So was it in broad daylight that the murder scene was enacted in full, in the prayer meeting?
: Maybe it was
: If Ramayan-da were here, he'd have supported me
: *Nothing begins and nothing ends*
: But the zombie will wear green clothes then
: Look here, it's very important for one point to be made absolutely clear
: Before that, hear this too, that I don't like to make such a fuss about Titumir any more. Just as he was after the English, as a Muslim he was after the Hindus too
: Amazing—Ramayan-da had told me in advance that at the time of danger you'd say exactly this
: Your Ramayan-da has a short circuit
: Are you saying incorrect information was provided?
: To say it properly, it was in order to distort public taste
: But the zombie's final dialogue has not been delivered
: It doesn't awaken except at night, master—unless it's dark

: It's gone on for too long, let us say the dialogues on its behalf
: Isn't scoundrel the word?
: We don't bother about words and so on—the bourgeois do
: *Politics is the last resort of a scoundrel*
: One should also add that he will deliver this part wearing a green shirt—as it was done during the murder of Gandhi Maharaj
: Both green and yellow, in stripes
: The colors will gleam
: Although it was his responsibility to awaken the zombie, and it was he who killed it in the end
: With his blunt knife—a penknife—which he used to keep in his pocket
: But at that time, who gave it the green shirt to wear— why did they give it?
: That's the mystery—must ask Ramayan-da
: I don't think he knows . . . and does he know everything or what—a fount of knowledge
: So then we have reached the conclusion that Gandhi Maharaj wished that we divulge the secret
: Now that we have said so much, one has to go back and think
: In that case, the whole carnage has to be brought forward
: Yes, along the edges of the circle
: In the distance and from a corner
: Yes, exactly so. Two shackles tying the neck to the feet. In the distance and inside

The man from before, wearing a long, green coat looks at them even more suspiciously and crosses from the right side to the left. The next moment, a dark green van comes and stops behind them. The metal door of the van opens. The rattling sound of the door being opened.

The miraculous Phantom and his beautiful companion

It was three minutes past midnight. Autumn. Nine days remained before the commencement of Durga Puja. In a tiny room in Santoshpur bazaar, near Metiabruz, a twenty- or twenty-one-year-old girl stitched away on a sewing machine, making a red checked T-shirt. Her shoulders almost touched her hands as she hunched forward, doing her work with great care. Her eyes weary and fingers stiff after a whole day's hard labor, the stitching went awry, and in every fiber of her being she knew she would have to pay the price for it. She had been working for almost eighteen hours and this was her fourth shirt. Of course, a little time went into bathing and meals. She had an arrangement with a shop in Lindsay Street. She got about two-and-a-half rupees per shirt, although the shop charged its customers eighteen rupees. Behind her, a few yards away, stood Phantom, the superhero. Wearing something like striped underpants, a pistol on his hip, blazing eyes and a massive body, he brought peace wherever he went, his faithful dog always behind him. Tell me: what's the name of Phantom's dog? Yellowish light hovered now on the muscles of Phantom—symbol of the defeat of evildoers and the nurturing of goodfolk. The light came from a thin candle placed beside the girl's sewing machine. All along, between them, between the ever-stitching girl and

Phantom, all along, a page from *Anandabazar Patrika* swayed in the gentle breeze—it fluttered in the breeze—a companion to the matrimonial page: "Seeking a female friend to spend my retirement with, age between eighteen and twenty-two, must be beautiful." The newspaper page swayed in the gentle breeze, cut out from *Anandabazar Patrika*—I have been seeing so many strange desires and wishes seeking fulfillment in your much-publicized newspaper advertisements—job-land-flat-matrimonial-tutor-pen-pal—and so another new desire is now added: Seeking a female friend. Some sought openly, the language used: "Seeking a female friend." In last Sunday's paper, at least two dozen advertisers sought female friends or companions. One of them explained the reason for his desire in this way: "A cheerful, golden-voiced female friend, free of all inhibitions, to fill an industrialist's days of retirement with song and unfettered joy." The other advertisers did not explain their need, but if unfettered joy was a permissible reason, then, it can be borne in mind, that is because there's not an iota of matrimonial intent . . . So there's no end to the desires and wishes seeking fulfillment, especially when, as the saying goes: if you put money on the table you can even get tiger's milk in this country.

"Hey—have Mohun Bagan depended mainly on Prasun all this time? I think so! During last Saturday's big match, while struggling against the other team, Prasun pulled his hamstring. Throwing supporters into deep gloom, and notwithstanding his strong reluctance to do so, he had to leave the field to rest. There have been four games since then, and in all four matches, it was clear that, without Prasun Bannerjee, Mohun Bagan were simply floundering."

Visible in the background, close by, was the old bullock, fettered. It had a bad wound on its shoulder. Flies kept sitting on the wound and the bullock kept trying to drive away the flies with swipes of its tail.

Free of everyday tiredness and fatigue, the great mighty one, Phantom, combining in his person rebel and ruler, beyond competition, transcending all social regulations and prohibitions. In this way, slowly, without anyone knowing it, the seeds of romantic rebellion are sown within us. It goes without saying, that this symbol of freedom, Phantom . . .

In 1961, Tarzan books were removed from the library of a school in California on the complaint that he was living together unlawfully with Jane, without marrying her, and Tarzan fans from different parts of the world—they were a few million in number—were shocked. Quite a few teenage boys and girls in Europe and America went on a hunger strike. A debate began. Scholars went into action. Poring through the pages, they proved that Tarzan and Jane were married in 1915 in *The Return of Tarzan*. A large number of people in the world heaved a sigh of relief, many began dancing in the open as they took to the streets, threw parties, fountains of booze flowed, and a holiday was declared in schools and colleges on the occasion of this festival. This created such an immense demand for Tarzan books that the publishers were unable to meet it, even after working the press all day to print new editions.

All the supernatural impossibilities that we can't ever render possible lay in the palm of his hand, and were performed with ease. Through the media of films, television, and comics, this protean prophet is transformed into one of the cult figures of this age—he keeps rescuing beautiful Jane from the alligator's jaws, the female body with scantily concealed breasts and buttocks, Jane . . . He was He-Man, captivating the modern age, a supernatural sex symbol . . .

A short distance from the bungalow was a forest, dense with sal trees. There was a stream beside the forest, and across the water a clump of kaash, almost touching the bank. The water was about knee-deep. The bed of the stream consisted of sand and pebbles. Their jeep stood nearby.

Light was rising steadily over the sky, trees, and earth. The come-for-fun babu and bibi were sleeping inside the bungalow. They'd sleep until ten or eleven in the morning. After lunch, the jeep would set off toward Calcutta. The hill-boy comes to sell chickens and milk to babus in the dak bungalow. Learning that babu-bibi would not open the door before ten, he felt dejected. They had danced naked all night long . . . in boisterous drunken revelry . . . only went to sleep at dawn . . .

Temptation

Sin

Destruction

Is the Formula, all right

Check it out

At about midnight on Saturday, a youth named Motilal was driving a jeep and entering Calcutta via Howrah Bridge. Beside him was a young woman, Aloka, twenty-one, and on the rear seat was Rajinder Singh. There was a gentle breeze and winter was setting in. Rajinder thought: Will you have the suit collected from Band Box Dry Cleaners? The missus, having just finished dinner, was applying cream on her face and chewing a cardamom pod. She asked: Cardamom, want one? That's when the accident happened. As the jeep turned at the Brabourne Road intersection, it suddenly banged into a concrete post. Going out of control, it then banged into another post nearby. The front of the jeep was badly smashed. There had been a loud crashing sound, people from all directions came running, although there weren't many people at that time of night. The first to arrive was a rickshaw-wallah, wearing striped underpants. He was at the roadside, making rotis on a stove after a full day of work, his body exhausted. All his rotis were burnt to cinders. A large piece of glass had pierced Aloka Ghoshal's throat. At first, nobody in any of the cars passing by wanted to get involved in any unnecessary hassle, they kept speeding past, merely craning their necks to size up the situation. A little later, a Punjabi taxi driver was forcibly stopped. After the three injured persons were taken to PG Hospital, Aloka Ghoshal was declared dead. The other two persons left the hospital after primary medical care and went off to inform the deceased's family. They did not return. Later, the police found out that all the identity details provided by them were false. The mystery deepened in the city. Who were they? Where had they gone? Who was the girl? The number plate on the jeep was from Bihar. Both the men had been wearing expensive clothes. Their faces looked tired, as if they hadn't slept all night. The girl's face too. The nurse had seen wads of bills in the tall man's wallet. The girl wore an expensive silk sari, but it was crumpled all over. A new blouse, brand new, a bit too tight, it looked as if it had been bought recently, it smelled new. Dirt on her neck. A new bra. Three petticoats under the sari, the top one made of silk, a bright red, that was new too, and of the two underneath, the bottom one was quite old, the stitching had come apart in a few places.

In this way, exactly this happened, but

the story could also be different—that is to say, the girl

did not die at all then—

After reading the advertisement in the *Anandabazar Patrika*, she called the specified phone number with trembling hands. She was given the address of an apartment on Camac Street and a time to arrive. The girl hesitated at first, but finally she went. Here, needless to say, the description of the girl's family situation is left out—readers, you already know about all that. She had no other option besides this. The gentleman advertiser—actually he was over forty years of age and had a thirteen-year-old son—saw the girl, her fresh, dark-skinned virginal body and figure—everything in this city is second-hand—damn—he craved a flower exactly like her. Actually the man—Arunangshu Dutta Choudhury, industrialist—despite being of his class, was somewhat different—he had a master's degree in economics, had lived for several years in the United States, kept himself informed about everything in the contemporary world, walked to Rabindra Sadan cultural center at dawn on the birthday of spiritual leader Gurudev Rabindranath Tagore, wearing a sparkling dhuti-punjabi and parking his car at a distance, and, most of all, he had read Marx and adhered to his philosophy too, especially Eurocommunism. He knew that millions of people in Calcutta lived in bastis, and it pricked his conscience to keep a poor girl as an object of pleasure merely with the power of his money, without giving anything in return. Simply identifying the man by his class—was an oversimplification . . .

Given his elite credentials, his gentlemanly conduct, and the fact that he was also good-looking, ordinary girls would definitely fall in love with him. And this girl's youthfulness and fickle mind, she had no notion at all about life's dilemmas, whatever she knew came only from watching cheap Hindi films and imitating them

. . . I'm terribly lonely . . . *too lonely* . . .

. . . *Hold your tongue and let me*

love . . .

An ancient garden-house with a huge compound, a tennis court behind the bungalow, a badminton court on the left, a red pathway of crushed brick in the middle, a spacious dining hall, at least six hundred square feet, with antique furniture, a piano, paintings on the wall—in the middle, a Kashmiri carpet spanning about two hundred square feet.

The man pulled the handle on the door of the cellar, there were expensive bottles of Scotch whiskey inside . . . and bottles of cognac and wine

The man, Arunangshu Dutta Choudhury, was pouring whiskey from the bottle for the girl . . .

The man: Mister Writer, *I am so sorry for you*, will you ever be able to think and fathom what side I will take, and at what stage, when the time of killing arrives . . . *Think about it, Writer*

And then, from behind the scenes, Ramayan Chamar blazes up, a terrifying pair of eyes sunk deep beneath his forehead, the region between his thighs covered with angry red sores, part his legs and take a look, you'll see it all . . . how much longer, how many more days, with these people

Lord you showed me the way
Didn't show the road

> Popular belief has it that Rome was founded by the sons of Mars, Romulus and Remus. A she-wolf suckled the newly-born twins—yes, a she-wolf . . .
> Alas, unknown to us
> Both our hands
> Got scorched sometime

In '47, after becoming the Governor of West Bengal, Chakravarthi Rajagopalachari had said in a meeting, *"Poetry is in Bengal's air."* Actually, he did not say this after hearing any Bengali poetry, it was his personal assistant who had advised him to say it. The two body parts of the two Bengals were then, like a mutilated goat, gasping in the hope of a little bit of oxygen. As if according to plan, a people were consigned to becoming permanent refugees. A few hundred thousand people huddled together like animals on the streets and pavements, and in train stations. He heard poetry in Bengal's sky and air then.

All thieves have two to four associates who help them blow up the stolen money. The whole country was partitioned among ten or twenty fortunate people. Cupboard, wardrobe, sofa, dressing-table, cot, radio, television, fridge, the collected works of Rabindranath Tagore, Bankura horse, and compensation for property in the other Bengal—so much is needed to stay alive—colored Puja supplements to match your heart's desire—*Anandalok*—let me send the cook to buy some meat—

"Did you have any booze today, pal . . ."
Get lost, bastard

Thanks to a conspiracy of two or three people, a people, an entire people became permanent refugees. That was called Independence . . . for the greater interest . . .

Forget all this talk about the country, mister— wear silk clothes and recite the Gita every morning, especially the second chapter.

Father was seriously ill once. He was cured of his ailment after wearing an amulet given by a sadhu baba. After recovering from his illness, Father's faith in religious mendicants increased tremendously. One day, while returning through a forest, he saw a sanyasi with matted hair sitting under a tree on the wayside, a sacred fire lit beside him. After making obeisance, he sat down in the dirt with the man. There were mutual introductions. His name was Jungli Baba. Father brought the sanyasi, Jungli Baba, home that very day and kept him there. His sacred fire burned all day and through the night in the veranda adjoining the living room. Finally, when word got around of the pretty maidservant becoming pregnant, Jungli Baba disappeared.

I massaged Jungli Baba's legs.

It was the time of nationwide elections, the last day for the filing of nomination papers. Astrologers were panting. For the last two months, they hadn't even had time to breathe. An old astrologer of long standing in Kalighat, said: "Brother, until yesterday it was so bad that I didn't even get time to empty my bowels. Members of all the parties were crowded into my house, whether Marxist or non-Marxist, sometimes openly and sometimes secretly. Some people came by car in the middle of the night so that other people wouldn't see them. They demanded that I tell them the most auspicious time to file the nomination papers after studying their horoscopes and determining the various planetary influences on their zodiac signs. This is the scene throughout India, mister, not just in West Bengal." The sale of gemstones associated with various planets skyrocketed. A former Member of Parliament from south India declared that he won the elections because of the blessings of the Lord of Tirupati. At the very moment when he went to file his nomination papers, with clock-work precision, a grand puja was performed in the temple at Tirupati, the priests loudly chanting mantras, praying for his victory. After all, it was because of the blessings of the Lord of Tirupati that he had been able to get elected as many as three times.

Continuously, the sound of the black van
Continuously, the newspapers full of reports about Dalits
burned alive
in Bihar, Madhya Pradesh, Andhra Pradesh
and
through the chimney of Kali Mata Rice Mill
wisps of smoke emanate   continuously

His ashrams were spread across the world, the number of people outside India who knew him was ten times the number of those in India who knew him. His teachings were translated into twenty or twenty-five languages and printed, with pictures, in five-color offset. If his picture was hung in a room, holy ash flowed from it. He had a massive Sunmica-top secretary desk, at which beautiful women sat illuminating the room. As soon as I arrived, Baba told me the name of the book I had been reading on the train and put a pinch of dust in my hand, I saw it transformed into two huge, sticky-sweet Ganguram ros-sogollas. The foreign disciples were all seated, rows and rows of them, waiting for a bit of dust off his feet.

Here a Bengali calendar, printed in five-color, has to be imagined, with a picture of bathing gopinis, Lord Krishna's female friends, and him stealing their clothes. It could not be printed for lack of money.

Baba's sadhana practice was somewhat different. He didn't say that the body was perishable, rather he had discovered that God dwelt within the body. His theory about the body was very interesting. A huge hall. The walls were sparkling white. Incense burned inside, in the dim light the entire hall was half lit and half in shadow. On the pretext of showing our devotion to the Divine, about a dozen of us male and female disciples entered the room. Opposite every male disciple was a female disciple. As soon as we entered the room, all of us disciples began pulling at the thin, saffron-colored gowns of the female disciples. Tore at them. Baba had said, "Tear it away with all your strength. Tear away any undergarments inside." And so, with utmost haste, we tore away everything. And who doesn't like to tear off women's clothes? The girls became enraged. They too began tearing away our gowns. That's just what we wanted. In delight, snippets of Bombay film songs erupted. And then we got down to business. Baba said, "Scratch and bite a little. That will enhance the pleasure." We did that. We groped, fondled, and scuffled for as long as we could. We broke into a sweat, our bodies were drenched. We continued our sadhana practice thus, until we were exhausted.

A difficult face, dark-skinned, savage-looking. The two eyes, gray like steel. The nose a lump of flesh. Thick lips. As he walked along, he did not budge an inch if anyone came in his way. His wife had been taken away at night by the babus who came to the bungalow for an outing. He had cut up and killed a babu with an ax. There was a murder trial against him.

Drought. The earth gasping. Eleven-thousand-volt electric cables spanning the sky, floating like a net in the void. The loud screeches of a bird. A long road of black tar. Looking to the fields, as far as the eye could see were rugged, wretched faces, here and there were tiny patches of the dark green fields of the fortunate few—all the remaining ones, scattered everywhere, were gray and yellow—

A predawn moon in the sky. The temple lies in faint darkness. A peace flag at the top. Goddess Lakshmi's owl flies off the branch of a hibiscus bush.

". . . Forget about nation and suchlike, mister—wear silk clothes and recite the Gita every morning, especially the second chapter."

A boatman stands, wearing a netted vest over a green-checked lungi. Near the bank, a barber shop and a tea shop. Two long, thin planks are laid, a crowd of people clamber in. Brown, red, green, and blue saris come most frequently to sight. A baby on someone's shoulder, the older child held in the left arm. They climb aboard the steamer, walking hurriedly over the narrow gangway, shouting loudly at their respective folks to hurry . . . a people, an entire people, become refugees like this . . .

A shining pair of steel handcuffs hangs on the wall, newly acquired, and a thirty-four-year-old portrait—quite unclear, faded . . .

"What's up, dada—shall we
show our might?"

A little sibling for Monu in the womb. Monu's mother went from house to house in the village, doing the household chores and husking the grain. The affluent folk in the countryside still did not eat mill-polished rice. In her pregnant condition, Monu's mother boils the paddy, dries it in the sun, stamps the husking pedal and wonders: "Why don't I die, death will bring an end to all troubles . . ."

Lord Ramakrishna said: "The world is a whole onion. Peel away the skin—all your life, peel away the skin—and until the end you'll find nothing. The world is a veil of illusion."

"I sent my thirteen-year-old girl to the babu's house to work. For food to eat. The youngest son of the house got her pregnant. And then he tries to pay us off, to keep quiet. Don't the bastards have mothers and sisters at home . . ."

The gentleman drank a gulp from the glass in his hand, one could observe the descent of the drink down his gullet . . .

Refugees hoped for assistance. There shouldn't be a clamor for relief until an all-India committee is constituted—they hadn't been taught that

The paunch juts out half an arm's length. It bounces like a balloon filled with water

Some boys and girls were spotted in the casuarina grove, entwined in unbecoming conduct, and when the local administration was informed about the incident, they knocked their hands to their foreheads—"What can we do, sir—everything's God's wish—call Him . . ."

He was a very good boy. Obeyed his parents. Whenever he traveled by bus and passed Kalighat, he knocked his knuckles on his forehead in obeisance and said a prayer addressed to the Goddess Kali. He never squandered his money on cigarettes, and he knew, he came to know, that everything, everything about our life, is contained in the Vedas.

Swearing in of ministry delayed on astrologer's advice

Barun Sengupta: New Delhi, January 10, 1980

Friday, January 11, was not a suitable date for all concerned. Consequently, the ministry will not be sworn-in on Friday. The swearing in will take place as soon as an auspicious date is determined. It is believed that it was on the advice of a highly respected astrologer that, at the last minute, the Indian democracy's date of swearing in was delayed.

The wife of a very senior civil servant, she had terrific influence in the neighborhood. She used to phone and ask for a car to be sent from the Writers' Building so she could go shopping in New Market in the afternoon. A theft had supposedly taken place in her house and her tobacco box, inlaid with silver, was missing. Standing in front of an audience of a few female neighbors, she grabbed the right hand of the servant girl and shoved it into a pan of boiling oil. The thirteen-year-old girl screamed in pain and fainted. No one uttered a word. The servants and maidservants have gone too far, they'll steal but never admit it . . .

Whose mother? You don't know the mother? She's each and everyone's mother—the thief's mother, the ruffian's mother, the black-marketeer's mother, the goonda's mother, the gentleman's mother. There—the sattu-wallah who sits under the shirish tree, sattu basket and shiny washed brass plates arranged in a little bit of cleaned-up space, around whom is a crowd of rickshaw-wallahs under the blazing noon sun—she's his mother too, and again, also industrialist J. J. Birla's. An old bakul tree. Flowered through the night. Fresh bakul flowers and poisonous ant colonies all around the roots.

Bedana Dasi
"I don't-want don't-want don't-want, dear
This measured-out love of yours."

Calcutta at dawn: the first tram. A widow, attired in silk—her son was an officer of substance—is on her way to bathe in the Ganga, the sacred stainless steel waterpot in her hand. Near the steps of the Jagannath Ghat, a paunchy, non-Bengali businessman, his two hands joined at his chest, eyes shut in pious worship of Rama-Sita. A band of scruffy looking urchin kids surrounds him, he throws a rupee coin toward Mother Ganga . . . a whole rupee coin.

On February 12, 1978, this age's most noteworthy sacred fire ceremony was conducted at the Sabarmati riverbank in Ahmedabad. Only four million rupees were spent on it. The organizer was the former queen mother of Baroda, Shanta Devi. For sacred fire offerings, 32,000 kilos of pure ghee, 500,000 liters of pure milk, 250 quintals of fine-grade rice, 200 sacks of sugar, 60 bags of daal and 300 sacks of wheat were used. The purpose of the sacred fire ceremony: (1) increase in wealth and power; (2) removal of scarcities in commodities of daily necessity; (3) increase in food production; (4) bringing back peace and love into the minds of people. Politicians Atal Bihari Vajpayee and Raj Narain left important meetings in order to participate in the ceremony, they flew there.

Ghosts
Jagdalpur, Bastar, March 11, 1980: UNI News

Recently, a youth from the Muria Adivasi community here was taking his pregnant wife to the hospital. Two nurses from the hospital had already been to the village and examined the girl and told her that there were twin babies in her womb, and that one baby was dead. Unless she was operated upon to remove the dead fetus, she would die. Her husband was therefore taking her to the hospital. On the way, he encountered a group of people from his own village. After hearing about the matter, they said: "Good heavens! In that case, the dead child in the womb has become a ghost by now. It will kill you too at any moment. You must kill the ghost before it leaves the womb. If you burn your wife, the ghost too will burn to death." So the man did just that. He burnt his wife to death. No one heeded the wails and screams of the unfortunate woman.

In this part of the manuscript, there's a statement by the boy who died after being beaten for being a pickpocket, the one whom we thrashed until his balls burst, he died in the hospital that very evening—

"From the time I was a child, I grew up just like the cows, goats, ducks, and hens. Until I was ten years old, I had never eaten my fill—do you know that? Like the dogs on the streets—the kids on the pavement grow up like that, and so we too grew up. How they grow up, what they eat, and how they survive—you babu folk will never be able to understand all that."

Morning descends on Calcutta. Sunlight hits Howrah Bridge. The streets awaken. The two banks of the river become visible.

It's very cold in Darjeeling. Tourists arrive in droves to savor and relish the cold.

"Do you know that a large number of refugees who came around 1947 have not been able to make anything of their lives . . ."

He wears saffron silk. Wears a turban on his head, in the style of Vivekananda. A watch on his wrist. The shiny-faced aristocratic sadhu said:

"Our ideology is Vedic communism. We too refer to Marx, to communism, we ask people to read Karl Marx. We say, where Marx ends, that's where we begin. We have said what Marx was unable to say. And Marxism is not something new. All of it is contained in our Vedas. Our ideology is Vedic communism."

Kasim Ali roams the countryside with a bamboo-shearing knife, for two and a half rupees, he castrates bulls.

Soliloquy

"Our goal is Vedic communism. Where Marx ends, that's where we begin . . . And if we carry on like this, even Mao's dad won't be capable of making revolution in this country. . . what . . . why . . . isn't that right . . ."

Bangladesh will supply shoe uppers worth 40.5 million rupees to India. An agreement to this effect was signed in New Delhi today. The tall and hefty Punjabi refugee of military appearance, who settled in Bhowanipore, wears a dark-colored shirt, and lounges on a string cot, sipping milky tea and shaking his legs

"Oye, *dil mein chakku maar diya* . . ."

The engine of the car parked right out front roars

Soundtrack completely mute

The silent rats of midnight. The silent rats of midnight chewed and destroyed everything.

Who eats these rats . . .

Time. Time consumes paper. And insects. For that matter, it even consumes the sun.

They eat whatever's left over after the meal. The blood sample's been taken, it has to be tested, got to know what's wrong. Actually, his blood is their food. They need his blood in order to survive.

They are not content with just the blood. They also eat the brains in his head. Scrape it out and eat it. Bones, marrow, fingers—the heel of the pen.

However much they attempted to finish him off, he kept preparing for the future. Staying up night after night, refusing to be used. The human face parallels the way the mind functions. Yes, doctor, I have found my future, which is inextricably linked to the past. As long as people are continuously told exactly what they want to hear, on and on, no one will know that beneath this mask, under the skull, are all the hidden things, all the forbidden doors. People will ask, why do you express your views in this way? Every person consumes what he loves, pressing it with his fingers . . . the neck, blood. His temperament was thus—either fraudulent, or support against fraud. Those who have openly protested against your lot's social system and been punished—those who you say do not deserve to live in society, are sick and depraved, supporting all of them,

protesting against the severe injustice done to them,

we wish to declare:

Be prepared . . . a sticky future is on its way

Ghost voter

"I'll eat the bones, the flesh too I'll eat
And with the skin I'll make the drum beat."

The witches' dance of *Macbeth* begins everywhere

All the way to the bait, the line, and the bobber, at first flat, and then slowly slanting, became immersed in the water. A colorful dragonfly appeared and began hovering near the float.

At about a quarter past nine at night, in the vicinity of the Jorabagan police station, near Posta Bazar, four youths, with daggers, razor blades, and revolvers concealed under shawls, set out to extort money. They entered a fancy restaurant by the roadside. It doubled as a country-liquor den at night. The boss tried to satisfy them with two bottles and an honorarium of a hundred rupees in cash. They did not cause a disturbance, but while leaving, they picked up some large bills from the cash register. Stepping outside, they caught hold of a woman. She was young, and was going by on a rickshaw. Brandishing a dagger, they removed her earrings, necklace, and bracelet. A long-haired youth, who was laughing loudly, apparently also openly groped and fondled her. The girl began to scream. A Nepali driver was passing by along the road at that moment. When he tried to fight them with his bare hands, one of them shot him in the head. He fell right there, his brains spilled out.

The girl screamed even louder, with one tug they undid her sari. At that moment, two police constables were grinding chewing tobacco in their palms and chatting about their joys and sorrows. They suddenly saw a woman clad in only a blouse and petticoat running along the road in terror, screaming for help. Chasing her were the mastaans, cleavers, and revolvers in hand. Stunned, they moved to the side of the road. The miscreant youths fired two shots in the air and slipped down an alley. Ten minutes later, after things became quiet, people from the neighborhood came out one by one and began talking loudly about the incident. Some of them lit cigarettes.

The kingfisher perched precariously on a thin bamboo, it was bent down like a bow, the shadow of the jamrul trees fell on the riverbank, a lot, a lot of it

---

Nepal Nag

Sushil Das, a peon in Calcutta University, was fired for concealing his educational qualifications while applying for his job. When corruption and fraud is spreading rapidly all over the country, in such a situation, for sheer survival, was it such an unforgivable crime to obtain a peon's job by concealing his BA degree? Have the authorities thought even once about dire poverty and the trauma of unemployment—in this country—as a result of which a youth was compelled to deny his own hard-earned qualification?

Sushil Das

"Punish me, but I beg you not to fire me."

University

"The matter is indeed unfortunate, nevertheless action has to be taken according to the law."

Amit, Partha, Moloy

"Shivlal Yadav will be able to set the ball spinning, won't he . . ."

Ramayan Chamar

"We mete out the punishment that the law is unable to

deliver. We make the ruling class aware that they do not have impunity."

Panu Mallick

"Mister, you've advanced greatly toward revolution, instead of all that, come now, make balls of dough and sit at the pond with a rod to catch punti fish, it'll be useful."

The area near Udaipur, in Tripura. They work in a brick kiln. Fourteen to eighteen hours of work, the wages two or three rupees. Tiny huts to live in. Eight or nine people stay in each one. Twenty-year-old Taru Munda and her husband, and nearby, eighteen-year-old Dhuniya Oraon and her father and brother. As per the agreement, after nine at night, the labor recruiting boss turns up, together with his sidekicks. In front of the husband, father and brother *redacted*   No means of protest, they would lose their jobs.

Giant ants were swarming on the packet of bait laid down near the fishing rod. There was nothing that these huge black ants did not eat. They ate dead cows and goats, they wouldn't even spare a dead man if they found one.

The peasant's wife sits beside the tarred road with figs, banana flowers, banana stems, and a few bundles of spinach. She has not rid herself of the habit of putting the ghomta over her head. A pair of doe-like eyes, a loose purple blouse full of grease stains, a coarse white nine-yard sari, which looks like a jute sack, wound around her.

Dirty, long unwashed. It's clear that she has been driven to the roadside by hunger. When customers haggle over her prices, she gets nervous and shrinks into herself. And you, the most junior sahib in the office, in the morning, after the cup of hot tea made by your wife, wearing a punjabi of fine cotton over an even finer batik-print lungi and combing your hair, you set out for the market. Hearing that a bundle of spinach is ten paise, you think she's asking for too much.

"It's ten paise for four or five bundles . . ."

"Are you crazy?"

"What?"

"Don't you know she gathered those few bundles of spinach after standing all afternoon and evening in waist-deep water, braving snakes and such?"

"We never shy away from the responsibility of building revolutionary violence in response to retaliatory violence."

The Mishirjis had rights over all fertile land. The Mishirjis had the right to the first crop from the orchards. The Mishirjis were also entitled to the beautiful maidens. According to the "dola" system in Bhojpur, a newlywed woman had to spend her wedding night with the zamindar. The Mishirjis were the zamindars in the villages. Even in the twentieth century, during the seventies, this system continued to exist in one form or another, perhaps in a slightly different way. The behavior that the peasant was subject to from the brahmins and zamindars—when he got the opportunity, the peasant conducted himself in exactly the same way with the Dalits. Exploitation and upper-caste nobility go, in this way, side by side, hand in hand . . .

Rape of women or caste oppression is only a pretext, the key question here is which class secures its economic rights, and how

---

Tensions mounted, the Hindus wanted to build a temple there, and the Muslims a mosque. A specific class of people, on both sides, suddenly became very clever. God-fearing people removed themselves far away. On both sides, some ten people were killed furtively. Going to Line No. 3 basti, I saw the Hindus as well as the Muslims were terrified. House after house was shuttered and empty. They had left their homes and fled. Large tiled roofs had been smashed. Marks of bomb explosions on the walls of the huts. The women fell to weeping: "How can we live here, we'll be killed!" Some local progressive folk, from both communities, proposed that the green flag from the mosque and the idol from the temple both be removed.

The situation grew extremely tense. The police arrived. They came and took away people on the grounds of injuring religious sentiments. The police superintendent said: "These extremists are out to whip up communal tension. They are trying to introduce violent politics in this country of nonviolence by violating temples and mosques."

In the very country in which the ideal of nonviolence is noisily propagated—the violence and terror hidden at every level of society erupts powerfully . . .

"It's getting too political, Mr. Writer, beware,

Even the walls   have ears . . ."

Several films about the Ramayana had been made under Vijay Bhatt's direction. The role of Lord Rama was played by Prem Adib, and Sita was played by Shobhana Samarth. *The real India lies in villages* . . . and the duo of Prem and Shobhana drove a particular class of people crazy in these villages. In some parts, Prem Adib was hailed as an incarnation of Lord Rama. Seeing his image, the audience threw flowers and coins in the direction of the screen. Some folks went on a fast before and then went for a "darshan"—or propitious viewing—of the film, dressed in saffron silk and with pious thoughts in mind. Once, during the shooting, a south Indian businessman arrived on set, paid obeisance by prostrating himself in front of Lord Rama, and sought blessings for success in his line of business. He was expecting to be awarded a contract that day. On another day, Prem was leaving at the end of the day's shooting, he was wearing trousers, and he had also had a bit to drink. Just then, an aristocratic Marathi gentleman came running frantically, requesting "Lord Rama" to kindly visit his hovel, as his wife wouldn't take no for an answer. Prem tried his best to explain, but the gentleman would not let him go, his car was waiting outside. He had to go to the dressing room, take off his shirt and trousers, and don the costume and makeup of Lord Rama. Stepping out of the car at the house, the wig-and-costume-clad Prem saw it was no hovel but a huge palace, with some five hundred maidservants ready to garland him. He was made to sit on a throne. Incense and lamps were lit and a prayer service was performed. Priests performed a puja. Only after the whole assembled mass of people had touched his feet and received blessings of wealth and sons was Prem allowed to leave.

"Hey, do hyenas like to eat jaggery? Why else do they run off with the jaggery pots?"

They are chamar by caste, and that's why seventy-year-old Jagdev has to pay obeisance to the child of the zamindar babu. And then the child, the two-year-old child, pisses gushingly on his face. He can't say anything, he pretends that this thing, this zamindar-offspring-urine, is as good as sacred Ganga water. Or else he wouldn't get work as a day laborer in the babu's house. And the response is given by his son Ramayan: "The bomb-making business has even reached the village."

"I have never eaten such tasty meat before. Yes, rattle-snake meat—imported from abroad—tastes like manna from heaven if cooked well."

In the South Arcot district of Tamil Nadu, in the hilly Kalrayan area, the practice of mortgaging wives is still prevalent. When money is borrowed, the moneylender takes away the debtor's wife in mortgage, and until the last penny of the loan and interest is repaid, he does not give the wife back. While in mortgage, she may bear the children of the owner—and that is common—and in that case, the recipient of the loan is responsible for the care and upbringing of the children. The wife cannot do any-thing, not even feed the baby milk from her breasts for that matter, she only has to serve her new lord, she has to close off her mind. That is the rule.

The rose bush has to be pruned from time to time. It won't grow unless the plant's dry and dead branches are cut off. It's also advisable to cut the branches near the base, a few inches above the soil. All kinds of insects, of various species, infest the rose bush and keep attacking it. Spray pesticide as soon as you spot any, or else they'll finish off the whole rose garden—your precious rose garden.

Drying her hair under the hair dryer after a shampoo, the missus moves toward the puja room to light incense. A huge lorry, overturned on the road, is visible from the window.

"Tell me, what's the most widely acceptable identity of
the pro-people culture?

The buxom film heroine Sandhya Roy, in a red-bordered
sari, carrying water in the crook of her arm, going on a
pilgrimage to Tarakeswar, right?"

The table itself is moving away, all the time, slowly,
I fell with a bang,
all activity stopped.

No,
Absolutely all right
Normal food. Normal bath. No sugar.
No-oh blood pressure.

On that day, Ramayan Chamar and others had stopped working in protest against the tyranny of the owner of the Mediyabari Tea Estate. The owner had been a sympathizer of the undivided communist party at one time . . . There's some basis for your economic demands, but why a "demand," why not "prayer," this egotism is not correct, brother . . . He arrived at a decision regarding their demands: he refused to yield. Ramayan and company were also obstinate: "Our right to strike—that must be accepted." Matters were tense. Bombs were thrown at the coolie quarters that night. One hut after another caught fire. The workers realized their plight and ran away. They tied up the two watchmen, and then they dragged out another suspect. Pandemonium ensued. The police arrived and arrested Ramayan. The disturbance spread to other tea gardens. People arrived with bows and arrows, with spears and rods, and fell upon the police to free Ramayan. Some carried axes. They gheraoed the police station. They didn't even allow the officer-in-charge to go out to piss. The police swung their lathis blindly. They fired tear-gas shells. They fired in the air. The people retreated a bit. But they did not flee. The police advanced once, and then the mob did. In the darkness of night—bows and arrows went into action. Then word got out that Ramayan Chamar had been beaten and killed inside the police station. The news spread. The mob was incensed. Breach of peace. Kerosene was splashed and fires were lit. Finally, the police received orders over the wireless to fire at the violent mob.

However progressive foreign policy is, the determiners of the destiny of developing countries, supported by the socialist powers, carry out the most feudal practices in their own countries. Here, saying even a word against the current government's undemocratic policies is prohibited. The funny thing is that the working class in socialist countries is also not allowed to know anything about all the oppressions happening within their own countries.

But
Ramayan Chamar's tale is an
even longer, even more complicated tale . . .

Chewing paan, he takes a lick of lime, takes out a match-
stick and cleans his teeth, the tip of the stick bears the red
of lime and catechu—
— "You've come to find out about the neighborhood, isn't
it?"
— "Yes."
— "Then listen," he pokes his teeth again with the red-
tipped matchstick, "you know, in our neighborhood . . ."
— "Yes?"
— "There aren't any lunatics."
— "Is that so?"
— "There aren't any drunkards."
— "How's that?"
— "No beggars here."
— "Amazing!"
— "No one ever committed suicide."
— "Incredible!"
— "Nothing involving women, no wife pouring kerosene
over herself, no virgin or widow getting pregnant."
—"It's simply Ramrajya!"
— "Yes, there are no Naxalites . . ."
— "And definitely no CPI(M) either!"
— "No."
— "Tell me more."
— "We don't spread rumors, we don't heed gossip
either . . ."

Just then, in the middle of the questions and answers, with the recitation of Sukanta's poem "Rebellion and Rebellion Everywhere" playing in the puja pandal where the image of Goddess Durga was installed, the bell-bottoms-clad folk began pop-dancing—

To the rhythm of swaying hips
Is the mighty environment for action prepared

"We are all confirmed progeny of slaves, a hundred percent slaves—no mark on the throat, but the voting ink remains on our thumbs."

The washerwoman washes clothes
On the date palm she splays her toes

— "I too have to figure out what to eat with rice, brother-in-law. All of you are only concerned about television, fridge, safe-deposit locker, and bank balance . . . We too are deprived, have a sense of deprivation . . ."
— "Sure, you people also need to think, but you think about whether to eat mutton or chicken, about when you'll have a new car instead of the Ambassador . . . while we worry about whether we can get by with vegetarian fare for five days in the week, with fried potatoes and daal . . . And so it is . . ."
— "You exaggerate!"
— "Absolutely not, boudi, just try to find out how many times a week a middle-class family with children eats fish.

But you know what's funny—our maidservant, she comes from Canning, takes the 5:10 train every morning, she has an eighteen-day-old baby at home, she has to get by cooking once a day, if that. Have to fill their stomachs with whatever they can get—pumpkin, taro, spinach. And don't think those things are very cheap in the village. Can't feed the son, no milk in her breasts, but she has to sell her own cow's milk to the sweet shop, that's the money with which she'll buy flour to feed six or seven mouths. She envies babus like us who eat rice and daal twice a day. She also despises us for not providing her with so much as a piece of stale bread for morning tea—she thinks that if she found work with better-off folk, she'd get a piece or two of fish and meat once in a while, a few handfuls of leftovers on her plate from Sunday's biryani, and could ask for some of the babu's children's clothes which they'd outgrown . . ."

> In between, from the kitchen, the wife says excitedly, "Mister, even rice and daal is now only for the affluent—daal is six rupees a kilo. You're not being practical, change your thinking!"

Last Saturday, in the afternoon

The taxi bearing license plate WBT 9999 mysteriously disappeared after a hoodlum with a cleaver boarded it on Chittaranjan Avenue

Apparently, the detective branch of the police department is doing their best to find the taxi

G. Agarwala, the Assistant Commissioner of the detective department, announced

Did the taxi passenger really kill someone on Chittaranjan Avenue with a cleaver?

Was the blood-covered person taken to Medical College?

Did the taxi driver cross Lenin Sarani and escape down Jawaharlal Nehru Road, instead of handing the hoodlum over to the police?

"All these angles are being investigated in dee-taaa-il . . ."

A witness's complaint:

Despite having contacted the control room at Lalbazar police headquarters, the police did not pay any heed . . .

Was he pouring his heart out to his lover then, at that time . . . He was advised to phone the relevant police station himself and inform them . . . "I don't have the time now . . ." he was told

When Mr. Agarwala's attention was drawn to this matter, he said—

"The rule is that the control room itself shall immediately inform the local police station, and put out the information to everyone."

"But on the day of the incident, did the control room inform the respective police station about the disappearance of the rogue taxi?"

"The matter is being investiga-a-a-a-a-a-ted . . ."

"Questions please!"

"Why did the taxi driver escape with the hoodlum, and not hand him over to the police, when he had been threatened with a knife?"

"Why why why?"

"Why why wh-yyy?"

That means on Saturday afternoon

The driver of taxi number 9999 is also a rogue

A bloody cleaver
flashing at his back
Let these inconsistencies be investigated
In broad daylight . . . in the afternoon . . . in the open
Brandishing a cleaver, in front of so many people . . .
. . . .
The gentleman was dressed . . . like a gentleman
His hair was well-combed, brushed back
Sparkling clean-shaven jaw
And above all, a gentleman
Meaning, it was definitely a gentleman
Then . . .
Then what?

Unseen

In the early afternoon, in front of Metro Cinema
A knife brandished, ornaments snatched
Car stolen
A knock at the door at midnight
The schoolmaster's lovely wife
Taken away
Bank robbery   train robbery
"Mister, simply removing the train's fishplate
and selling these for two or three rupees—
If you venture into the interior, you'll
understand the plight of the country—
Everyone's out to fend for themselves, in one
way or another
It's utter anarchy, mister . . ."

We are in danger
we babus
who are neither here nor there . . .
That means we are really not safe anymore, boudi!
Our lives and possessions, our youthful desires,
wife-and-children, the chastity of mothers and sisters . . . everything . . . everything whatsoever . . .
Speak, Madam,
do say something—

Unseen, the public
"Where's the police—your police?"

Bombs drop on the courtyard. Bombs drop on the bedroom. Bombs drop on the bed. Three bull-like zombies
dragged his wife and laid her on the dining table.

> Unseen, Leader No. 1 cries out: "Beware—don't
> arouse the masses unnecessarily!"

> Unseen, Leader No. 2 cries out: "Everything's going
> to ruin. The red sun's not risen! No kingdom of
> heaven in the future! Beware! Ruin! Beware!"

> Unseen, the editor cries out: "Beware! Stand guard
> at the fence against obscenity. So that we can read
> together with our mothers and sisters . . ."

Amid all those cries, his wife lay supine, and then, right on
top of the table, they spring into action . . .

> "It's a real scene, mister   in my own house   my wife
> I'm journalist Patra from Orissa   I'm Patra, the journalist . . ."

Unseen, the intellectuals, with loud voices

"Set everything aside and speak
Speak like a gentleman
Even protest has to be
Expressed in proper language,
Doesn't it?"

"Setting everything aside—what shall I say, mister
In front of my very eyes
My own wife was . . ."

"Oh, this habit of you lot
Becoming agitated at the drop of a hat!"

He was stabbed in broad daylight for not giving an adequate puja donation, under the papaya tree outside his own house.   He's in the hospital

At dawn on Saturday, on Hyde Road, six or seven youths dragged a fifty-year-old gentleman belonging to a rival political party out of bed, threatening him with a sharp dagger. At 10 A.M. in the morning . . . "You've come to cast your vote haven't you? Your vote has already been cast, you can go home. There, at the curb of the lane on the left, next to the milk depot, look—we're treating everyone to Limca, do have some, sir." Jumping from the fifth floor of PG Hospital, Harimohan Das, retired headmaster, committed suicide. He had five sons and three daughters, but after he was admitted to the hospital no one came to enquire about him, no one at all.

A gang of mastaans. All of them entered the house, one after another. The girl—a case of rape. After that, her private parts were burned, little by little, using lit cigarettes, to their great delight. The girl lost consciousness and remained that way for sixteen days. The complaint stated that they did this after being incited by the leaders of a political party. At first, the police were unwilling to register the complaint.

The youth charged with murder was released very soon, for lack of evidence. No one came forward to testify against him. And there was such a carnival of bomb explosions to celebrate his release that the people in the locality were unable to stir out of their homes for three days and three nights. Bomb shrapnel hit the eyes of a seventy-year-old man. A few splinters could be removed from his left eye, the right eye is still . . .

The only son of a professor died in a nursing home. The injection that he was given in the emergency room was spurious, it was ineffective.

At a voting center in central Calcutta, around afternoon, as five to seven youths laughingly claimed the identities of women voters, the electoral officer said: "Fine, fine, everything's just fine, please cast your votes." The agent of the opposition party was, at that time, engrossed in probing his ears with a matchstick.

The accused, Gautam Roy, a.k.a. Bhulu, was killed in public, inside the courtroom, in broad daylight. It was stated that when the accused was about to enter the courtroom, some youths suddenly, and without any apparent provocation, fired at his head. This happened inside a crowded courtroom, in front of the judge.

A prior arrangement had been made between the engine driver and his coworkers—the train would slow down, and the looters would take away the coal. On the day of the accident, there was an altercation between all parties regarding the division of spoils. The coal-lifters were not willing to give more than forty rupees to the engine driver and twenty rupees each to the other workers. They were so preoccupied with the matter of their share that they did not even have time to look at the signal. And so the train collided head on with another train standing at the station. More than two hundred people were killed in the collision and about a thousand people were injured.

At dawn, the entire locality was surrounded, and a search for the criminals was initiated. Police entered and searched one house after another. An opposition leader declared with great perturbation that mothers and sisters had been dishonored. In the end, ten or twelve innocent youths were taken away, on the pretext of questioning.

A group of youths entered a voting center in the southern fringes of the city around evening, a sheaf of papers in their hands: "The sons-of-swine aren't coming, give us their ballot papers!" The officer smiled and accommodated their demand. Together, they stamped the ballot papers and stuffed them in the ballot box, and when the opposition party protested loudly, they said: "Don't shout, sir, be quiet. If you don't like it, go away, and if you make any trouble . . ." Well, there were a few rifle-bearing policemen standing outside.

As a result of using inferior quality cement, sand, and steel, and having the work overseen by an ordinary mason rather than a civil engineer, the house that an upper-division clerk constructed with his life's savings and bribes collapsed within two months, and the whole family was buried under the debris.

In a village in Nadia district, in West Bengal, all four

daughters of a gentleman consumed rat poison and . . . The saris that the gentleman bought for his daughters were extremely cheap, the girls did not like them.

There was a watch on the wrist, an expensive ring on a finger. As the train was about to leave . . . the entire arm from the elbow . . . using a sharp cleaver.

After he was released on bail, the criminal charged with murder went to the officer-in-charge of the police station and pleaded: "Let me keep the den." He had to be allowed to continue running the gambling and illicit liquor den. This was his livelihood. "Should the poor die?" he asked.

In a voting center in north Calcutta, a sixty-year old woman had come to cast her vote. A youth was joking around inside with the poll agent, his mouth full of paan, and smoking a cigarette. Seeing the woman, the youth asked her to stamp on a particular symbol. The woman said: "You are like my youngest son, dear. I know whom I should vote for." The boy (employing a particular demeanor) replied: "As soon as one gets married, kids are born, auntie, but politics is something else, so stamp where I tell you!" And then, in front of the electoral officer, he snatched away the paper, stamped on it, and put it into the ballot box. The agent of the opposition party was then gazing at the rafters on the ceiling.

Slowly, in the background, a light appears. It becomes bright. The whole world steadily comes to light.

> — "Stop shouting! Quiet! In a democracy, a couple of incidents like this always happen."
> — "I shouldn't shout?"
> — "No! Stop shouting! The neighboring country will hear it."

The masses are stunned. They keep saying: "But, but . . ."
—"Aren't you citizens of a great country . . . shame-
ful . . ."
— "But . . ."
— "There are no buts. There can't be. Be quiet.
Everything will be all right."
One person is very suspicious. Sniffing, she advances,
trying to get as close as she can.
— "Who are you, sister?"
— "Oh dear, brother-in-law—don't you recognize
me?"
She bares her arms, one after the other, five and five, ten
in all. Autumn sets in. Bell-metal gongs sound everywhere.
Hussain drew his picture in exactly this way, didn't he?

I'm Kali, when necessary
Krishna when necessary
A devotee of Rama, too, when necessary
Boons I grant, and offer sacrifices too, you see
Sometimes large-hearted and sometimes
Hitler-hearted . . .
Because Ashok Maharishi married my paternal
aunt's mother-in-law's
Maternal grandmother
I have glued his wheel to the country
With Fevicol.

Everyone bows their head and pays obeisance. The light
washes over their heads.
Some unruly rogues lower their heads and mutter, perhaps the Goddess's fishy odor had entered their noses . . .
"Tell me, oh tell me, Mother, why so much blood?"

The drop scene comes down. Shehnai music spiked
with cabaret
The child dances, the mother dances, the ministers
and bureaucrats dance
The hoe dances, the spoon dances, pots and pitchers
dance
Dear Mother, Firozini, let's see you dance
Let's see you just dance, and dance

Everyone looks askance. The police come running to
enquire about the meaning of all these words. He feels
threatened, and he starts singing a self-authored folk song,
in Runa Laila's voice—

Whenever I go to the riverbank at the rear
Mister Bleeder, the fount of knowledge
Lifts up his clothes and pees
Gushingly he pees

But why's "Bleeder" in the song? The minister comes running. The leader himself comes running from the party
office—

Politics in the name of Art
is not permitted

Keeping in mind the tune and rhythm, he then changes
"Bleeder" into "new son-in-law"—

The new son-in-law is a fount of knowledge
He pees in his pants

Gushingly does he pee
Whenever I go to the riverbank at the rear

From nearby, someone remarks: "Isn't this going in another direction?" Another person responds: "Let that be, this is much safer than politics. And politics now means left-ist politics—it's the fashion now. But there's never any obscenity in folk music."
The police and the public twirl their moustaches
Tapping to the beat, they enjoy the sacred arts

"Do you know what's the most ancient substance found on Calcutta's soil? A six-million-year-old oyster shell, nothing else, just this shell, a shell."

So who decides?

Smiling, Boudi puts her hand on the shiny turntable and asks, in jest: "Begum Akhtar or Bob Dylan?" And then, at once . . . The Chowdhurys had a huge, old mansion. A huge, green phonograph cone attached to a small box-like windup gramophone . . . "*Bajubandha khule khule jaay* . . ." A dog with its face to the cone. Faiyaz Khan sahib on a 78-rpm record, singing the raga Darbari Kanara. A gale breaks out, making the sky look distressed. Sitting alone in the darkened veranda, and listening to the just-acquired Faiyaz Khan sahib. Standing on the veranda, hunched forward with her head bent down, Ranu-di looks at the gale blowing outside. Ranu-di had just begun to wear saris. "*Bajubandha khule khule jaay* . . ." Feel like laughing now. And then, just then, he saw—why is the dog white? Like Ranu-di's neck—white. Definitely an English dog? Its ears hang down. Has a collar round his neck. Boudi's sister, Nandu, entered and said: "What was the song you mentioned—'Oh milk-maid sister' . . . ?" "No!" "I rummaged through all the old records, we don't have anything like that. Haven't ever heard the name of Bedana Dasi. I found an old record of Dilip Roy." She blows the dust off the record. "'Drums resound on the battlefield' . . . Shall I play that?" He looks directly into her eyes. "With every wish, I swing in bliss, I'm a wild-flower, dear . . ." But she didn't mention it was Kanan Devi's record. Nandu was completing her MA in psychology that year, she was very keen to take up research on the attitudes of slum-dwellers . . . A lot of dirt has accumulated on the neck. Get terrible prickly heat these days. Someone has said that if the prickly heat's bad, one should see a doctor.

Just like race horses have pedigree—who's the sire, who's the mother—similarly, old merchant families have genealogical tables, the family background, so to speak. Robi Thakur had it too, it was published recently—want to see? They've got a copy at the library of our own recreation center. It's on the strength of such pedigrees that people get jobs. "Who do you have, boy? I say, did your grandpa retire as district magistrate—or at least a minor official in some government department? Do you have any family background—which college did you graduate from? Just a degree—there are so many people with BAs and MAs tramping the streets of the city. Nothing comes of that. At least get a letter of recommendation from someone of position—or can't you get even that?"

The officer-in-charge dictates

— "Before he was killed, the man was wearing a dirty pair of pajamas, torn at the cuffs—a saffron-brown khadi punjabi, black-framed spectacles on his nose—"
— "Shall I write saffron-brown?"
— "Not exactly saffron-brown, when it fades, saffron-brown becomes a dull color."
— "So what shall I write?"
— [Scratching his head] "No point bothering about all that, write saffron-brown."
— "But the color's not saffron-brown."
— "I can't express in language what exactly the color is—colors can be so complicated . . ."
— "Had a book in his hand."
— "Which book was it?"
— "It was . . ."
— "The title on it was *Non-violence*, the author was Manik Bandopadhyay."
— "Everything's getting mixed up—the book *Non-Violence* was not supposed to be in his hand—apparently they don't believe in nonviolent politics—by custom, it should be a book of poems by Sukanta Bhattacharya."
— "Perhaps he wasn't able to obtain that . . ."
— "Keep quiet. Is it really necessary to lay so much emphasis on the book?"

Lord Ramakrishna shines bright in the picture
Lying with his head on Mother Kali's lap

The cuntry advances, the people get more than their

salaries, just like the neighbor's wife was better than the wife in one's own home. The lowly, paan-chewing clerk at the Writers' Building takes a lick of the lime and tells the man beside him: "You know Mukherjee—when the lights are turned off, all are equal. Everyone gets aroused by exciting things." The freshly-recruited boy—he's also an intellectual, who writes in little magazines to boot— replies: "Do you know, Sen-da, there's a play by Brecht about a soldier who returns home after war to find that a smuggler has gotten his girlfriend pregnant. He doesn't get alarmed by this, instead he too seduces someone else's wife and runs off with her." But Sen does not like all this intellectual talk, he pretends to ignore the callow youth. "Forget about your Brecht, remember what happened in our own Mohsin Building about a year and a half back . . . in the darkness of twilight, a forty-year-old hag had a fourth-class staff member who was her son's age . . . it's the same thing, tell your Brecht to learn from us . . ." He gets annoyed, seeing someone standing at his table clutching a file, he waves his hand: "Can't do all that now . . . it's tiffin break . . . Come later, boy . . ."

— "Bengalis are done for. Getting screwed everywhere in India."
— "Bound to happen, too . . . What else can you expect when we fuck each other in the ass."
— "If only Subhas babu had arrived that day, together with the Indian National Army, then you'd have known . . ."

A large rooster was feeding near the heap. Enormous, black-and-brown in color, the comb on his head a bright red. Half running, half flying, he jumped and climbed to the top of the heap. And then, ensconcing himself comfortably there, swelled his throat and began crowing in victorious pride . . . cuck-koo-roo-koo-koo. A plump white hen came flying and took her place beside him, and the two of them—with their fierce claws—began scratching the dirt on the heap, began crowing and cackling and the distance keeps increasing . . .

Ranu-di: "You can't deny that among middle-class folk like you and me—even if there are only very few—some people have realized that the affluence of ten percent of society is paid for by the hardship of ninety percent of the people. They realize that perhaps it's not right. Are compelled to realize. But until now, they have not been able to overcome the delusion of fine words like elections, democracy, human rights and so on—perhaps it would be quite accurate to express it like that."

Unseen, Ramayan

"Your trade union movement, party politics, private property, wages-profit-production, industrial relations, self-reliance—the complex developments associated with your economic evolution, remain mere complicated words in our consciousness, they don't exist in reality"

Fundamental rights and suchlike are the talk of a specific class of people. They lack any meaning until the common people in our country—who never bother about such things, nor shall they do so in the future—attain aware-ness. No one will go to court on the grounds that, by the imposition of Emergency, he has lost his right to speech, he can't even think about the rudimentary aspects of this. For the majority of the people, democracy means going to cast their vote, the question of whether one is able to vote, or of how he is compelled to sell his freedom to vote—such matters are not transparent to him in the normal course of things.

Ramayan Chamar

"The High Court and the Supreme Court are for mon-eyed folk
The police and administration are for the folk with money
Parallel to the court case, the bosses use the police, use the administration, to harass and torment. From '74 until today, the police camp hasn't left the colony for even a day, can you imagine that—and Section 144 too"

For the majority of the educated and semi-educated peo-ple, who have been kept in such conditions according to a plan—whether you speak of autocracy or fundamental rights—the fact remains that all these are merely words devoid of meaning; and our ruling class takes advantage of the opportunity to the fullest—our own weapons wound us.

Ramayan Chamar

"On a dark night, a thatch-roofed village house was set on fire, thanks to the links between the landlord and the police, and we became the accused, whether or not we had anything to do with it

"A village boy suddenly went off somewhere one day. His father was bribed to file a complaint with the police that we had kidnapped him. Of course, soon enough, the lost boy returned merrily, but the case dragged on, and we had to be present for the court hearings

"My wife was kept in the police lockup all night—do you know why? She had apparently stolen and drunk the babu's milk"

It is becoming very clear that to keep the hegemony unchallenged, people's helplessness and impotence has to be ensured and perpetuated. Don't dare protest, the one who bears it, lives—this sermon must be broadcast everywhere.

Ramayan Chamar

"Can you imagine, for the last year and a half, not a drop of the allotted kerosene oil has come. The tea estate manager's brother is the kerosene oil dealer of this locality. We have been living in darkness for a year and a half"

Because most of the people in our country are illiterate, they have an innate weakness when it comes to the printed word. Whenever they see something in print, they believe it is divine truth. The people who have monopoly over literature and culture know very well about this weakness of the largely illiterate people of our country.

Diary, which was written ten years ago

Not merely left or right politics, my battle is against anything connected with every kind of establishment—which suppresses people and does not let them be fully human.

As he writes the letter, he yearns for a cigarette. While smoking a cigarette he also smokes two beedis, which is very common with him. Searching for the beedis, he sees the back cover of a weekly magazine lying on the table—a clothing company's advertisement. What magnificent colors in the advertisement—the chap is wearing a gorgeous shirt and almost-naked girls are falling all over him. Even a laboring man, whether or not he knows how to read and write, is supposed to be drawn to this advertisement. His servant boy too will most definitely see the advertisement while dusting the table and, for sure, his twelve-year-old daughter as well. All the bosses who paid to get such advertisements printed were the ones who reviled his writing as lacking in basic decency. He was apparently, through his writing—let's take the description of the incident relating to the advertisement—poisoning society and wholesome culture. They do say that, but so also do those who ought to be thinking about, evaluating, and considering the description. Perhaps most people can't think for themselves. They are content to get by relying on others' thinking, which is something corresponding to their likes, at least in this chapter of the social system . . .

The society lives in the middle-ages, can you change

society, mister, with ten or twenty schools and colleges
and two or four factories?

The zombie pops out
from behind the green curtain

"Yes, we shall take advantage of just this, misters, exactly
like we did earlier. We'll set the CPI(M) against the Naxalites and set the Naxalites against the CPI(M)—there'll
be fratricide between the shits, and then we'll come to
power—ha ha ha."

The first wife looks like fire
The middle wife a blessing
The last wife's a working cunt
She shags by secretly glancing

— "Tell me, the reference to the first wife, middle wife
and last wife—what's the meaning of all this?"
— "That's my question too."
— "I see you highlight social exploitation in your writing,
but the conflict does not have a clear face, it's almost as if
there's no analysis at all . . ."
— "Perhaps there's a lot that still remains unclear despite
all the supposed awareness . . ."

Just past the house, the rawk, past the rawk the road
Confabulation all around
Visible in a long shot
a handcart bearing corpses,
goes from Baranagar towards the Ganga

"The newspapers are for the babus doing politics and for the bhadralok working in offices. We don't read all that." An open, overflowing drain on the narrow dark alley in Pathuriaghata. Wasn't it in some lane in Pathuriaghata that Saratchandra found Kironmoyi? Bihari works in the flour-mill—"Forget about a bonus, I don't get even my wages on time. Whether or not our girls and boys even have underwear to hide their shame, does that in any way affect the babus' pleasure-seeking lives?" Who do you mean when you say babus? "People exactly like you." Bihari spits, and then says, "Those who spend hundreds of thousands of rupees every Durga Puja on lights, mics, pandals, and fireworks. Here, in Line No. 31 basti, most of the people are workers in small workshops and factories, rickshaw-pullers, it's where the day laborers live." There's a quarrel at the water-tap. Bihari takes a burnt-out beedi and tries to light it a few times. Failing, looking directly into my eyes, he says, "Please give me a cigarette. My mouth's gone rotten from smoking beedis." Bihari's wife makes paper packets with old newspapers and works as a part-time maidservant in two homes. Their twelve-year-old son has just started working in the coal-briquette factory, carrying a sack of briquettes on his head, to deliver from house to house. In a corner of the one-room house, a bunch of night-flowering jasmine is spread out on a wet gamcha. A seven-year-old girl—wearing a dirty, torn dress—makes garlands. Her jutting spine can be clearly seen through the opening of the buttonless dress. Bihari says: "This is my middle daughter. Do you want to hear? She goes in the evening with her brother, Kartik, to Notun Bazar to sell garlands. For ten to fifteen paise a piece. People haggle a lot, they look for the cheapest price. Three for four annas. Has to pay eight annas a week to the police, or else they won't let her sit in the market. But that's not all . . ." Bihari takes a few deep puffs of the cigarette. "Do you know what happened one day? A babu passing by on a rickshaw took as many as eight garlands and got back into the rickshaw and went off in the direction of Sonagachi. Because she's still a child, she couldn't understand properly at first. But once she began to shout, not so loudly though, the rickshaw had already turned down some lane." The man spat again.

> Hearing the girl shout, people gathered. A babu in freshly-laundered clothes aired his viewpoint: "All these girls are rascals. Full of lies. They cheat people. A girl like that passed off a rotten egg to me once. She's hidden the money somewhere. Pull off her underwear and look!"

Notun Bazar comes into view. I observe myself as I buy garlands with my wife and her two sisters. The girl squats on her haunches. Her buttonless back is clearly visible, her spine juts out. My two sisters-in-law on both sides, one in a *Love Story* dress, the other in an *Ek Duuje Ke Liye* salwar-kameez—my three-hundred-rupee printed-silk wife behind us . . . "You tell me, can you get a decent sari—one that can be worn to go out sometimes—for less than two hundred fifty to three hundred rupees nowadays? Tell me . . . After all, I'm not asking for a thousand- or thousand-five-hundred-rupee sari like the bourgeois girls of Ballygunge and Gariahat—I too know a little bit about people's hardship and suffering . . . don't I? Tell me . . ."

A close-up of a grain-seller in Sealdah comes into focus: "Aren't you a bonus-receiving babu? You get a bonus of a thousand or a thousand and a half, and while buying eggplant for a kilo a rupee, you say— Hey, you're asking too much, boy—fine eggplant's selling for eighty paise a kilo."

At Gariahat crossing, written on a neon-lit shop: "Please don't embarrass us by asking for cotton handloom saris." And at the crossing of Hatibagan market, in a ready-made garments store, hangs an advertisement in big letters: "Limited Stock. Come with your ration card and pick up an original *Love Story* frock here."

"Ranu-di, for me Marxism is not a rigid ideology. Rather, it is a living philosophical inspiration. The dialectical inspiration of the analysis is what brings out its secret meaning. It does not confine us, does not keep us static, in one place. It takes us to the sky, but with feet planted firmly on the ground."

Now, in such a situation, the Naxalite youth who introduced himself thus, comes to Joba's house to hide there. Joba is the name of a whore who lives in Sonagachi. This Naxalite youth, on whose smoothly-shaved cheek even a fly would skid, who wears a watermelon-colored punjabi—he actually wanted to be a poet too, at one time—this poet-cum-Naxalite-cum-debutante boy would, in the first instance, abuse his father, calling him an animal for siring him, and in the second instance, weep in memory of his father and flood the stage. Wouldn't be bad to lay out a revolutionary play like this, with Sartre's respectable prostitute by one's side. (After all, how many people have read Sartre?) Please tell me, dear reader, how great would that be?

Scenes from a cyclone

A heated exchange began between the minister of health, the minister of disaster management and relief, the chief secretary, and the district collector regarding the precise number of deaths. A week after the cyclone, the chief secretary announced that the dead numbered ninety-three. Immediately, the minister of health declared: "No, the number is one hundred forty-eight. I have visited the affected areas. I can present the names and addresses of the dead persons if necessary." When the minister of health openly challenged the statement of the chief secretary in this manner, the chief minister was not in the capital, but was traveling in north Bengal on party work. Consequently, no one else wanted to open their mouths until he returned. There were only mutterings in chamber after chamber. The district collector alone continued to issue statements unilaterally: The government's position, that only about ninety persons died, was incorrect. The minister of health was unable to give the correct figure. "Actually, the number of dead exceeds two hundred. Cholera and gastroenteritis are spreading rapidly in the affected areas, about fifty-six people have lost their lives, and yet the health department has sent neither doctors nor preventive medicines. There is no coordination between the officers of different departments in the Writers' Building, no one pays any heed to anything. Everyone carries on according to their own whims and fancies." Hearing the district collector's complaint, the minister of health was incensed: "All this is a conspiracy against me. Death can occur through three means—first, through cholera; second, through gastroenteritis; and third, through consuming contaminated food. Besides, people also die per usual. The fifty-six persons that the district collector declared dead—can he provide any evidence that all of them died of gastroenteritis? I challenge him: if he can prove it, I shall quit office." Calling another press conference, he announced: "No one went anywhere, mister, while I went from village to village and saw everything with my own eyes. Let a commission of inquiry be instituted to determine exactly how many people died of gastroenteritis, and I shall accept the report. Actually, people have died because of lack of relief supplies, which does not fall into the purview of the department of health. And the district collector is an idler." Immediately after the announcement, there was an uproar among the ministers. They split into three or four camps and began issuing statements according to their own positions. The relief minister and the minister for municipal affairs issued separate statements from their respective chambers regarding the number of deaths. Journalists began running from one chamber in the Writers' Building to another, collecting press releases. The final press release was issued by the chief secretary. He said: "The chief minister is now traveling in north Bengal on party work. Until his return, howsoever many statements may be issued, none of them can be considered to be correct." He was continuously shouting and screaming over the phone. He was very infuriated with the union leaders of a particular region. Matters went very far.

There, one can see—dogs are eating corpses, decomposed corpses are being found even nine days after the cyclone. A mother with a tightly-clasped child in the crook of one arm, a broken branch of a tree in the other. Mother and son, bodies bloated, a terrible stench all around. Beside the lake, one can see a dog tearing away and eating a little girl's decomposed body. Lying dead, all of them, for nine days and nine nights. The government's speedboats shuttle around here and there, the roar of the engines of the racing VIP boats

— "Are there parties where you live?"
— "Parties?"
— "The ones who say, 'Vote for us.'"
— "Yes, there are babus."
— "Do people go?"
— "People go when there's a meeting."
— "Don't you go?"
— "No . . . I went to Calcutta once, a long time ago, the babus took me."
— "Did they give you money?"
— "Who gives money . . . but they did give us rotis . . ."
— "Which party?"
— "I don't know, sir—how can you expect us to know all that?"

"You see me as a business executive, don't you? A huge office, air-conditioning, expensive furniture, a pretty secretary, a hefty check at the end of the month. But this is the tiger's cage of the whole circus—heavy steel rods on the outside, no way out. Only work and more work. And responsibilities. It's been ages since I looked at the sky. Trees and greenery? Look, I've arranged cacti and leafy plants in brass tubs in the drawing room."

Babus' houses are built in the city, the man works as a mason's assistant. Been doing that for the last twenty years. Carts bricks on his head all day long, at night he snores on a jute mat spread on the damp earth. His home is in Canning. Gets one day off a week, and after receiving his wages, he goes to visit his family. Look, there he goes, look—

"I don't need to know what Marx said, tell me what Jyoti Basu says. Don't try to bring in foreigners at the slightest pretext, look at the soil of your own country instead—"

"I had a teashop at the bus stand. It was taken down. Started another shop on a curb in the neighborhood, but the number of people buying on credit began to exceed those paying each day. It soon became a den for the neighborhood's hooligans, those wayward and emerging mastaan boys, who sat on the wobbly bench all day long. I got angry a couple of times. They threatened me in return: 'This is public land—you don't pay taxes, you think you'll get away with free income? If you make too much noise, we'll kick you out.' Another person advised me: 'Do you think the shop can run merely by selling tea? Sell booze. The nighttime customers are the real customers . . .' So I'm thinking of selling booze now."

— "And you?"
— "Cine-journalist."

— "Doesn't that mean you write features about whether Uttam Kumar picks his teeth after eating, or which side Rakhee likes to sleep on?"

— "Yes, I write that, because that's what people want to know. The public shows greater enthusiasm for reading about all this, rather than your revolutionary stuff . . ."

— "I don't believe that."

— "I say this from my twenty years of experience as a journalist. People are more keen to know about celebrity gossip pertaining to Uttam Kumar than about China's political situation after Mao's death. And we survive by selling all those news stories. And so our newspaper sells too."

— "Even now, in 1981?"

— "Definitely."

— "In all these years, haven't people attained a minimum level of political awareness?"

— "That's for you to think about. Do you remember that the publication of various obscene sex magazines shot up like anything in West Bengal at the very time of the Naxalite movement? Let me tell you a story, a story from our own profession of journalism. The police recovered a girl's dead body from Dhakuria Lake. It looked like a case of murder. I reported the news. 'The dead body of an unidentified woman was recovered from the lake yesterday. From the injuries to the body, the police suspect it to be a homicide. Nobody has been arrested yet.' Our rival newspaper printed in bold letters on the front page: 'Lovely Lady's Dead Body in Lake—City Agitated.' After that a one-and-a-half column story, half crime report and half something akin to a thriller. The editor called me and said: 'What do you think you're doing? The rival newspaper's beat us. Has the ink in your pen run completely dry, or what?'"

The publishing medium of the arts
and the social system
which uses the media
for serving their interests . . .
A mouse races
over the lines

All of us know that, among the birds, the eagle and the vulture are the ones that fly the highest in the sky. We read in the papers that quite a few planes are damaged each year by vulture strikes. That a pony was born of a calf, that the sahibs love to eat daal and chochchori—some papers lovingly publish such news, using bold type, right on the front page. That the crow was not behind any other bird in the matter of flying high—I read this story in the newspaper the other day. When members of an expedition set out on a Himalayan trek, besides all their supplies and the sherpas, the companions accompanying them were crows. Greedy for food, a crow can easily fly to an altitude of nineteen or twenty thousand feet. The crow is a very strange creature. It can eat anything—from dead, decomposed rats to murgh musallam—with equal relish. This incident happened fifty-five years ago. The Everest expedition was on. The members of the expedition were setting up camp, one after another. They reached an altitude of 27,000 feet. No sign of anything living. The climbers had masks on their faces and oxygen cylinders strapped to their backs. Only ice everywhere. The temperature steadily fell below zero degrees Celsius. At this altitude, even in that frightening environment, the climbers saw a bird. Jet black in color, the sun's rays gleaming on its body. Greedy for food, a crow hovered behind them that day. So think about what a creature the crow is!

When we find it very difficult to give a donation of five rupees to the party fund, they laughingly donate one hundred rupees. The dadas in the neighborhood who are into politics mind their ways a bit. When we go around the houses to collect donations, we are invited inside and requested to sit. Offered tea. They eagerly ask about what we do, how far we've studied, and so on. And then before we can ask, they take out a crisp fifty-rupee note and give it to us with a soft smile: "I can't give any more than this today, brother . . ."

The young beggar girl stands on the pavement on Chowringhee and gazes with astonishment at all the captivating things in the stores—all these things, so many things, what do people need them for? The young wife had come to beg, a nice body, smallpox scars on her face. From her womb would the future hoodlum—begotten by a babu—be born. The unbearable length of desolate Mahatma Gandhi Road would be left behind.

Future hoodlum
Yeh haath nahi, phansi ka phanda hai

You must hear Beethoven's Fifth Symphony here, conducted by Toscanini, if you can find a copy. Of course, listening to the Ninth would be the best, the hair on your head will stand on end. To understand the difference, and to remember it, it's also necessary to hear Mendelssohn and Schubert, here, in this environment . . . A lifetime's perspiration will break out on your body, you'll keep perspiring.

— "What you write—shouldn't one be able to understand it?"
— "A story about Picasso used to be in circulation at one time. An American youth came to Paris for a visit. He met a beautiful young woman. After they became intimate, the youth took the girl to his hotel room. Switching off the lights, he was unable to locate the appropriate parts in the appropriate places. The boy became terribly angry. Seeing his rage, the girl smiled and said: 'This was bound to happen, after all, I am Picasso's model . . .'"

A thousand multiplied by a thousand

From the drops of blood that trickled down to earth from the body of the battling Raktabeej, ever new Raktabeejs were born, and they joined the battle immediately. Their battle cries resounded in the air and sky. Although Chamunda Devi was bewildered, she did not pause. Without letting the contagious drops of blood fall to the earth, she sucked them up to her heart's content—so that the multiplication of Raktabeej offspring could be brought to an end.

In the course of all this, everything is coming true. Water flows under water, all the houses are being inundated speedily. They appear to tremble beneath the water. After a while, he advances. The road in front is entirely submerged, a powerful current of flowing water, chest deep.

Ranu-di's laugh, just then, at that very moment . . . After that, he is alone again. A day without rain, but stormy winds, sitting beneath the Monument, peanuts—absent-mindedly breaking the shells. That day, on that very day, under the Monument, some people . . . Reporters find an opening: "Altercation between two Naxalite groups under Shahid Minar on the issue of the May Day program venue!" All the bright neon signs at the cinema theater explode one after another, making splashes of sound. A sandstorm blows, while in front, all the people from the light of some erstwhile dawn, who buy garments of colors that match the advertisements. Darkness descends in its own way. In every direction, far below the honeycomb-like apartment blocks, the open drains of bastis and densely-packed tin roofs. "Everything exchangeable for money is exchanged"—a signboard hangs in front of mysterious buildings. He bravely pushes the door and enters . . . The pages torn out from the diary slip out and begin to flutter, then fly—although inside that mysterious room there is a gentle, cool breeze. The pages of the diary flutter and fly uncontrollably and chaotically, on and on, impossible to retrieve them, titters of the heavily made-up and lipstick-smeared Ranu-di's laughter, in the mild darkness.

At the end of the text, he, the writer, carries an unknown dead body on his shoulder, wrapped in a white sheet. So, did anyone die in this piece of writing? He carts and brings the dead body that's completely covered in the white sheet to the middle of the text, lays it on a table. Lying outside are the torn slippers he has removed, covered in dust, they compose another picture.

Unseen, the devotional chanting becomes a roar

Surrendering everything, with heart and mind
I shall most definitely be a slave girl
Oh de-e-e-e-e-ar
Don't ask questions
never ask questions
eat and live, get fucked in the ass
Ask questions and you'll go to jail
One nation, one life, unity
The masses of great India awaken

Sidestepping all this tumult and rumbling, the one in the dirty longcloth punjabi and knee-length dhuti, who seeks to live free of hassles, advances. Lakshmi and Satyanarayan puja performed regularly at home, at least one lottery ticket every month, as a rule . . . "Do you know, if you are caught taking bribes, your job's gone . . ." "I'll die, sir, I'll be completely finished, my children will die of starvation . . ."

Ranu-di

It's terribly hot today. Goats and cows on the field move to the shade under trees. There's a traffic jam in Sealdah. Just now, a man wearing a brown lungi went by under our window, tugging at a rope tied to a goat. The goat was bleating, *beanh, beanh*, it did not want to move. The man was hitting it with a stick. It must definitely be snowing in Darjeeling now. The clock tower in the jailhouse rings, *dong, dong,* it's two o'clock. An unrecognizable youth stands at the end of the road and waves toward our window, trying to convey something. I open the window a bit to hear. A stream of sunlight enters the room and at once we hear: "Leave the house and come down quickly, an earthquake's going to strike any minute!" The meaning of the words does not sink in immediately. I see an old beggar lying beneath our veranda, in the patch of shade. Beside him are a box and a staff. A stray dog sniffs the old man's face suspiciously. Craning my neck from the window upstairs, my head half in and half out, I can see. I can see the dog sniffing the old man's gray mustache and beard. The boy wearing punjabi-pajama, the unrecognizable boy—screams out once again at that moment. "Come down at once, there's going to be an earthquake right now!" From here, I can clearly see the boy's frantic gesticulations, the veins popping out on his throat as he screams.

Then, the future hoodlum, Ramayan Chamar, the girl from Metiabruz, as well as the writer, all of them together, all the same characters, begin screaming in complaint—

Ramayan Chamar

"I'm from Arrah in north Bihar. I was supposed to work in fields and farms. But you turned me into a tea-garden coolie."

The girl from Metiabruz

"What you've done to me . . . what's it called . . . it isn't complete, that's it, why don't you make me clearer, ple-a-se"

Future hoodlum, coming on to the stage

"At the time of the riots—am I alive or did I die?"

Phantom

"My character is not at all clear, how will people recognize me . . ."

Writer

"Whatever happened to me, where exactly am I?"

Go to the end of the text, there you'll see the bulb being removed from the table lamp on the writing table, the writer's member being inserted, and the switch being turned on, nearby the characters from Guernica have grabbed space and squatted. All of you know that the last ten pages are devoted entirely to a description of the storm, like in *The Tempest*. There, neither the characters nor the incidents are under the writer's control, they have determined their destinies by themselves . . . only the storm in the last ten pages, only the massacre, which indicates a change in the weather.

Unseen

The chorus of the Greek play emerges

One nation, one life, unity
The masses of great India awaken

A vulture from Antigone's crematorium comes flying. In

a rented flat on Camac Street, father and son begin quarreling over a girl. A bayonet is thrust into the chest of the most impartial clerk. Those who had nothing whatsoever to lose realize they're losing nothing. Who does what, who has which role—nothing can be understood clearly.

The characters are then no longer porters carrying the writer's luggage, it is the characters who set about controlling the writer. Oppression begins everywhere. The police step down from the Guernica. The description of just that in the last ten pages. And, of course, obviously, in such a narration, there are no paragraphs.

"It's funny, Ranu-di, that literature is a lie through which we try to understand the truth, at least the intelligible truth . . . I have an old habit of marking the text while reading books—three or four months ago, I had read a book on social economy, actually it was four interviews, or I should say more accurately, conversations between a famous sociologist and four persons, all of nearly the same caliber, and I had marked the text—now I find that almost every mark was made emotionally—in the wrong sense—and quite a bit of the elaboration and explanation too—or to say it correctly, a simple, straightforward ability to corroborate the complex subject, according to my own preference—I had done that, I don't mind admitting that now. Reading through a few pages of the book, I'm having to think anew now, about the issues raised in it— and also about the markings on the pages. I'm thinking, I've been biting my pen for a long time, the truth is that this arrogance on my part of writing Ramayan Chamar's tale is also only a pretense, an attempt to go close to the intelligible truth—where I myself am the impediment—but not to reach."

A hullabaloo begins everywhere
Far away, country-bombs rain down on Lenin Sarani
Thus, in all the commotion, who said what
Can't be heard clearly anymore

The cuntry advances through all this. Revolutionary thoughts as well as Shani worship increase dramatically. Science and palmistry become mutual rivals. An electronic watch around the wrist, and exactly six inches above that, the amulet of Baba Taraknath. The cuntry advances. Through the English-medium schools, the cut and style of clothes, marriage ceremonies and Happy Birthdays, through penciled eyebrows and free mixing with girls, the cuntry advances. Father speedily goes from being "Bapi" to "Dad." Mother, father, brother, sister, boyfriend, girlfriend, all of them together, in unison, get down on the dance floor. Hips swing and gyrate in a particular animal-like way. Seeing the vast jiggling field reaching from between the mother's breasts down to below her navel, the boy's friends put fingers to mouth and whistle, mother lovingly pinches their cheeks and says: "You naughty boys!" Modernity—fierce modernity, not to be outdone by the developed races. The cuntry advances.

This part must be read keeping in mind what the average per capita consumption of ninety-five percent of the people is, those who live permanently below the poverty line

---

Ramayan Chamar

"For the last year and a half, not a drop of kerosene reached the tea garden, can you imagine that? The brother of the tea-garden manager is the kerosene dealer, and our quarrel is with the manager. For a year and a half, we have been living in darkness, bribes have also been paid to the village council to make sure they don't do anything untoward. There was an announcement that the kerosene van was looted by someone while it was on its way to the tea garden, and that the delivery of kerosene was discontinued for that reason."

The home commissioner announced that the police had undertaken large-scale search operations since yesterday night in the concerned areas and recovered three thousand country-bombs and eight thousand quintals of explosives. They believe a huge quantity of illegal firearms is in existence across the country. They have discovered many secret arms-making workshops. A total of 20,370 illegal firearms, including rifles, guns, and pistols, were seized in a single day. According to the police, this figure does not include pipe-guns, cleavers, knives, and axes.

The zombie emerges from behind the green curtain

"We'll set the CPI(M) against the Naxalites and set the Naxalites against the CPI(M)—there'll be fratricide between the shits, and then we'll come to power—ha ha ha."

The first wife looks like fire
The middle wife a blessing
The last wife's a working cunt
She shags by secretly glancing

Ranu-di

"Everyone has one weak point or another . . . don't they?"

The neighborhood grandpa

"Nowadays boys reach puberty by the time they are twelve years old . . . See the furor at the neighborhood curb . . . the girls' school is about to let out now, you see . . ."

Phantom

"By strewing grains of wheat, I can get any domesticated hen to the bakul-lined alley, keeping at a safe distance. When I'm gnawing on that chicken's leg later that night— together with the necessary drinks—and when I think of how I lured it in, I'm unable to contain my laughter!"

The youth whose decapitated body will be found in the drain

On the 4:56 A.M. local train, a wagon full of pitchers of toddy goes to Calcutta, and from the 11:13 A.M. down train, professors from Calcutta, clad in dhutis with hanging pleats, disembark on their way to the local college—all the calculations are correct, aren't they?

The babu, umbrella in hand, who was run over by a bus

"Why do you try to write about what you don't know or understand, mister? Just think once about where the country is headed, day by day . . . It would have been different if Subhas Bose, together with the Indian National Army, could have entered the country that day . . ."

Ramayan Chamar

Unable to bear the torments of the hoodlums—extorting donations night and day—we've registered a few dozen police complaints. But the police station must surely have been displeased with our complaints because they only conducted a nominal inquiry, and did not find any evidence to support the complaints.

The officer-in-charge of the police station

"No untoward incident has occurred in the last twenty-four hours."

A Dalit leader from Bihar

"Between 1975 and 1980, there have been 56,596 incidents of oppression of Dalits, 1,852 people were killed, and 1,941 women raped. These are the government's figures. According to nongovernmental sources, the number of incidents is ten times greater. There are thousands of incidents of oppression that do not even find any mention in the newspapers."

Father

"Remove your watch and ring, son. Because I have seen with my own eyes, just as the train was about to leave, how an arm was severed at the elbow through the window of the train compartment, using a cleaver . . ."

Mother

"I'm touching the bel leaf blessed by Baba Taraknath to your head . . . keep it in your pocket, son. The picture of

Sai Baba is in the suitcase . . . Put it on your desk as soon as you reach . . . You'll see, son, there'll be no more danger or difficulty then."

An inspector on probation was informed over the phone at about 4 P.M. in the afternoon that there was a dead body inside a public toilet, with the face smashed in. It could not be identified. Later, the information was conveyed to the police. The dead body was removed at about 7:30 P.M. The tram conductor kept saying with a weepy face that he was forcibly pushed off the tram, and that kerosene was splashed and the tram was set on fire. They stood on the edge of the pavement and silently watched the front car of the tram being reduced to ashes. Killing, rioting, and looting began and spread across a very large area.

Leader

"A great evil power is at work in the country. Unparalleled goondaism has started all over the country . . ."

Clerk

"Do you understand—actually a world war is needed, or else military rule . . . otherwise nothing will happen . . ."

Diary

All the waters become one, there are connections between all the rivers . . .

The girl selling spinach on the roadside

"All the babus who work in offices, who walk with squeaking shoes . . . they take out a stick at the slightest pretext and torment us."

The Naxalite youth whose decomposed body would be found

"If India was a genuine democracy based on adult franchise, would the workers, peasants, and poor employees, who comprise ninety-five percent of the population, ever vote for the tiny minority to rule over them?"

The youth sitting at the rawk

"Quite sexy, really . . . When she walks along the road, swinging her hips, then, I swear on my mother, drums thunder in my chest."

Mother-and-child [Adhar Jena's wife]

"To be able to eat two handfuls twice a day . . . for fifteen days this month there was no cooking . . . And you want to play the husband?"

Jean-Paul Sartre

I saw the starving child die before my eyes. That's why the dilemma in the novel, *Nausea*, is now extremely irrelevant.

Mister Leader, who's built a house after having retired from politics

"Forget all this talk about the country, mister, wear silk clothes and recite the Gita every morning, especially the second chapter . . ."

Writer

"Remember this person—earlier he used to talk about revolution, now he goes around clad in khadi. Meanwhile, he's got a minibus permit. He shaves very carefully every morning. He unfailingly buys a 400-gram cut of fresh fish from the market. Just look at him, he has the demeanor of a most responsible citizen."

A reader, sotto voce

"What's this, mister . . . You're describing your own face . . . pipe down for heaven's sake . . ."

The very person described, clad in a lungi, shopping bag in hand, turns around suddenly, he confronts the writer:

> "Neither CPI(M) nor Naxalite, you occupy such a nice, opportunity-seeking halfway house, evading all responsibilities—fine fuckery, boy . . ."

A flat attaché case in the room, the stuff had been stored inside that. Filling up the box very carefully with the dynamite now, the lid was shut and fastened with tape. Now came the wooden clothespin and battery. Power would come from the battery—and the clothespin would function as a switch—meaning, at the right time, it would draw out the current from the battery . . .

> "By talking about deprived people
> You have taken literature to a nauseating place."

Hands trembling, the blasting cap was in place. One

mistake and the whole bloody country would explode to high heavens. Holding his breath, he took out a cable from the dynamite and joined it to the wooden clothespin. He attached another cable with extreme caution. Now there was only a small piece of plastic remaining on the path of the electric current.

"You are fickle-minded, perverted. And you have also cleverly laid out the rationale for the perversion."

A small hole inside the piece of plastic, he slid the string through that. He tied one end tightly and put the other end through a narrow hole already made earlier in the attaché case. It jutted out beneath the handle. Making a loop on the string, he cut off the remaining portion. If a finger was inserted into the loop and it was tugged, there would be an immediate explosion.

"After so long, you'll surely admit you have failed . . ."

He stuffed some papers inside the attaché case now— right on top, he kept Manik's *Non-Violence*, with a wry smile—so that the explosives couldn't be seen, so that even if the bag had to be opened for some reason, no one would suspect anything.

The dead body wrapped in a white sheet lay in the same way, in the middle of the whole incident. Whose dead body was it, why was it here, no one thought it necessary to open the sheet and look, no one even inquired. The soundtrack's completely silent. On television, the physical gyrations of Hindi films become excessive.

Writer

In the last scene, he will be seen with the terrifying dog that he had always wanted to feed poison to and kill.

Police officer

"The complaint against us, that for a 'consideration' we refrain from catching the real culprit, is not correct. Whenever we arrest someone for murder, assault and bomb-throwing, we find that he belongs to some trade union or another. There's continuous pressure from the top to release him . . . So tell me, what can we do . . ."

Ranu-di

"Look, look, see how the two plump pigeons sitting on the tile roof of Aru's cowshed clasp beaks and make love!"

Munia's dad

"Steel will be made in the furnace. Rolling will be done in the mill. But the contract labor shall remain contract labor, they will not be made permanent workers."

Munia's mother

"Smoked ganja again, have you—oh—don't you have any shame, may fire scorch the face of such a man."

Rabindranath

"How much money the babus have . . . bundles and bundles of notes . . ."

Maidservant

"Your smile clings to my melody."

College boy

"Irrespective of whether I do well in my studies or not, if an English newspaper is subscribed to at home, even today, here in the city fringes, in this locality, people talk to you respectfully—that's why I take an English newspaper."

Youth sitting on the rawk

"I'll toil on your behalf during elections. But I must get a minibus permit."

Diary

Quite naturally, it is people's wealth that's noticed, but look beyond the surface, there's deprivation everywhere, cries of distress and suffocation . . .

Ramakrishna

"The issue is climbing to the roof . . . you can do that using a staircase, or by climbing up a rope, or even by going up an unsanded bamboo pole."

Naxalite youth

"Our leaders get enraged with their nation when they don't get the votes. But once they get the votes, their love for the nation returns immediately."

Lover

"Whatever you may say, a woman's skin, her figure and her heavenly mystique is more significant than any other truth."

Herbert Marcuse

"Revolution does not mean merely a formal change in the social system, but a transformation of people's thinking, outlook, their innate faculties, objectives, and value system . . ."

Youth

"Shivlal Yadav's spin is going to work, isn't it . . ."

Drunk officer, whose wife flirts with the boss

"I swear on my mother, I don't like anything . . . *Believe me, I never wanted to be born.*"

Grandma

"No! You shouldn't let your feet touch the dog—his ancestor had accompanied Yudhishthira to heaven . . ."

Diary

When middle-class patriots come into contact with any Marxist thinking, their alienation from their roots has been seen to become steadily evident. Again, when they sought to maintain at least that connection, politically they kept pursuing only utmost confusion . . .

Bharatchandra

"Who thinks of tomorrow, everyone dies today
Afraid of getting pregnant, yet does it with hubby"

Naxalite youth whose body would be found in the drain

"We never shy away from the responsibility of building revolutionary violence in response to retaliatory
violence."

He wore deep green, a glittering star on the shoulder, an
automatic rifle in his hands. The prohibited military camp
was in one corner of the city, fenced off with barbed wire.
Everything was enveloped in the unknown and the mysterious . . .

— "Hey, want to come along to Calcutta in the procession? There's a meeting in the Maidan . . ."
— "Fuck the meeting. You just want to make us
walk! Return by train, without tickets . . . and let the
conductor catch me and put me in the lockup, right?"

Samar Sen

"I want to eat fruit but I cut the tree too—that's not
possible. I'll be a communist and yet be afraid of bad
omens—that's not possible. It is not possible to manipulate
the accounts of history. It is because it took us so long to
learn this truth that we see the crushing of aspirations
now, and our sons and daughters are beyond our control."

Charandas Baul

"My body was like a crematorium
Guru came and with a mantra
made it a flower emporium"

Tapasi, Mita, Krishna

"First the prospective groom's father and paternal uncle came, then the maternal uncles, and then the groom himself, together with his friends. All of them have to be offered sweets. And you know how expensive sweets are. After all, one can't offer them the four-anna sweets."

Ghost voter

"I'll eat the bones, the flesh too I'll eat
And with the skin, I'll make the drum beat"

Ashok Rudra

"No, it isn't there, it's really not there, nowhere in the world is there a booklovers' paradise like the books quarter of College Street. I sometimes get angry with the Bengali poets. Such ingrates they are—not a single poem has anyone written in praise of this beautiful and joyful books quarter . . ."

Maidservant

"I sent my thirteen-year-old girl to the babu's house to work. For food to eat. The youngest son of the house got her pregnant. And then he offers us money. Don't the bastards have mothers and sisters at home . . ."

Diary

All the problems of the whole country are tied up in knots and have reached such a stage that memorized incantations, yoga, hatha yoga, karate, socialism, Gandhism, Marxism-Leninism, Jyoti Basu, Sai Baba—nothing's going to come of all that. Day by day, the people . . . Just think about it . . . Getting agitated about everything, they want to get agitated . . .

Naxalite youth

"All this petit bourgeois whining and sniveling
Do something . . . anything"

Diary

It is the human who touches humans the most, and nothing else . . . It is only by overcoming weaknesses through small battles that you can move ahead to fight the big battle . . . Yes, only humans . . .

Yesterday was the third day of the disturbance. The group of rioting youths rained stones and bricks on the police. A second group began looting in other parts. Vandalism erupted. One warehouse after another was set on fire. The police fought a pitched battle with a few thousand youths all night. But yesterday, the police were fully prepared from the start. With their faces entirely masked and carrying riot shields, they confronted the rioters. Some policemen, wearing metal helmets on their heads, could be seen charging toward the youths. A press photographer reported that he had seen the rioters break down the door and enter the house of an affluent family. It's said that an unruly mob entered one house after another. The news spread like wildfire. The police officers were unable to restrain themselves . . . It was reported that to pacify the situation and to placate the rioters, a team of three MLAs got together and visited the disturbed area. The objective was to appeal for peace. The mob threw stones and broke the windshield of their jeep . . .

> Dog show, chrysanthemum exhibition, horse racing, the receptionist's bloodred lipstick-bearing lips and plunging neckline, the half-domestic girl in front of the cinema hall, the sharebroker, protest processions, Akashvani Calcutta: "I say to our farmer brothers, Sri Ramakrishna had said that after you have one or two children, you should live together like brother and sister."

Evaluating the gravity of the situation, a state of emergency was declared throughout the country. It was stated in the announcement that during the Emergency, all the rights of the citizens would be rescinded. Under these circumstances, the public should desist from going to court. Of course, in the announcement there was an assurance that the state of emergency was only a temporary arrangement. As soon as the rioters were suppressed, it would be lifted. Until then, everyone should act according to the law. Under no circumstances should Section 144 be violated or protest processions be taken out. Later, through radio broadcast, it was also clarified that the declaration of emergency did not mean imposition of martial law. The broadcast was immediately followed by military music.

When the announcement was being broadcast over the radio, the army had already moved into all the important places with assault rifles. Admittedly, in some places they faced stiff resistance, but in the very beginning the army and the police together were able to occupy the central offices of the agitating organizations, unanticipated.

Arriving here, taken aback, our Panu—hey, it's our Panu Mullick—screamed out: "I say, where did our cuntrymen go . . ." Saying so, bitter and annoyed, he slipped out of the opening in the broken wall and went off to the fields to do his business, his red, half-dirty gamcha on his shoulder

---

In an announcement, the Ministry of Home Affairs declared that all trade union activities in the country were now prohibited. The spokesperson remonstrated that the enemies of democracy were pushing the country toward civil war. He said: "We are not carrying out a military coup. Neither do we wish to impose any undemocratic autocracy. No military council has been instituted in place of the constitutionally valid administrative apparatus. The only task of the emergency is to restore law and order in the country. It is only those persons who are endangering national security who have been taken into custody."

In the back projection will be a woman, standing, the one who wears a dirty sari and brings toddy from Canning in an earthen pitcher—that she has to lose her honor to the home guard and policemen, and even the ticket checker, for not being able to pay the bribe asked for—she has accepted this as her normal fate

Immediately after the declaration of the state of emergency, curfew was imposed for an indefinite period. Shoot-on-sight orders were put into effect. Normal life was turned upside down. Shops and establishments were shut down. Military patrols were stationed at airports and in all the important places in the country. The whole country came under the control of the army in an orderly fashion. No one made the least noise anymore.

O mind, ignorant of the grand plan
Shyama's no ordinary girl, you know
Clad in the raiment of clouds
Sometimes she appears as a fellow

The monkey now climbs to the top of the arithmetical bamboo. The slippery bamboo and the funny monkey, who climbs up four feet, and then slides down five feet . . .

— "I am Captain Nemo, I escaped midway from the enemy's submarine and have now come to land. The funny thing is that my submarine runs not on oil but on seaweed. My propeller too was made using three-and-a-half-thousand-year-old marine algae that I had collected. Take me to the one among you who is most organic. I don't have any time to waste."
— "Some trouble with women or what, mister? If there's a woman involved in this, then the matter can be understood using one's brains, but if it's got to do with politics then you are destined to be in great trouble."
— "It's not about a woman, it has to do with a three-and-a-half-thousand-year-old seabed, a bit like the chaotic

justice undersea. I've been drawn to marine botany for a long time. I love to sprinkle fresh green algae on my food too."
— "The man's stark mad!"
— "Yes, before setting off into orbit I'd like to chew a piece of green algae. Take me to your nearest launching pad."

After that, the man would be compelled to reenact Christ's death. As he's about to die, a woman wearing a blue cloak would hold the Christ, whom he actually wanted to create, but for lack of imagination couldn't, and over the mic, one would keep hearing the final gasps of the companionless man on his journey to death. This would be relayed by microphone and the whole country would be made to hear it, on and on, which was the punishment for thinking without limits. The final gasps would go on getting transformed into the horrible mechanical sound of a crane, the horrible noise would grow louder and louder until it exploded with a horrendous bang at the edge of the audience's hearing, and the curtain would come down slowly, as was meant to be. In the final scene, he would be seen together with the terrifying black creature, the zombie, which he had wanted again and again to poison and kill.

Ramayan Chamar's final words to the writer:

"Mister, even the dog on the street bares its fangs when it's kicked,
And you're a *human being* . . ."

After a time, everything would turn cold. No one would utter even a word that might be considered politically wayward. Only one kind of politics would be in operation then—one nation—one leader. Bombs would rain on the neighborhood in broad daylight. Satta dens would emerge in rawk after rawk. The bomb-making business would reach even the village. The progressive bureaucrat would sit on his chair and shake his legs: "What's it to me—I shall pledge complete allegiance to whichever government comes at any time. After all, I have to keep my job." He'll keep laughing—like the knight laughs in *The Seventh Seal*.

The monkey will then keep climbing to the top of the arithmetical bamboo—the slippery bamboo and the funny monkey.

The moon will cast light upon the earth. Everywhere, drops of dew will rain down. The temperature will drop far below freezing. The streets will become dangerously slick. Nothing else on earth will be awake except for crickets. But the headless bodies of youths will continue to be found in the drains of Calcutta.

WHEN COLOR IS A WARNING SIGN

BI-COLOR ON THE COVER

Lantern in hand, Manthara enters the women's inner quarters, which lie in darkness. She will entice Kaikeyi. Instigate her. And then, right then, one sees in the hazy light, a thin, dark-skinned home guard stop a cargo truck and take money. On the book's cover, printed using a zinc-block, is an exact reproduction of the photograph in the way it was printed in the newspaper—if you look carefully, you'll notice a kind of weary look, a vague sign of poverty in the face and eyes—the man was the kind who had difficulty providing for his family. Below that is printed in 18-point type: "The victim of this social system, undivided, has been apprehended in a divided way"—again, he is also the means to perpetuate this social system, this creature, a sacrificial lamb—perhaps he will have to be finished off somewhere in this text . . . somewhere, perhaps . . .

No Sex Please
We are Indian
Because
India Has No Sex
India Has Charaibeti

Although nowadays
boys reach puberty
by the time they are eight or ten years old
and naked women's pictures are printed
even on the packets of firecrackers and sparklers meant
for children
Nonetheless
NO SEX PLEASE
WE ARE INDIAN
INDIA HAS NO SEX
INDIA HAS CHARAIBETI
Choo-kitkit choo-kitkit choo-kitkit

NO

SEX

Newspapers have been chewed up and eaten alive in this text. A lot of visible and invisible debt, both national and international. Parallel to Gautam Buddha, the founder of Buddhism, is scholar Ramram Basu, and the André Bretons become one with composer Rupchand Pakshi, with and without admixture. Many contemporary writings in Bangla and English have been used, with a tendency to twist, crush pitilessly, harshly too, as if ripping the skin off a body. Donning various forms, they have arrived, and on the plaster of color and lines, straight and topsy-turvy, the bits and pieces of the gilded border have become an inseparable part of this collective collage. For this variegated feast, I acknowledge my debt with gratitude. They are flesh and blood. And my salutations for the flesh and blood . . . Yes, salutations.

SUBIMAL MISRA

A Composition in the Bengali Language

WHEN
COLOR
IS
A WARNING SIGN

Published
in the metropolis of Calcutta
in 1984

Lantern in hand, Manthara enters the women's inner quarters, which lie in darkness. She will entice Kaikeyi. Instigate her. And then, right then, one sees in the hazy light, a thin, dark-skinned home guard stop a cargo truck and take money. On the book's cover, printed using a zinc-block, is an exact reproduction of the photograph in the way it was printed in the newspaper—if you observe carefully, you'll notice a kind of weary look, a vague sign of poverty in the face and eyes—the man was the sort who had difficulty providing for his family. Below that is printed in 18-point type: "The victim of this social system, undivided, has been apprehended in a divided way"—again, he is also the means to perpetuate this social system, this creature, a sacrificial lamb—perhaps he will have to be finished off somewhere in this text . . . somewhere, perhaps . . .

The writer held out a test tube. Look at this dust. This is cinnabar. A brilliant red is made from this. But in the light, the color takes on a blackish hue. I'm trying to make a kind of red that won't turn black even when brought to light. I don't know whether it can be done, nevertheless I'm trying. And what's the harm in hanging on to the belief that it can be done?

Prostrated before the factory
village and city conjoined
after this
boys will be made in the factory

The man's a donkey. The man
doesn't dream

While being offered to the flames, an extremely beautiful maiden's knees, bones, and torso—they had to be quite fatty—used to be laid out on the altar. A square altar, and on that, pieces of flesh and clippings of hair. On top of that, a layer of skin, stiff, sometimes thin. The interior of the altar used to be decorated with the deep-red liver, the yellow brain inside the head and the intestines. Fat, that's why the knees used to burn so fiercely . . . sometimes they would burn deep, to the bone. And these flames were considered an auspicious sign. We received the term "petit bourgeois morality."

Once there was an argument between the king of the gods, Zeus, and his wife Hera, about whether it was man or woman who enjoyed the pleasure of sexual union more. Hera's view was that it was man. Zeus held that it was woman. They gave the responsibility of deciding to Tiresias. He explained logically that the woman's enjoyment was nine times greater than the man's. Hera grew angry when she heard this and turned him blind. Rocking in joy, Zeus granted him a boon of long life. He now roams around in this text, pronouncing prophecies about the future. He has a hand in the genetic tests and experiments that are conducted to make the people of the Third World impotent.

One night, when a husband and wife were seated in bed, a camel made a sound. Hearing it, the wife asked the husband, "Who made that sound?" The husband said, "A camil." "What was that?" asked the wife. The husband replied, "Camil." Hearing this, hitting her head with her hand, the wife recited the following shloka: "*King na karoti virdhiyadi rooshtah, king na karoti sa eb hi tushtah. Ooshtre loompati ramba yamba tasmayi dutta vipulanitamba.*" The meaning of the shloka was that proof that the Almighty can do anything when enraged—and do anything when pleased—lies in the fact that such an illiterate idiot, who mispronounces even the word camel, is granted to me, while I, beautiful and full of fine qualities, am granted to him. As soon as he heard his wife's statement, his conscience awakened, he was seized with self-hate, shame, and self-condemnation. He, Kalidas, resolved to give up his life and left for the forest that very night. Entering the immense forest, full of wild animals and wrapped in dense darkness, he, who was running hither and thither, utterly at a loss, became endowed with divine knowledge, by virtue of the merits of many lives, upon hearing the mantra of Blue Saraswati chanted, even as he slept, by a self-realized sage who lived in this forest in a hut made of leaves, and then not being able to see on account of the darkness, he sat on the corpse of a menstruating Chandal girl who had hung herself, and in that deep night began chanting the mantra with great devotion, with a resolve not to rise until he attained sadhana, even if he perished in the process.

Once, while traveling from Varanasi to Uruvela, the Buddha came upon a band of youths. They were picnicking together with their wives. One among them was unmarried and had brought along his paramour. But the girl took some of the youth's possessions and ran away. Everyone then began to search for her. Coming upon the Buddha, they asked him whether he had seen the girl. Hearing everything, the Buddha replied: "What is it you search for? Instead of looking for this woman, don't you think it is better for you to search for your own self?" In order to understand the Buddha's views about the absence of self, it is necessary to know this story. The person who completely denies a separate self advises someone else to search for his own self. These two apparently contradictory views are resolved if the difference between the self which has to be denied and the self which has to be searched for is understood clearly.

Casuarina Avenue. Under the immense trees were cars with their windows up, and there was only a mysterious darkness everywhere. Everything was enveloped in mist. Every now and then, suddenly, a tittering laughter erupted from the ground glass windows when they were momentarily opened. Only—a few boys, bare-bodied even on this winter night, ran around collecting beer bottles thrown from cars. On one boy's body there was only a jute sack worn like a coat. Every now and then, they rubbed their hands together to keep themselves warm. They had collected seventy or eighty beer bottles so far. As the night advanced, there would be more. "Look . . . look! That fatty has made the girl lie down on the back seat . . ." It was long past eleven at night. I would like to examine once again the oft repeated quote attributed to Darwin. Tonight itself if possible. Yes, the monkey—it was sitting on the German sahib's bookshelf, and in its hand was a human skull. The monkey was gazing at it with a very thoughtful look. Reader, do you think I'm very jealous— the jealousy of nonfulfillment—what do you think, sir? I forgot to mention, some Bihari folk had even made a fire with twigs on the Victoria Memorial grounds. They sat around the fire warming themselves in the winter night.

Long hair continuously narrows and then thickens upon the upper part of the rectangle. Stands up. In excitement. The brownish-red color will be added here. The complete list of sex offences is known to many. *Polygamy is a tendency in man.* Not all are mentioned in this text. For instance, the color purple. Who on earth would openly keep it company?

From an alert writer, the reader expects that there will be a discussion on why, in certain social conditions, people express moral laxity. It is also expected that he will provide an explanation. In this kind of writing, there's a socialist significance, and the writer is only responsible for explaining that aspect. It's difficult to accept that he provides only tasty descriptions of sexual behavior in the text—that he doesn't provide a basic social explanation. Without saying anything more, the objective of presenting such a sign can be easily guessed.

In a society in which individual earning is the sole means of gaining recognition, where poverty and deprivation bring disregard and denial, the artist's independence is bound to be pushed in a perverted direction.

The reader who seeks to become one with the times and tries to advance in this pursuit does not find what he is looking for in the popular stream of stories and novels. For him, the story has to convey many-more-things besides the story. And it is through these many-more-things that the real character of a writer can be discerned. Notwithstanding all the information and statistics pertaining to a country or a society that are easily available in books and are published in newspapers, it is in these many-more-things of a story that some truths are contained ever more clearly—the effort is made to do just that. It's because of the trustworthiness of a writer's effort that a piece of text is simultaneously story, history, proclama tion, and personal diary. The carrying capacity of a text can be stretched as far as man's thinking and imagination can reach and ascend. In the normal course of things, in the eyes of an unpracticed reader, it may well appear complex and entirely doomed. A story or a novel is not merely a form of art, it is also a medium of expression of a personality. On the other hand, a writer is not merely a social theorist or a sophisticated political thinker. The conscience of an independent writer submits only to truth and truth alone. And in that sense, it is the task of a writer to raise all kinds of questions, on all sides, and to always evaluate the possibility of alternative realities. Let us learn to recognize our own likes outside of the likes imposed upon us.

Some days ago, I visited the famous French painter, Henri Matisse, to sit for a portrait, and I had a discussion with him about the purpose of art. As Matisse was feeling somewhat unwell, he was working in a semi-reclining position. He asked his secretary to fetch an elephant. The girl brought an African statue. The elephant had been sculpted as if it were in an intoxicated state. Matisse asked me whether I liked it. I said, "Yes."

"Doesn't something about this strike you as unusual?" he asked.

I replied: "No."

"It doesn't strike me either. But look carefully. Not just its trunk, but even the tusks are raised too high."

A fool came and said: "The tusks can never be raised so high. The sculpture is not at all realistic."

The next time the artist worked according to the man's instructions. Matisse asked his secretary to bring the second elephant. This was an extremely ordinary figure.

Matisse said: "Do you see, the tusks are in the right place now. Everything's according to the rules. But now there's no art . . ."

"Guru, I've seen A-class, B-class, C-class, and several classes of wackos in my life. For that matter, I've seen golden wackos, blue wackos, and orange wackos—but I've never seen such a Z-class pure-white wacko in my life."

Having had a bit to drink the previous night, I woke up late. It was about nine o'clock then. Even before I could have my tea, I got the news that someone was waiting in the sitting room to meet me. I felt annoyed that I couldn't even sip my tea in peace. I went and saw an extremely skinny-looking youth, wearing rather shabby clothes. We sat staring at each other for a few seconds. I realized he was finding it difficult to succinctly frame what he wanted to say. He had never been in such a situation before. After some time, he did open his mouth, but as if in a stupor. Need a job. A mother and several younger brothers and sisters at home, et cetera, can't survive without a job. I grew thoughtful and was about to give a suitably noncommittal reply—but I was not at all prepared for what happened next. Like a spring, the boy left his chair and shot toward my legs, he fell on his knees and threw himself at my feet. "Please do something . . . anything whatsoever . . . or else . . . or else I shall do something terrible . . . I'll become bad . . ."

Many days have passed. I could not, or rather did not do anything about getting the boy a job. I didn't even remember. I don't know whether he found a job or not. Nor have I tried to find out if he's turned bad. Not finding out is the safest. Because if I learn that he has joined the numbers-game operation, or has become a wagon-breaker and is looting freight trains, then, at that very moment, I would feel the jab of a thorn within me—a thorn that wouldn't be easy to pluck out. It wasn't possible to worry about such things in the midst of one's own myriad responsibilities and problems.

The people of the country ask in loud voices:
"What's the main problem before us now?"
The country's leader, the Big Boss, shouts:
"Vanaspati mixed with the fat of cow and pig.
Poverty, unemployment, illiteracy—all that's for later.
Save vanaspati first—save caste."

"You can shoot and kill me, but you can't make me surrender. I fight for the exploited, I protect the honor of women. This land shall one day belong to the ones who plow it. Even if you people kill me, this will come to be. Behind me, many more like me are lining up. They shall come—they will come—they will keep coming." He writes this once again, anew, from *Ramayan Chamar*; all his life he'll keep writing the words, as a preface to his writing.

The cameraman keeps taking pictures. Pictures of the person killed in the explosion. Dead or injured? Torn slippers and shreds of a saffron-colored punjabi scattered here and there. Who knows where the shoulder bag is, the books and papers inside it are strewn everywhere. Papers fly in the wind. One book still emits smoke, its pages smoldering. The pen had been thrown out of the pocket, who knows where the head had flown, myriad cracks in the spectacle lenses. But they didn't break. Someone had fondly given him a brightly colored apple to eat, it was rolling on the ground. But isn't it said that writers don't eat apples? A dream? Of course it's a dream. There was an asbestos roof overhead, a big chunk of it lay in pieces on the railway track. The rail station was the background. It was one minute past twelve on the clock hanging over the platform. And the explosion had therefore taken place then, at one minute past twelve. In this text. Blood had accumulated in various places. Blackish. Mop and bucket in hand, the sweeper had begun to wipe away the stains of stale blood from the walls and the floor. The frame, the entire frame is like this. The cameraman keeps taking pictures.

SNACK SHOPS SURROUND THE COUNTRY LIQUOR BAR

It's begun, the movie's begun
The Hema Malinis will dance—
Pran & Co.
will flash daggers
The Bruce Lees will show off their karate prowess
And an all-India people's leader
Will remove his underwear and act wacky
As a bonus, there's
Miss India's nude cabaret dance
Ninety paise to sit on the straw laid upon the ground
For the babus in trousers there are chairs with cushions
A whole section of them.
Come, see my cuntry
Jis Desh Mein Ganga Behti Hai
There's cabaret, there are fight scenes
There's Rajesh Khanna and there's Rajneesh
There's unrestrained sexuality
and the politics of women's rape
The law for the poor and the law for the wealthy
The parliament of shoe-flinging
There's the historic speech of 1947 by Nehru-ji
Black marketeers shall be caught
And hung from the nearest lamppost
There's man licking man's vomit in the throes of hunger
In broad daylight
The scene does not strike anyone's conscience
There's a red-sun branded image of struggling folk
A lively A-class cinema show for flood relief
Perverted sex and red-light districts of women's freedom
How Jean-Luc Godard blends with
Cherabanda Raju's thoughts
The procession to Tarakeshwar

Carrying water on the shoulder
The world's longest spell of darkness
Men and women in unbridled preparations,
Outside family life
There's the twenty-first century
How, paradoxically, in building a state in a socialist mold
The rich get richer and the poor get poorer
A film about all that
Murder, mayhem, Rabindrasangeet[6]
The story of the Maruti car, elucidation of the Gita
Even the voice of my Mao Tse Tung
There's everything, everything whatsoever
Now for you, in full Eastmancolor

Nanda ate palm fritters
and began to dance

COME, LET US NOW
EMBARK UPON A RED-LIGHT TOUR,
VIA CHAMPATALA TO HARKATA GALI

Raising a furor, the members of the opposition raced forward. One person posted up in a corner and aimed his
gold thread-embellished nagrai slipper at the speaker's
nose. Crying, "What a disaster," the members from the
government-side rushed toward the speaker's table and
surrounded him. A scuffle ensued, punjabis were clutched,
paunches were pinched, dhutis fastened around waists
were undone. "Hit the guy with shoes, hit him!"—a roar

---

6   Songs composed by Nobel Laureate Rabindranath Tagore

erupted. Two women members stood up: "Come, let's also join the scuffle, for life's sake!" Another person supported them: "We must, or else we won't be able to save our dignity." The woman in a sleeveless blouse tied the anchal of her sari around her waist, and then she picked up a slipper lying on the carpet with her left hand. A fat government-sider tore the speech papers of the skinny opposition-sider into shreds and kept flinging them up into the air. A feminine slipper landed with a smack on someone's cheek. Trees, flowers, and creepers in exquisite golden handiwork over brown. An aesthetic member said: "Excellent, oh beautiful one! When there are so many surprises in the showcase, wonder what the warehouse will be like!" (The member has to be asked later what "showcase" and "warehouse" mean.) Bits of paper flew in the air inside the circular chamber—pieces of protesting papers. Shreds of the sugar scam, shreds of the fodder scam, shreds of the blanket scam, even the My Marx scam. In a flash, the woman with the sleeveless blouse pinched the cheek of a woman with plucked eyebrows and said: "It's necessary, Rekha-di, it's all necessary for life." The face of the woman named Rekha-di became flushed, the speaker saw what had transpired. The speaker, making his somber face even more somber, kept saying, "It will be decided tomorrow whether or not it is appropriate to use the term 'goondaism.' Everything is adjourned today."

THE FEAST JUST AFTER

On Saturday afternoon, on the last day of the monsoon session of the legislative assembly, the honorable speaker invited the MLAs to lunch. The menu: chicken biryani, murgh musallam, fried fish, palm-fruit sandesh, and ice cream. There was also an arrangement for spirits, however, that was not made public—it wouldn't do to put that in writing. People could satisfy their needs furtively and they could openly participate in the session as long as they wiped their mouths with a handkerchief. Everything is democratic, it's a question of democratic rights. One person states the governmental view while eating. It was a very modest lunch, bearing in mind the talk of imminent famine in the country and the crop failure for two successive years. Chewing a chicken leg, gravy trickling down from his mouth, an opposition member's view: "I did drought relief, and after that, for a long time I have been prepared to engage in flood relief, but why are there no floods in this state? What will we fight for then?" Finally the government and opposition members cooled down, slowly they sat down beside one another, maintaining peace and harmony while they were all busy eating. "At least at this time there ought to be . . ." "Yes, at this time . . ." The way to Harkata Gali via Champatala, sometimes turning toward Murgihata, and sometimes to the Great Departure.

CABARET SHALL CONTINUE

Staff Reporter: Cabaret shall continue in the government-run Great Eastern Hotel. It could not be discontinued. The state tourism minister stated this in a written reply in the legislative assembly on Thursday. He further added that the India Tourism Development Corporation would open a five-star hotel on Chowringhee and there would be cabaret shows there, too.

An immense ship on the peaceful ocean. Bits of clouds floated in the sky. The captain sat with his eye on the most modern weather-monitoring instruments, a lazy moment, there was no warning of any kind anywhere. No possibility of any deluge, people were getting on with their activities, eating, sleeping, and running around, nothing unusual was showing up on the radar. And then, in front of their eyes, in a trice, everything turned topsy-turvy, there came a thundering storm that made the sky tremble. An electric storm. But for just a few moments, then everything ceased. Everything was placid again, the sky and air turned peaceful. Seeing that everything was in order, the captain of the ship heaved a sigh of relief, and suddenly there was an announcement over the intercom. They learned that by now time had advanced by at least twenty years. A radio program from the year 2003 was being broadcast. The loose end of a gorgeous sari—its anchal—floated on to the television screen. Boiling and bubbling, with red and blue drops of steam. Deep red, mixed with deep green. Past, present, and future were all conjoined, illusory, erroneous. The girl's mother walked around clad in the miniest of miniskirts, chemical war broke out steadily in the northeast corner. Who is whose father, who is whose mother, and who is still brother and sister. The ravishing woman stands solitarily at the seashore. Some said the Goddess Ambika herself had come down from Mount Kailash to trick her offspring, while in the opinion of some others she was a water-sprite, and yet others had seen her before, in Champatala, standing on the road, soliciting customers. Only a long-bearded fellow, a sailor from the east, in disguise, knows her identity. And Number One knows. She's nobody else, merely an abandoned woman who's left the confines of family and society, who, donning a sad face, looks at the sea. This planet's aboriginal folk had to be reproved by her. She'll come to the pages of the text as soon as she's called, she'll perform a cabaret as soon as she's asked to. Please be a bit patient, you lot, because this will happen, will definitely happen—it has to happen.

NUMBER ONE

Just as in a conventional detective story we are used to seeing an exceptionally strong-cum-clever hero, the hero of this story too is no less than that, although, of course, one needs to be able to identify him clearly. Just like in Hindi films, where Amitabh Bachchan can battle hundreds of people simultaneously, similarly, the hero of this story, Number One, also equals a hundred. He could have been a bit like James Bond, but he became a Hindi film hero. Fate, everything is fate. And how convenient the water and wind in India! Look carefully, he is constantly accompanied by a secret agent who's neither male nor female—twenty-first century citizenship. Foiling the conspiracies of various kinds of villains, placing the risk of every kind of danger upon his head, our hero jumps from the top of the Writers' Building toward the countryside—he'll fall, fall, and perhaps perform a somersault, but he won't die. He's a Hanuman by race, instituted ages ago in the stiff pages of the Ramayana, immortal is he through the four ages, Satya, Treta, Dwapara, and Kali. And all the furor is about him, about his activities, the one who knew that if his tail were set alight he'd really create pandemonium in Lanka.

My garden worth thousands of rupees was eaten by a goat worth five quarters

In the course of writing, I gave the manuscript to Nirmal-da of College Street to read and he later sent me his valuable opinion by letter. Nirmal Gupta was in his fifties, his sideburns were entirely gray, he ran a serious little magazine called *Eikhon*, it sold about a thousand copies. After reading his letter, as I was wondering whether I could write afresh, in a simpler way—as I was grappling with the subject—I saw to my surprise that Nirmal-da too was becoming entangled in the text, he was becoming another incident and clearly the complexity was continuously growing, multifarious, and more, what I have never thought also emerges clearly, page after page.

NIRMAL-DA'S LETTER

I am never elated about your writing, and it is quite difficult to suddenly come to any conclusion regarding you. Again, the question of outright rejection does not arise because some aspect or another haunts me, and it occurs to me that perhaps there could also be this kind of writing. In your writing, there are no such things as sequential events, it appears outwardly to be only floating images and to my eyes quite disconnected. Employing selected clippings from newspapers, an amalgam of politics and sex—something that mixes everything together. I won't say that I was fully able to accept the writing. That's because there are so many of your angles here that are of a combative nature—as well as the ignoring of these same questions—demolishing popular beliefs, arriving at an unpredictable conclusion, which apparently is not even a conclusion. It's not certain where the writer wants to go, or at least it's unclear—I became confused reading it, and I have no hesitation in saying that most of the time I am confused by your writing. You have a tendency to debate everything, in some parts mixing a bit of French humor—there's no certainty anywhere, no care to reach a conclusion—this apparent cynicism compels me to be confused. In the middle of disciplinelessness, sometimes discipline peeps in, although discovering it is arduous. And this has to be searched for amid the wrecking of form, the use of elegiac language and ongoing experimentation. Throughout the writing there is a predilection toward investigation at work, a continuous search, which is at the same time sensational too. While it attracts me a bit, it's good to admit that it doesn't attract me that much.

MUCH LATER, FOR ANOTHER KIND OF POLITICS

Reading Nirmal Gupta's letter, the writer becomes very dejected. He sets out despite the afternoon sun. A Sunday afternoon in July, not many people on the street. He will just not be at peace until he writes a suitable reply, convey- ing exactly what he thinks. He keeps walking along Park Street, toward the old cemetery, he buys beedis at a shop below the Asiatic Society. Long beedis, with red string, his favorite. As evening turns to night, he buys and eats telebhaja, the famous telebhaja from Hanif's, at the curb-side on Circular Road. True to form, he gets heartburn soon after that. He searches frantically for an antacid. As he searches, he feels terribly sick. In the drawer, in the box, under the bed—nowhere does he find the antacid tablet. That's how he loses all his things, doesn't he? Hadn't he lost, just like this, all the news-clippings pertaining to the ninth Asiad—which would have gone very well with this text? Suddenly he finds a whole haritaki fruit. Is the haritaki a symbol, in this text? Putting it into his mouth, he sits down to write a reply; as is his habit, he writes a first draft in his diary. It is past midnight then. He doesn't vomit that night. Needless to say, the very next day he overcomes his sadness and sits down again to write, with new zeal. That piece of his is reproduced here exactly.

REPLY TO NIRMAL-DA'S CRITIQUE, WHICH WASN'T SENT

The needs of the reader who makes an effort to become one with the times are not met merely by the popu-lar stream of stories and novels. For him the story has to convey many-more-things beside the story. And it is through these many-more-things that the real character of the writer can be discerned. Consider all the informa-tion and statistics pertaining to a country or a society that are easily available in books and are published in news-papers. Some truths are contained ever more clearly in the many-more-things of a story, the effort is made to do just that. It's because of the trustworthiness of the writer's effort that a piece of text is simultaneously story, history, proclamation and personal diary. The carrying capacity of the text can be stretched as far as man's thinking and imagination can reach and ascend. In the normal course of things, in the eyes of the unpracticed reader, it may well appear complex and entirely doomed. A story or a novel is not merely a form of art, it is also a medium of expression of a personality. On the other hand, the writer is not merely a social theorist or sophisticated political thinker. The conscience of the independent writer submits only to truth and truth alone. And in that sense, it is the task of a writer to raise all kinds of questions, on all sides . . . and to always evaluate the possibility of alternative realities. Let us be able to recognize our own likes outside of the likes imposed upon us.

TWENTY YEARS ON THE CHARGE OF STEALING A FEW PIECES OF CLOTH

On a winter's night in 1979, under cover of darkness, a family of approximately five half-naked adivasis had allegedly stolen a few pieces of expensive silk from the courtyard of a locally-influential person. Standing in the witness box, they admitted that they did not know that the pieces of cloth were so expensive. They were sentenced by the Raigarh sessions court. A welfare association filed an appeal on their behalf in the Madhya Pradesh high court. After eleven months, the Jabalpur bench of the high court gave the order for their release. They were arrested again after a few days by the Jashpur police, on a subsequent complaint by the same person. Apparently, they had now stolen mopping cloths and were roaming around wearing these. The pieces of cloth worn around their waists were identified as stolen goods. The old case was registered anew in court; they went back to jail. In Indian democracy, they were now sentenced to twenty years of rigorous imprisonment on the charge of stealing a few pieces of cloth. Although they were granted bail by the court, owing to the absence of the concerned officials, even their bail was repeatedly delayed. Finally, there wasn't anyone to pay the bail. Who knows why the welfare association washed its hands of the matter.

YOUTH'S CORPSE

The body of Neelabja Roy, a.k.a. Neelu, a second-year student of Bengal Engineering College in Shibpur, and a hostel resident, was recovered from the Ganga on Thursday evening. The body of our Neelu, Neelabja Roy, had decomposed completely by then. His eyes had been gouged out. The police stated that at dawn on Wednesday, someone had come to call on him and he had set out immediately. Clad only in his vest and pajamas, he had gone toward the Ganga. His toothbrush and a tin of Monkey brand red tooth powder were in his hands. He did not return. After the body was recovered it was sent for autopsy. The viscera would apparently also be examined. A major difference of opinion arose between the local police and the river traffic police on the question of who, or who all, had come to call on him, and why the student had gone to the riverbank. In the view of the local police, this was clearly suicide, while the river police held that this was a result of young love. A roommate of Neelu's reported: "The boy had a bad habit, whenever he saw injustice he would immediately start arguing with the people concerned."

DOG'S DOINGS

An adroit dog that was an expert at snatching the hand-bags of beautiful young women suddenly appeared in the town of Seville, in Spain. It was a huge dog, and one with some pedigree to boot—a German Shepherd. It used to snatch the handbags of beautiful women with its teeth and run away in a flash. The police said that the dog had troubled some twelve to fourteen women in this way—but they were simply unable to catch the animal. He did not pay any attention to little girls or elderly women, but as soon as he spotted a beautiful young woman, he leapt into action. Especially with those who were dressed in red, and those who liked the color red. The police advised that in order to be safe from this danger, for the time being, for a few days, it was better not to wear red garments or bright red lipstick. It was not possible to say when or from where the menace might next arrive.

A FULFILLED LIFE, O MOTHER

My father drowned while performing tarpan[7] at dawn on Mahalaya in Babughat. The news was published the next day in the newspaper. The report stated: Eight lifesavers and two police boats began patrolling as early as five in the morning. We read that with astonishment. Where indeed were those boats that could have saved my drowning father! He drowned in front of the helpless eyes of my mother. The driver had left the car and had gone to have a

---

7   A Hindu ritual where people "offer water" to the gods and departed members of their family to "quench their thirst."

cup of tea. A bare-bodied man, wearing a checked lungi, was standing near the riverbank. He said to my mother: "If you give me all your jewelry right now, I can give it a try." My mother was somewhat startled at the proposal, she couldn't decide what she ought to do, because she was wearing almost seventy to eighty thousand rupees worth of jewelry on her. Another man, also bare-bodied and lungi-clad, warned my mother: "Don't give it to him, he'll swim underwater and slip away." In practical terms, it was too late. One boat, lifeboat No. 2, arrived ten minutes later. With folded hands, my mother pleaded with them to do something. The answer: "We don't have divers in our boat. There's nothing to be done at this moment." My mother ran around in a frenzy, like a lunatic she ran to the river traffic police. "Please save him in whichever way possible, I fall at your feet . . ."—but the officer-in-charge informed her that he could do nothing, they had not yet received any order regarding this. Since then, we've been waiting confoundedly for my father's dead body to surface; it's been three days now.

SKY-CLAD

Preliminary investigations have revealed that every liter of water from the Damodar River contains a thousand to fifteen hundred milligrams of phenol. In the view of experts, only 0.01 mg of phenol in a liter of water can be tolerated by humans. If there is phenol and mercury in excess of that, a process of slow poisoning begins in the consumer's body. The poison has a harmful effect on the human nervous system. Through prolonged use of the water, the coordination of the body's vital organs is affected, the joints become stiff, and the movement of the hands, legs, face and head is affected. The person slowly sinks toward a painful death. No apparent ailment is detected. The condition of the Damodar river today is a result of the discharge of chemicals and other polluting substances into the water by factories in Bihar and West Bengal.

FATHER AND SON WERE PLAYING CAROM

At about two in the afternoon on Sunday, in the vicinity of Entally police station, bomb-throwing and brandishing of razors broke out between a father and son in the course of playing carom. It spread to the entire locality very quickly. The police fired four rounds of live ammunition and also seven rounds of tear gas in order to bring the situation under control. A rice-vending woman was killed in the crossfire. There was a quarrel between the father and son about cheating while playing carom. After a few heated exchanges, they became incensed and the enraged father slashed his son's cheek with a razor. The police had to rush to the spot to restore order. Both sides began attacking the police. Stones and bricks were thrown. Bombs rained down. According to the police report, one junior officer and seventeen police personnel were injured in the altercation. Both father and son are now in the hospital with critical injuries.

MURDER, RAPE, AND HIGHWAY ROBBERY OCCUR FREQUENTLY IN THIS COUNTRY, WHY RAISE SUCH A HULLABALOO ABOUT IT?

A band of about forty people from the Thakur community attacked Babu Bigha village in Bihar under the cover of darkness. Babu Bigha was a predominantly Dalit village. There had been a long-standing tension between the Dalits and the thakur moneylenders and zamindars. The Dalits were no longer willing to work under the begar system. On the night in question, the thakurs caught and raped each and every woman in the village to avenge this offence. It was only due to their noble magnanimity that they did not set fire to all the houses. An appeal concerning the incident was made to the supreme court by Dr. Jose Kannailal, the program director for Dalits. Dr. Kannailal complained in his appeal that, incited by a group of zamindars and mahajans, and with their unconcealed encouragement, some forty high-caste Hindus had attacked Babu Bigha at night. They did not spare anyone in the village, not even an infant on one woman's arm. The raiders snatched away a six-month-old child from its mother's bosom and smashed it against a stone. This stone was a Ramshila, bearing Shri Ramachandra's footprint, where the village folk worshipped daily. Blood thus mixed with the vermilion spread on it, dark-red blood. They also did not spare any girl or woman between four and seventy from sexual abuse. Among the rape victims were a four-year-old child as well as pregnant women. The child's name was Lalti, she was now in an unconscious state in the hospital. A few women suffered miscarriages just after being raped. One young woman just could not be brought under control and so the hair on her head was pulled out and one of her breasts was cut off with a sharp cleaver. Before that, the girl had badly bitten a man, and even gouged out another man's eye. More than a hundred people were injured in the violence unleashed upon the village and the condition of thirteen of them was serious. The injured were sent to the hospital in Sarmera for treatment. In shame and terror, the rape victims did not initially lodge any complaint. But later, everyone opened their mouths. The names of a few miscreants were specified in the complaint. But the Sarmera police did not give much importance to the matter. Such treatment of Dalits was a frequent occurrence. For that matter, the district's superintendent of police too did not initially agree to any investigation.

EVERY CHILD WILL BE TAUGHT IN SCHOOL

The hydrant tap was open and so the pavement on the roadside was brimming with flowing water. Two kids were splashing around in great delight in the brown river water. One was completely naked, the other's only cover was a pair of elastic-less underpants. Just observe these boys with their jutting ribs—looking just like plucked chickens . . . "Who are you to call my mother lame duck, stupid fucker, I'll ___ your mother." The other throws the first boy to the ground and presses his head down in the gushing flow of the Ganga's water: "Serves you right—your dad's a whore-chaser, everyone knows that your mother enlisted her name in the whore register . . ." The tire of a bus with the tiger logo was getting stuck in molten pitch. The bank officer's wife was taking her child, Bubun, from kindergarten back to their apartment. There was kohl on Bubun's lovely eyes, a blue ribbon on her head and her hair was in a bob-cut. Hearing the talk of the two naked boys frolicking in the water from the hydrant, she came to a halt and devoured their actions and gestures with wide eyes. "Chhee chhee, you shouldn't hear all that bad talk, dear . . . You don't know, they're basti boys." . . . A rickshaw-puller parked his rickshaw beneath a luxuriant gulmohar tree and was fanning himself by twirling his gamcha around. The sun beat down mercilessly on the desolate street.

BADSHAH BEGUM JHAM-JHAMA-JHAM

Most of the male youths of the village drove van-rickshaws. The rest were agricultural laborers. Some tended paan gardens. There were no male youths left in Hamidnagar village, almost everyone was in the hospital, some were in jail or in police custody, the rest had fled. There were only three rifle-bearing police constables sitting on a bench. And all around, one after another, were mud houses burnt to cinders. Maniruddin's house was set on fire last Wednesday morning. A few hundred people had surrounded the hamlet from all sides and then set it ablaze. They threw fistfuls of dry chilies into the fire. About twelve people had locked themselves inside Maniruddin's house, they were trembling in fear. As soon as they stepped out of the house, coughing, they would be beaten with lathis. Maniruddin's mother, seventy-year-old Mariam Bibi, was hunched in a corner of a room on the second floor. She was thrown out of the window. She was still alive. A neighbor, Salehan Bibi, had bravely avoided the incensed mob and given her water to drink. No one saw Mariam Bibi after that—neither the police nor the village folk. Three days later, Mariam's body was spotted floating in the river. A dog was tearing away at her stomach and eating it, her bloated innards were spilling out. That morning, a total of twelve persons had hidden themselves in that accursed house to save their lives.

Most of them were now in the hospital. Either burnt or concussed by lathis. Among them was also a one-and-half-year-old baby girl, Habiba Khatun. Three persons died the following day, they were Abdul Latif, Sheikh Karim, and Hatem. After Maniruddin's house was burnt, the mob looted the house of Sheikh Yasin. Some youths held down his daughter in the room and destroyed her honor in front of her father. The girl is still unconscious, she is in the district hospital. Asma Khatun and Salehan Bibi managed to escape. Salehan was Maniruddin's sister-in-law. When the arson began, she was nearby. She said: "Escaping somehow from the fire, I ran to the police station across the lake. It was nine in the morning then. The big babu was there. I said: 'Come at once, the Hindus have burnt down the entire neighborhood.' The OC stared at me blankly, he said: 'Can't go now. There are no cars. The daughter-in-law of the zamindar has hanged herself. I'll go after seeing her first. You go on ahead.'" Salehan reported that the babus from the police station did finally arrive at around five in the evening. Everything was over by then. Hamidnagar had become a graveyard. The officer-in-charge of the police station was not present on Friday afternoon. The second officer was present. He was queried:

Some seven persons have been apprehended. A picket is in place. It's the old Hindu-Muslim quarrel, mister . . . it keeps happening.

"When did the police receive the information, and when did the police arrive on scene?"

"As soon as we could go, you know . . ."

"Was the incident purely communal—how did it start?"

"I'm unable to tell you about that, the big babu can tell you . . ."

"People say the trouble was over cutting railway cables. About who'll cut cables from which area, that was how it began. Apparently, some Muslim youths had forcibly entered a Hindu area and were cutting the railway cables. After all, ordinary peaceful people can't do all this. It seems mastaans with the power of their gangs are behind such activities. It's about occupying territory. What does the police station's report say about this?"

"I don't know anything about that, the big babu knows . . ."

"When will the big babu be back?"

"How would I know that, only the big babu knows."

THE BODY—WHERE'S THE BODY?

On Saturday morning, Tararani Bhuiyan, Manasi Dasi, Tarubala, and five children were killed while foraging coal from the garbage hillock in Dhapa. They were buried under a thirty-foot high heap of garbage. Like every day, on this day too at around nine in the morning, small children and womenfolk went to the garbage hillock on the Dhapa dumping ground to forage for coal. The group dug a hole and burrowed their way in. Suddenly, there was a loud noise and the garbage hillock collapsed. Only one woman, Angurbala Dasi, survived, as most of her body lay outside the heap. Seven of those who died were from Pagladanga, Tararani alone was from Mathpukur. One can see a bulldozer searching for the dead bodies under the thirty-foot-high garbage hillock. Three or four squads of police arrived and skillfully cordoned off the entire area. A few thousand people from the bastis of Mathpukur and the surrounding areas—emaciated, naked, half-naked, curious, and agitated—stood outside the police cordon. The news reached the fire department around noon. They rushed to the accident site and, using hoes to move the earth, began the rescue work. But it wasn't possible to move a thirty- or thirty-two-foot-high hillock of earth using spades and hoes. The Municipal Corporation then arranged for a bulldozer to be sent from Palmer Bazar. Now the Corporation workers' eyes were trained on the jaws of the bulldozer. As it dug into the earth, tiny baskets emerged now and then. It was with just such baskets that early in the morning, a group of living humans had dug a hole like rats and entered it to forage pieces of coal. Suddenly the public shouts. A leg emerges from the earthen hillock and then disappears. The bulldozer is then moved away and they begin digging the earth with spades. After about five minutes, the body of a woman of about twenty emerges, a crumpled lump wrapped in torn rags. The officers keep saying: "There, we've found a body!" The public races toward the spot to identify it. On the other side, across the mud road, sitting beside another crumpled lump of a body wrapped in rags, is her father, an eighty-year-old man with shining white hair. The name of the body is Tarubala. Mother of five children. She had left in the morning, like every day, to forage for coal. If they sold the coal, they would get about three rupees in the evening. With that she could feed her children. Someone said that Tarubala had told her youngest daughter that, for the coming puja, she would buy her a toy. The girl sits on a pile of dirt and puts handfuls of earth into her mouth. Earth—yes, earth. With astonished eyes, she gazes fixedly at the crows flying around chaotically. All around her are many crows, and a couple of sparrows. After searching continuously until eight in the evening, the fire brigade personnel and the officer-in-charge of Tiljala police station are drenched with perspiration: There are no more bodies buried under the earth. If there are, we'll look into that later. Police cordoned off the garbage hillock. The basti-dwellers frequently come to the garbage hillock to forage for coal. Someone says: "They are prepared to take any kind of risk for just two handfuls of rice." "This dangerous garbage hillock causes accidents but it also provides a handful to eat once a day," says the white-haired eighty-year-old man, sitting beside his dead daughter's body. He knows that this kind of accident has occurred several times at another garbage hillock, near Dunlop Bridge, and that many people have died, everyone in the locality knows about it. He says: "What will we people do—what will we eat? Would anyone willingly go to do such work, babu, only to die?"

THE RULE OF PEASANTS SHALL BE ESTABLISHED

THE RIGHTS OF DESTITUTE FOLK SHALL BE PROCLAIMED

The inauguration ceremony of the new building of the Ita-nagar Village Council office, in Gorubathan No. 2 Block, was to take place today. The date had been fixed after consulting the almanac. Boys, old men, women, and men, everybody had been crowding there since morning. The village council office building had been beautifully decorated with red and blue paper garlands. An elevated dais had been set up in the field in front. A massive pandal had been erected. The elected head of the village council was running around busily in a punjabi with exquisite embroidery of colored threads, holding the end of the pleat of his fine dhuti, fanlike in his hand, and calling out loudly to people. He issued instructions, one after another. His bootlickers and subordinates were bustling around. Some bare-chested men with gamchas on their shoulders stood in front, rubbing their hands. They wanted to catch the pradhan's attention. Furrowing his brow, he indifferently issued a few instructions and bits of advice to them too. Two people ran to lay out the tarpaulin sheet, it was covered in dust. The peasants and other nonentities of the village would sit there. Some others went to arrange chairs and benches. The former zamindar, Roychoudhary babu, would come, the teachers of the high school too, and many more influential people as well. The chairs and benches were for them. The chairman of the block development council arrived then, accompanied by the village council administrator. Avoiding the crowd of poor village folk, the administrator led the esteemed chairman and moved ahead to show him the village council office and the dais erected for the program. The head of the village council was rubbing his hands nervously, inquiring whether all the arrangements were in order and requesting a careful scrutiny. The chairman went around and surveyed everything. He pointed out a couple of flaws in the decoration of the stage. Hearing the loud noise of static on the mic, he issued the order: "That won't do, hey, change that right now!" After that, he went directly to check the food arrangements. If this was not handled well . . . nobody would be satisfied. The time for the inauguration steadily neared. Government officers had started arriving in ones and twos. Jeeps and cars formed a line on the village's mud road. Everyone held handkerchiefs to their noses because of the dust being kicked up everywhere. It would definitely lead to dust allergy. The block development officer and the subdivisional officer arrived one after another. But there was no sign of him, the one who would inaugurate, the elected head of the district council. The officials had begun muttering quite a while back. The auspicious time window was passing. The officers looked at their watches every once in a while. About four hours after the scheduled time, the sabhadhipati's car was finally spotted. A jeep in front, and another one behind. The tricolor fluttered at the tip of the car's nose. As soon as he neared, the masses shouted out the victory chant: *Sabhadhipati Govardhan Purkait Ki Jai!* Hundreds of voices chanted back in reply: *Jai!* The girls in red-bordered saris blew conch shells with full gusto. The whole place resounded with the victory chant and the *poan-poan* of the conch shells. The block development officer assisted the sabhadhipati in getting out of the car. The officers came forward with smiling faces. The program dais was adjacent to the road. A printed silk sari had been laid out for the sabhadhipati to walk on. The colorful sari had been bought and kept for the purpose a long while back, on the advice of the village council officials. The volunteers stood next to one another and formed a chain by joining their hands to control the bursting crowd of village folk. The sabhadhipati slowly made his way to the dais. The subdivisional officer, block development officer, elected head of the village council, and chairman of the block development council ascended the dais after him. A girl wearing a *Love Story* frock planted a dot of sandalwood paste on the sabhadhipati's forehead, and after that began the ritual of garlanding him on behalf of various organizations. There was jostling over who would garland him first. The officials of the oldest youth club of the locality asserted that they should be asked to garland him first. The village council members protested this vociferously. That could simply not be permitted. It was the block development council's turn before anyone else, before anything else. After one or two exchanges it got physical. Finally, after the block development officer's intervention, both sides restrained themselves. After this, the name of each of the organizations was announced and the organization's representative came and placed a garland on the neck of the sabhadhipati. He was adorned with twenty-seven garlands, one after another. After that began the sabhadhipati's real task. The speech:

"Friends, on the auspicious occasion of the inauguration of the new building, we have come up with a special plan . . . We shall paint these new village council offices with the color that's on the walls of the Writers' Building in Calcutta because each one of these is a Writers' Building for the administration and management of village government . . ." Applause erupted from all sides. From the subdivisional officer, block development officer, to the elected head of the village council, everyone clapped their hands loudly and for a long time. In a corner under the dais, an emaciated man with a dirty gamcha on his shoulder spat on the ground and expressed his opinion through gnashed teeth: "Swindlers, the whole lot of them . . ." In all the noise of clapping his voice did not even reach the ears of the man beside him.

I've seen from my own experience that, irrespective of party, ninety percent of the elected representatives of the village council, block council, or district council are of a feudal mentality and from a particular opportunistic class—school and college teachers, quacks, briefless lawyers, contractors, bus owners, retired government employees, and quite a few influential persons, such as members of the managing committee of organizations like cooperative banks. The people of the whole area may be uneducated and illiterate, but most of these people belong to the educated class. After receiving self-government training, all these people understand everything about laws and their ramifications within two days, they are unwilling to think of any of the village folk as equal to them. Just like the erstwhile zamindars and landlords, they too have status—senior officers and officials, from the officers-in-charge of police stations to the ministers in the Writers' Building, dwell in their charmed circle. Whenever the opportunity arises, full of the pride of their own power, they will recite from memory Article 40 of the Constitution of India: *The State shall take steps to organize village councils and to endow them with such powers as may be necessary to enable them to function as units of self-government.* "I am a full-fledged, constitutionally empowered, elected representative of village government, a legally authorized controller. Every person of the region will be bound to act according to my instructions—there's no place here to get out of hand—do you understand?"

The color in the picture was once deep red, but has now faded and become pink in some places and in some places brown. On the other hand, even if the sheen of white has faded, it can be identified. If one looks patiently, one can discern all the images of wild animals in the pictures that have faded and become greenish. In some pictures there are axes, staffs, and fierce bows and arrows in people's hands. They are assembling in the Bengal, Bihar, and Orissa border region. A nilgai can be spotted in one place. One can see a herd of buffaloes racing ahead. There are a few people standing in the distance, with hands on their hips. Their appearance is stick-like, moustaches and beards on their faces, a striped pattern on their chests, and a red sign and a rope net in their hands. Why a rope net? What do these people want to trap? There, one can see the two birds of the Mundaka Upanishad, independent yet conjoined, companions on a peepal tree. One of them keeps pecking at the sweet and sour fruits of earthly life, the other is still.

THIS DIARY NOTE HAD BEEN WRITTEN EARLIER
WITHIN A NEWS-CLIPPING, IMPORTANT

Toward the beginning of his life as an artist, Rodin had made a human statue. It was so immaculate and realistic that people who saw it did not want to accept that it was his own work. They said: This is definitely modeled from a living man. He heard them, but he was indifferent. He did not say anything. After that, whenever he made any statue, he made it either larger or smaller than human size. That was Rodin.

QUESTION

A hunter went out from his shelter and after walking five kilometers due south, he killed a bear. Then, walking three kilometers in a westerly direction, he saw that the distance between the place where he killed the bear and his shelter still remained the same. What was the color of the bear?

THE BEAR'S COLOR

The atom bomb is prehistoric now. Human violence is no longer limited to cobalt bombs or neutron bombs. Using nuclear power to melt the ice in the polar regions and inundate an enemy country, creating earthquakes, causing sea storms, changing the course of rivers to stop them from flowing toward an enemy country, driving away clouds from the sky and stopping rainfall to create famine-like conditions, destroying the ozone layer and initiating a gigantic mass murder through the release of the sun's ultraviolet rays . . . the capability to attack using laser and death rays has now come into human hands and people are searching for pretexts to use these on enemy countries.

PASCAL, FROM BEHIND THE SCENES

Man is just a trivial creature, the weakest creature in all of nature. However, although trivial, he is a conscious creature. Nature does not have to prepare to engage in warfare in order to destroy him. He can be destroyed in a breath. Yet, even while standing at the edge of death, man is greater than nature, because man has known death through his awareness.

I was sleeping peacefully in my room at night. Suddenly there was loud screaming and weeping. I woke up. I furtively went and stood on the veranda. There had been no lights on the street for a long time. Nevertheless, one could clearly make out that about five people had surrounded a youth. The lane was desolate. The boy was plaintively trying to prove his innocence. The others were repeatedly accusing him in muted tones. Looking at my watch, I saw it was half past one. Could I do something? I called on the gentleman in the adjacent flat. He was a senior government officer. Although it was cold, I was sweating profusely. He stared at me with sleepy eyes. And then he told me slowly:

"Go to sleep. Shut the doors and windows properly before you go to sleep." He shut and latched his door noisily. Just after that, the silence of the dark night effaced the boy's voice. The shadows on all sides moved away swiftly. For some time, a tear-drenched melancholy tone hovered over the road. And then there was silence. All the doors and windows of the large apartment block were shut. The entire housing complex was still. After staying up for a long while, I went to sleep at some point. It was very late when I woke up in the morning. Stepping out, I heard a lot of talk. Two mechanic boys slept at night in a garage across the road. They peeped through the slit between the doors and saw everything. They did not come out either, in fear. Sometime after the people disappeared, they ventured out bravely and took the wounded boy to hospital, carrying him in their arms. The boy's life was saved because he received treatment in time. Hearing about it, I wanted to have another cup of tea. I heaved a sigh of relief.

I lit another cigarette. As I sipped the tea, I told the person beside me: "Do you know, I saw everything clearly last night." In an indifferent tone, the unshaven man beside said: "Everyone saw it. Turning off the lights . . . from a narrow slit of the window shutter . . . everyone. The murderers knew well that none of the babus from the apartment blocks would come out. Not even after a thousand screams. They picked the place well."

Democracy doesn't fill the belly, that's why democratic socialism came to our country—hooray for d e m o c r a t i c   s o c i a l i s m.

At first, a drop of rain fell exactly in the middle of his forehead and it was cold—at this sudden assault he looked once at the sky and advanced straight toward the rawk ahead—there, the rawk is visible—don't you know the rawk . . . he advances.

"In your first book, you wrote that even if you believed in Marxism, you couldn't believe in civilization—what do you think about the conflict between Marxism and civilization?"

The matter, at least to me, is about disbelieving the entire value system of this bourgeois society. A civilization in which the relation between one man and another rests only on the commodity market, competitive exploitation and oppression—I shit on the face of this civilization.

After that, one evening, when he had crossed the age of forty and was touching forty-five, he saw he was standing atop an enormous wooden platform, the waiting masses from all sides advanced, he was brought in front of the stocks—and at such a time, quite suddenly, the heroine of this story, in tight jeans and round-necked T-shirt, appears hurriedly on the question-and-answer page and begins to sway her body. Yes, *sexy*. This saves him from the impending stocks. She, the heroine, jumps up and climbs on to a high branch and our hero, No.1, begins to pull at her leg from below. After this, the two of them somersault and begin to wander on the grass and then start singing a full-throated duet. This is not the end of the incident—in the mood of the song, the hero takes off his shirt and the heroine hops on to the hood of a moving jeep and begins to deliver a speech on women's freedom. The spectators watch, they watch and nod their heads and are rapt. The stocks are forgotten for the time being.

A narrow crack like this and, in the silence, the sound of something collapsing. It is dawn, from the tap comes the sound of the landlord cleaning his tongue. He gets up between a quarter to five and five, he does sit-ups on the roof wearing a red loincloth, eats gram left to soak overnight in water with slivers of ginger, and then chewing it elaborately, he says: "You are a nocturnal creature, mister, when people go to sleep at eleven at night, you sit down with a book. Pay attention to your health, mister, let my electric bill be less, isn't it written in the scriptures, *shariram adyam*? What, am I not right?" The man's sister, dark-skinned, has recently bought a new pair of go-go goggles. She's an MA student in history at Rabindra Bharati University. She punctiliously performs Shiva Puja—"I'll get my sister married with thirty tolas of gold, why don't you find me a good groom, a gold merchant, but the horoscopes must match." He was satisfied with milkless tea. As he sips tea, he hears: "There's no water even to wash after going to the toilet—please leave the tap now, *my maharani . . .*" People can keep running away from themselves, but until when, and for how long? . . . There's Soviet Russia . . . planning to send the spacecraft Vega into outer space, fitted with the most modern instruments. The Vega project is designed to collect all the relevant data regarding planet Venus and Hailey's comet. Monetary offerings are religiously made and pilfered at the Sitala shrine. He never likes the chatter in cities about the purity of village life. The bastis and huge buildings in the cities are not the last word, the peculiarity and multidimensionality of thinking is also a part of it. Sipping the last of the tea, he lights a cigarette. Just opposite the lane are the tin and tile roofs of the basti. Beside the small shops selling sundry items and veggie fritters, a two-arm-lengths-wide mud road enters the basti, after a few houses one finds a tin-sheet workshop, noise emanates from there, day and night. When it rains, capsized paper boats and heaps of excreta float by together from the basti to the main road. Yes, he cannot plow the farmland and harvest the crop, but for sure he can plow the inertness of the mind and harvest the light of freedom—as much as is possible for him . . . It's great, carry on . . . and who doesn't know that once inertness enters the mind, that same inertness continues to bring darkness in the social, economic, and political spheres too.

How he lolls languidly and spouts wisdom—
I swear on my mother, the whoreson
has enthusiasm . . .

Akashvani Kolkata. An important announcement. Those who collected deworming syrup from Howrah Hospital today are warned not to give the syrup to their children. Instead of deworming medicine, carbolic acid, which is a poison, was distributed. It can kill the children if it is consumed. We have warned you in advance—if someone dies, we are not responsible . . . Yes. And there's a flood of foreigners entering our country. Barbed wire fences are being erected along the border between Bangladesh and West Bengal in order to stop the illegal entry of foreigners. Earlier, there had been talk of erecting a concrete wall, but that was an expensive affair; so instead there will be 3,300 kilometers of barbed wire fencing.

UNSEEN, NUMBER ONE

Do we live in a civilized country? Some years ago, a group of people were blinded in a Bihar jail. But who did this, why they did it, what punishment they received, or whether they were at all punished—nothing is known. A few saffron-clad men and women were beaten to death in broad daylight in Gariahat. Who committed this act and what did the investigation find—we have no clue about that either. A village in West Dinajpur was surrounded by a band of attackers and people were hacked to death. Who does all this, day after day, does it in the face of our democracy? Why aren't they unmasked, why are their antisocial misdeeds not exposed, where's the impediment—who is the impediment? A boy set foot in Calcutta for the first time. The taxi he was in broke down on Howrah Bridge. Without a second thought, he got out to push the taxi, and he never came back. There was no grill over a drain-hole. That new visitor to Calcutta fell in and dropped into the water below. The police abused the public works department: Why didn't they install the grill? The public works department retorted, blaming the police: Yes, we installed them, but they are being stolen, the police are not apprehending the thieves. Thereafter, all was silent and still.

Uncle-in-law sits on niece-in-law's lap

On September 12, when the demon Rahu was in the twentieth planetary aspect (it was an inauspicious time of the day then), a lame colleague of mine went out to drink tea during tiffin break and was run over by a Mercedes Benz. The man was a great believer in astrology. Just the previous month, he had bought a gemstone for a substantial amount. The car ran him over on an empty street. The bhadramahila who was driving the car fled the scene. The traffic police and well-meaning pedestrians put the man into a taxi and took him to the hospital. The taxi driver was muttering, this was his first trip of the day and here he was having to take on such a fare . . . The doctor in the emergency department of the hospital said: "Oh, this is a simple matter—why are you so worried—everything will be all right. So many are run over every day." Later, in the course of conversation, I learnt that it was our colleague's lame leg that was broken. There was to be no treatment of his leg that night, as no doctor could attend to him until the next afternoon. We became angry and swore at a nurse. We told one doctor: "Bastard, what the hell—we'll make you forget your father's name!" But even after such treatment, they did not pay any heed. Finally, twisting and stretching his body theatrically, a callow-youth-of-a-doctor came forth and said: "Come, let's plaster your leg." But the lame man was saved by a power outage just then. At once, the callow youth declared that he could not plaster the leg on the pretext of insufficient light. The doctors went out in groups and were strolling up and down the veranda, discussing whether or not they should go to Madhupur during Durga Puja. Finally, one doctor took pity and somehow applied the plaster cast in the darkness. And thus was the day spent. The next day, blood began oozing out of the broken leg. A pretty-looking nurse was passing by. I went up to her and inquired. "Oh it's quite common. Don't worry about it." Saying so, she went away, swaying her hips. From the next evening, our lame colleague began having convulsions and experienced difficulty breathing. By night, his condition began to get worse. The callow-youth-of-a-doctor suspected that the lame man must have contracted tetanus and so he should immediately be transferred to the Infectious Diseases Hospital. But because of a shortage of X-ray plates and the disappearance of the technicians, no X-ray had been taken on that day either. Seeing all this, the callow-youth-of-a-doctor changed his mind, and all of them began to debate whether he should be transferred to some other department instead of being taken to the Infectious Diseases Hospital. They argued with and shouted at each other for a long time. The callow-youth-of-a-doctor could be seen leaving in a huff. In the end, no X-ray was done until the next morning. The patient was unconscious by then. At noon, the neurologist was called, but he could not be located in person until the following afternoon. He had apparently signed out and gone to see the Vishwakarma Puja. A fat doctor came instead of him, and he said: "The X-ray plate is bad. Nothing can be discerned." He asked us: "Is this the patient's leg or arm?" Our lame colleague had died by then. The gemstone had brought this on. This was a result of not consulting a good astrologer and consulting a quack astrologer instead. He prescribed incorrect gems and the lame fellow gave up his life as a result. One cannot afford to be miserly in such matters, even if the expense is considerable one should always consult an esteemed astrologer. The lame man's elder brother asked: "Who can stop fate?" The fat doctor said: "You are right. You are 100 percent correct, dada. What should we do?"

Gazing at the buttocks of a pretty-looking nurse, I began to wonder whether to vandalize the place. The lame man's younger brother was also gazing at her buttocks, he said: "Will brother return if we vandalize the place? Besides, vandalism is an undemocratic affair." Death was to blame, atonement was prohibited. A mild breeze arose from the generator exhaust. Most fragrant. Plant trees, save trees. One tree, one life. A group photo with farmers. Electricity had come to village after village. The landless were receiving homestead plots and agricultural land, they were getting water for irrigation. Thousands of health centers were being constructed. There were exhibitions in the cities, in the information centers, with news of multipronged progress. As soon as one entered, one's eyes fell on a huge picture of a farmer with a smiling face—a sickle in one hand, a bundle of paddy in the other. And what's the color of the paddy? Sparkling yellow-gold. Beside him is a female farmer, the picture has been taken in the style of a particular film heroine. A smiling face, a hand on the man's shoulder. Inundated with picture after picture—bank, school, healthcare center, a pukka house. Nearby, an advertisement for going across an unmanned level-crossing: cross the level-crossing only when you are certain that there's no train approaching from either direction. Reach your destination safely and go home smiling—South Eastern Railway. Even after evaluating all aspects of the existing situation, the social responsibility as a writer—which is not merely a visualization of reality, but demolishing that so-called reality and creating a new reality, for the creation of a new kind of tradition, the responsibility of helping to awaken others to thought and awareness employing literature and one's awareness . . . mine, Manjula's and mine, making love in the darkness at Eden Gardens—we were at the peak then—the police officer on duty had said candidly: "Why do you unnecessarily trouble yourself like this, you could have brought your bed along." Manjula was not alarmed the least bit, she continued to keep her hand wherever it was. She didn't allow me to remove my finger from there either, and not at all what could be called desperately—but in a very easy, habitual way—she said: "That's great, why don't you also try a bit, he won't mind it, my lover is very open-minded." I, Subrata, was being slain then. In exactly the same way, at the very beginning of the seventies, just as a twenty- or twenty-two-year-old boy was getting murdered, observing his blood spilling, a policeman just like this one, a constable, had said: "See the fellow's blood—it's just like paan spittle . . ."

Subrata had once written on the New Year: Manjula, you are my Goddess

---

Devdas was screened on television a few days ago. Manjula and a few of her friends were there, all of them were twenty or twenty-two years old, they laughed all the way through, especially during all the sad-coy scenes. From time to time, their commentary ran: "*How funny*—what do they think they're doing?" Later, I asked them and learned that they did not believe in love. In their eyes, all these affected, coy love dramas were something to laugh at. Boys like girls and girls like boys—a very normal matter—and when you like someone you are bound to go around and fondle, and so why such mushy and heavyweight dialogues? Love was something to do, not to talk about. "What do you say, dada? . . . Slept with someone yet?" "Shut up!" "Forget it pal, once the light's turned off, everyone's the same . . . I swear on my mother, the babe's hot." I wasn't in the mood, I said, "*Shut up!*" and left. "Did it have to be Manjula? What I mean is: with so many girls around, why did you have to do it with your youngest aunt?" "I fell in love, it was very manly—what's called a He-Man. Blatant sexuality, a healthy relationship between man and woman, romantic love-bliss, which was once the stuff of the English-wallahs' drawing rooms . . ." "Hey, it's going in—look! It's going in . . . There . . . Damn—it's in." The whole is made up of the mixture of one person's morality and another person's immorality. I recall that among all of Hitchcock's fifty-three films—Hitchcock, that ancient Englishman—*Psycho* is the only one where we see a woman clad only in a brassiere. What was gained from that? At first: the atmosphere, the place, and then a house, a room inside the house, that's how the story starts. But in which place, on which day, in which part of the day, at what time? Nothing is communicated clearly, and yet everything is. In the entire story, there's not a single situation or character with which you can identify. Was that necessary? Whatever could possibly take place in the story—at all times the opposite direction is taken. Nothing wished for is considered, everything is the opposite of what should happen. Isn't the subject everything—actually, how much can a piece of writing wound the reader, that's what needs to be reflected upon. Whether an atmosphere is created or a character, that isn't the issue, the real act is this cutting-into-fragments, this cinematic usage: how capable is he of being successful in his objective, whether he is able to create adequate pressure on the reader's mind. All the love scenes have been written like murder scenes, and all the murder scenes have been converted to have a love angle. The first part of the story creeps along merrily, hazy and mild, and in the second part a captivation arises, which is like a nightmare. Not being able to remain objective despite wanting to be so, taking a side which time and environment compel him to take. One wonders why, even after knowing about the facet of destruction of a self-centered narrative, he won't apply all kinds of mediums of art in the writing. Louis Aragon and company finally took refuge in the socialist camp—he considers the event very significant, but almost from the time he was born, he was disinterested in the experience of adolescence, or the form of acknowledging gratitude regarding workers' suffering. Who was it that had written, after Bishnu Dey's death, that while Sudhindranath gives importance only to the decadence of the elite class, the stream of egalitarian struggle is powerfully evoked in Bishnu Dey's poetry?

Her father, torn to shreds, food for foxes and vultures,
Slain in vain effort to quell roving pillagers.

*　　*　　*

Her mother, a wayfarer, on a primeval quest for food.
Famine arrives, astride the Ass of pestilential ferocity.

Cheat and charlatan swarm town and hamlet,
While marauders storm in with the monsoon flood's fury.

Beside the picture of deer-hunting, two people with shields
and swords in hand dance frenziedly. On one side, a bear
chases a thin-looking deer. A few men, drawn in black and
red, linger on the shore of a river.

MY EIGHTY-ONE-YEAR-OLD GRANDFATHER

Arthritis of the hip. The body has become bent. The torso
remains parallel to the ground. The two arms flutter like
vulture's wings while walking. A pot in one hand. Water
from the Ganga in the pot. The obligatory ritual bath and
subsequent mantra recitation, twice a day. Bare-chested,
the sparkling-white sacred thread flashes in reflected light.
He blows his nose noisily and wipes his fingers on his buttocks. A matriculate from the old days. He reads Cheiro
in English. He had bought all the books of Däniken. A
great fan. "That with the advancement of science, people
go less and less to the church or temple or mosque—isn't
true at all. Neither does one notice any deficiency of faith
in God. Your astronauts Borman, Lovell, and Anderson
could not forget God even when they were beyond the

earth's gravity. They read out from the Bible in the space vessel. There's nothing on earth that's new. Whatever has occurred in the past and whatever shall occur in the future is all predetermined and preplanned. No effort by man can change a predestined event. Is there life after death? Your science cannot provide an answer to this question. Religion provides the answer to the question which science cannot answer. Here, religion wins over science."

Religious Assembly in Poland
Warsaw, June 18, 1983

Pope John Paul presided over Mass at an immense religious gathering here yesterday evening. The congregation can be compared to the Kumbh Mela in India. The stadium, in which almost two million people had gathered and heard the pope's speech, belongs to the communists. The pope was seated on a golden throne beside a huge crucifix. He addressed the gathering. In the address was a call for dialogue toward the granting of complete citizen rights. It was a very grand affair. The faithful stood with a thousand golden cups in their hands. In front of the pope were cardinals and bishops. There were gold necklaces around everyone's necks. To the chanting of hymns, the pope poured wine into the golden cups and round loaves of bread were distributed. There was no shortage either in terms of grandeur or faith in the massive religious assembly in Poland. Everything was of gold, grandeur, faith, round bread—all of gold. A gold-ornamented religious ceremony in famine-afflicted Poland.

He could not scream either, his vocal chords had been cut, then

: "You're a graduate. You have a job. We need you. We will ask you some frank questions."

: "Speak."

: "Which party do you support?"

: "I'm not into parties and such kinds of political groupism."

: "Do you think there will be revolution one day in our country?"

: "Why do you ask me this? What do I know about it?"

: "All right then, but you would surely have heard the word 'revolution.' What do you understand by the term 'revolution'?"

: "Didn't I tell you, I don't understand anything of such subjects."

: "Fine, what about 'democratic socialism'?"

: "No!"

: "That's astonishing."

: "No, I've never heard about all that. I learned my lesson well once. I don't want to lose my job under any circumstances."

: "You were associated with an extremist political party during your student days . . ."

: "Look here, I don't remember anything about my student days. I don't even want to talk about this subject with you."

: "One more question, a nonpolitical one . . ."

: "Make it quick."

: "Your relationship with Manjula . . ."

: "Yes, it exists. I believe in free sex. Polygamy is a tendency in man. And why shouldn't I do it? Who in this country is pure? Everyone snatches what they want from life. Why should I be excluded? All this revolution, and so on, sounds nice, mister, but when you have to give up one meal and stay at home—when you have no more than a single pair of trousers to wear—then who comes to even look you up? Write it down, at one time I did a lot regarding revolution and so on. I stayed up at night and put up posters on walls. What did I gain from that? I had to escape from home day after day. I whiled away the day eating muri. I was a fool. Now I know that everything belongs to the one who has money. Even this revolution of yours can be bought for money, mister. It's an open field in front of you—loot and gulp in any way you can! Try to fuck around with idealism and you're dead."

ADDITION TO THE INTERVIEW

Nothing whatsoever is possible on the part of the individual in this social system—when people have easy access to any kind of realist experience, it's only then that the middle-class conscience finds calm and the solace of contentment.

The constitution could not be amended without getting two-thirds of a vote. Hitler got an ordinance promulgated by the president, and in the people's assembly the opposition members were muzzled with the threat that, unless they voted for him, they would be declared traitors. Silence. Fearing arrest, many did not participate in the voting. Those who participated were afraid of voting against, and thereby inviting trouble. Silence. Hitler easily got two-thirds of the votes, and on the strength of that the constitution was amended and his writ was turned into law. Silence. After that no session of the people's assembly took place at all. Not even for a single day in twelve years. Once again, silence.

THE PICTURE SPREADS AND OCCUPIES THE ENTIRE WALL

A band of advancing warriors moves toward a safe refuge. With them are elephants, and armed warriors on the backs of the elephants. Somewhat below are many birds, not a single one can fly. The picture of the warriors is full of white color, the birds are scattered with geometrical proficiency. One can only surmise that they are birds—it's not a realistic picture. In one place, a band of people has surrounded a white mammoth. So, has World War III started? Nearby stands a horseman blocking the road. The perimeter is cordoned off. Is this a trap? The big-tusked elephant has no rider. No howdah strapped on its back. But is the elephant a wild one, and is the scene one of laying a trap for elephants?

SOME TIME WITH MY NIECE PUPU

Pupu, let's see what you have inside your tummy! Show uncle! Let me pull it all out, one by one. About three broken blades in all. One Nataraj pencil. Some intestines. One bra that is now too small. A picture from a previous life, in which Pupu was a landlord's wife. She was, wasn't she? And so? Some crumpled five-rupee bills, a light-blue fragrant letter pad with "Go bird, tell him" written in golden watermark. A nose ring of the latest style. Two sanitary napkins. Nail clippers, made of steel, from abroad. A pair of earrings, possibly made of rolled gold. So there was fear of robbery and burglary at that time too. A pinch of aniseed. One bottle of pills. About three songs of Rabindra Sangeet. One can't discern whether it is three or five, it's not clear. An almost chewed-up skull of a twenty- or twenty-three-year-old youth.

At least two dozen popular songs from Bombay films.

A copy of *Devdas* with a torn cover.

A Nirodh condom, unopened. One bottle of nail polish.

FOUR-SIDED

One day God began to make wind blow from the east. It blew the whole day and night. With the wind came locusts, at dawn, wrapped in sunlight. They spread through the whole country—nothing green remained on the fields. Like this, exactly like this, is society . . . Yes, it changes. But the image of the hero does not change. He's written a two-volume novel about the nineteenth century. The subject being, in the previous century our forefathers were all drunken scoundrels. The novel is extremely popular. Selling like hotcakes. Was a bestseller for a year and a half. And on top of that, got the Bankim Puraskar award. If one could release one like that about Subroto and Manjula—that wouldn't be bad at all.

MANJULA AND SUBROTO'S CONVERSATION:
IN BESTSELLER STYLE

: "It won't do to forget that we're two characters in this text."

: "Whatever people want—is everything for us. Got to do it. What people want."
: "Been sent here. To the page of this text. For that purpose. That's it."
: "In that case what shall we do?"
: "What if we have sex. Let's go to bed. Lots of people will be happy."
: "A little bit of sad-sad as well. Some talk of the poor too. Added to it."
: "But which one first? Going naked to bed? Or going to bed and then getting naked . . ."
: "It's a problem."
: "There's no need to get philosophical. Our readers don't like it if it's too serious."
: "But it's great fun. They call it decadence."
: "While enjoying it fully."
: "Look, there's a person signaling something . . . look!"

Light explodes with a flash in the eyes. From the faraway jungles of the Terai, wind blows with a whoosh. There's a dust storm. The red crocodile breaks through the bluish eggshell, it awakens and roars: "Don't wake me, sister-fuckers—don't wake me up." The red crocodile must be fed now. Where will the red crocodile feed? Left, right, eat from wherever you can, strike and bite. Darkness every-where, the black-as-pitch darkness of the new moon night dedicated to the worship of Ratani Kali, everywhere.

FROM EHRENBURG'S WRITING, IN THE WAY IT HAD BEEN
NOTED DOWN IN THE DIARY

. . . Reading is also a creative pursuit, and readers are always reading something or other. I remember a gathering of readers of the novel *Storm*. Young students had read the critiques of the novel in advance. In trying to ape the professional critics, they blabbered more about the popular critiques than about the novel itself. All of a very pedestrian and general nature. There was a terrific argument at the end of the meeting. A war of words between two girls regarding the protagonist of the novel. One of them said: "I really want to meet a person like Sergei [the protagonist of *Storm*] in real life." The other girl's answer: "I can't figure out what you see in him! The man's simply useless, lacks personality." The two of them were of the same age, both had received their education in the same school and college, and what's more, on all other matters their viewpoints were of the same kind. But each one had read the novel with her own power of imagination, emotional experience and particularities of character. And thus were born two diametrically opposite Sergeis.

OPERATION FAUSTUS

Israel invaded Lebanon
America provided the ammunition
Provided the fighter planes
Several thousand Palestinian folk became refugees
America gave them dollars
Provided assistance for refugee relief
It's ten in the morning
While rubbing Keo Karpin hair oil on her head
I teach tenses to my niece Pupu
Tense is the most vital thing in English grammar

And then
One morning
While learning about the difference
Between past and past perfect tense
Pupu finally says:
Uncle, I'm not there.

MY INNER DILEMMA

A long-standing desire for a ceiling fan in the bedroom. But there was never any money left at the end of every month. Finally, when I couldn't take it anymore, I bought one a fortnight ago. In today's newspaper, the same fan company has advertised that a fifteen percent discount is being offered on their fans. That means the fan bought for three hundred and sixty rupees is now cheaper by more than fifty rupees. After seeing that, I felt terribly annoyed. Fifty rupees! I don't like the boring drone of talk about literature. Instead, let me now tell the story of a mosquito. This is the mosquito that at some time, unknown to me, sat on my left lung and punctured it, and sucked away everything of me—

This mosquito now flies over Victoria Memorial. It casts its shadow on the top of the Memorial. The color of the angel atop the Memorial changes, the shadow keeps spreading in the direction of the Maidan. Leaving behind the vast human settlement in the south, it began to steadily encircle the Maidan. The last of the day's sunlight there now, sticking to the leaves on trees. Moloy Bhattacharjee lies with his head on Chandana Sen's lap. This is the Moloy Bhattacharjee who stuffs Number Ten cigarettes in a Wills Navy Cut packet and lights them carefully in front of his lover to show that he smokes Wills—while rubbing his face and neck with a half-wet gamcha the whole evening. To get a reddish tinge. On the cheeks.

And this is the Chandana Sen who, even at the age of thirty-one, seeing the lack of effort from home toward getting her married, willingly or unwillingly, regularly feeds honey to the Moloy Bhattacharjees when darkness descends beneath the tree. But she isn't able to snag anyone. Now the mosquito goes and sits on Moloy Bhattacharjee's cheek. It lowers its proboscis and sucks it up, yes, that's right, blood. Then it flies off after some time. Chandana Sen looks at Moloy Bhattacharjee lying with his head on her lap, here, but despite the proximity he was not quite all there, from the corner of his eye, again and again, he looked intently at a buxom young woman walking with her blue sari blowing in the wind—the mosquito now flies northward, further north, and it then goes and sits on the elbow of a middle-aged conjurer who is performing for a thousand people beneath Shaheed Minar. This is the conjurer wearing a black achkan over a jet-black silk lungi, who speaks in a fabricated language made up of an amalgam of Bangla and Hindi. He makes a skull speak and tells simpleminded folk the way to reach the road to Ramrajya.

The mosquito sits on the conjurer's elbow and keeps sucking blood as the people gather around him. After a while, looking at the conjurer's face, they sense something, and then each one goes his own way—they keep leaving.

The mosquito flies off, and with it goes its shadow.

It goes and sits on the fleshy thigh of Jagmohan of Burrabazar. Now he, Jagmohan, with a telephone receiver in either hand, is engaged in a discussion about the share market. This is the Jagmohan who can discern at a glance gold and silver buried under ash, who buys government goats from the government, and sells them back to the same government with a one percent margin. The mosquito merrily sucks Jagmohan's blood through its proboscis. When its belly is full, it flies off—the mosquito flies away, taking the large shadow along. It comes and sits on Jhantu Kayal's shoulder in Baghbazar. Jhantu Kayal, who has fallen asleep in the stifling heat in the course of trying, in vain, to cool himself with a hand-fan after a whole day's backbreaking labor. This is the Jhantu Kayal who works twelve hours in a lathe-machine workshop in Bantra. At the end of the month he receives a salary of three hundred and forty-seven rupees. Returning at night with grease-blackened hands, he tears off pieces of roti and stuffs them into his mouth, labor-fatigued, his eyes close, swollen eyelids.

The mosquito goes and sits on his elbow, but there's no blood to suck there. It sits on his back, which is hard and bony, with leathery skin—it can't prick and insert its proboscis. It sits on the forehead, there's no flesh there, only protruding solid bone and forehead. Jhantu Kayal is fortunate. The mosquito then flies off. Again. Jet propellers on its wings. Sound. Speed. In the wings. Its body becomes heavy. The shadow keeps spreading. Of the jet propeller. The mosquito's shadow spreads across the entire Maidan—the martyr's pillar is in shadow, as is Gandhi on Park Street, and the stone angel atop Victoria Memorial. A gust of wind blows, clouds gather, the symbolic measure of the sun becomes small. No one can see or sense when it goes and sits with a quiet plop on the barrel of the pipe-gun held in the hands of an eighteen-year-old boy.

On the floor, taking up a lot of space
The faded yellow mark from the explosion

ON THE STREET ALL NIGHT
FOR GODARD

**A college girl who couldn't get
a ticket for Godard**

"What's there to worry, let's watch any other film and when we return home we can always say: I saw a Godard film."

A middle-aged cine-goer crazy about Hindi films

"Why should this be called cinema? Sit on the banks of the Ganga, count the waves and keep writing letters—no one will stop you. Where's the need to make a film?"

Discussion in the newspaper

In the evolution of film grammar, his contribution and influence are comparable only to that of Picasso in the fine arts . . . this film-maker is committed to serious cinema, bringing together the apparently conflicting poles of sexuality and politics.

A female feature-writer

The ordinary cine-goer was flabbergasted seeing Godard's

ARE YOU A MARXIST,
SUBIMAL BABU?

"Why do I say there's no difference whatsoever between the slogan, *Inquilab Zindabad!*, and the Hare-Krishna kirtan; why is there no difference between the so-called revolutionary movement's ritual process, that is, formal customs, and religious customs; I humbly ask the elite class of English-medium bhadralok, who are the hereditary guardians of our education and culture; and especially request the middle-class Marxist-Leninist geniuses to think about it."

I quote Binoy Ghosh here because, in the name of Marxism, I don't wish to remain confined to any stagnant water. In the decades of the sixties and seventies, the youth of various countries revolted in different ways against the current society, state and values. Behind the denial of the legacy of custom-bound tastes and education-culture was a dormant seed of social transformation, even though that is only in broad terms. Some think this is a kind of psychological malady, going astray—which is the polar opposite of the struggling films. What dismayed them most was the fifty-minute film, *Letter to Jane*. Perhaps seeing the film's name, they had hoped that the subject of the film would be the love story of some woman named Jane, and there'd be lots of sizzling sex. But when they saw there was none of that, they ran belligerently toward the cinema hall's manager . . .

A VIP in the inaugural ceremony

"I believe all the tickets for Godard's films sold out in just an hour and a half. From this one can understand that Calcutta's audience possesses cinematic awareness."

A conversation between the state government's spokesperson and a woman delegate on the agitation in front of the cinema hall before the screening of the film *Numero Deux*:

— "Tell me, what's so special about the film that makes the delegates so excited? This week, most of the time, the delegate seats remained unoccupied during the Godard films."

—"Don't you know, today's film is very hot. The whole of Calcutta knows, and you mean to say you don't? Tickets are being scalped for 50 rupees outside."

Reportage

mentality. I didn't exactly see it that way. In the context of the un-Marxist political leadership of our Marxist leaders, and the smugness, betrayal, and fulfillment of self-interest exhibited by the middle-class in the name of practicing Marxism—the term "struggling" is very synthetic and seems to be a slogan, no more than mere sound, coined by urban babus who have no relation whatsoever to the labor force. The beatnik poets, the angry generation, the pop singers or artists and directors who were thinking in a new way, could, if nothing else, wound the foundations of prevalent values a little bit. Such wounding is, of course, not everything, but it is needed first. With this is needed a struggling outlook, the assault should come from that rather than be superficial. In this context, those sparkling words of Ritwik Kumar Ghatak:

"In my artistic life, both actively and inactively, I understood that struggle must become the daily companion of the artist's life and even if any crisis temporarily engulfs the artist it should not lead to a complete defeat, that is to say, we must not surrender our conscience and mind during the crisis."

I don't know whether my writing is Marxist or not, but I do know that my fundamental inclination is to investigate.

But Godard doesn't make films for ordinary people. Nevertheless, why did the ordinary people of Calcutta spend the whole night on the streets, waiting for a ticket, even in this winter cold, braving such difficulties, why? What can the ordinary cine-goer get from his film?

A story in the Sunday supplement of a newspaper

Poor Godard. Trying to make a film do the work of an essay, he's scorched even the bones of the seasoned audience.

Editorial in a newspaper

What exceptional capability Godard has in making commercial films. If he had retreated a bit, people could have seen more naked flesh. In that respect he could have scored over any Western commercial filmmaker.

A critique in a Marxist publication

To explain, we can see that Marxism has been imposed on him, rather than its acceptance being the fruit of a historical process. He is against every kind of stasis, and hence, it was largely out of emotion that he supported the Chinese cultural revolution. In the middle

Until now, it is the search, rather than reaching a decision on anything, that I'm more enthusiastic about. I am always aware of my sense of incompleteness, and the inclination to search arises from this sense of incompleteness.

I look at two broad strata in society (the arrangement of strata is however not so easy and simple, rather it is quite complex and this is not the place for a discussion on that); a certain class is content with the progress of a few people, while most people, ordinary laboring folk, are merely a means for the progress of the few people. Today, there is an effort to build a society where the progress of the majority of people takes place. There is no end to artful analyses or opinions about this, and to the division into levels as well, but it is clear that my writing and the attempt of my writing is against those who in earlier times had the sole right over culture, and in favor of the excluded people.

In this context, it is necessary to state clearly that staying away from politics too seems to be a kind of political attitude. We are living in a situation that is changing rapidly, and actually changing each day.

Generally, we support the communists in those cases where there is a convergence of the film, Mao Tse Tung is quoted spontaneously: *Let a hundred flowers bloom, let a hundred thoughts develop.* French materialism and Sartre's existentialism make him elaborate upon and explain human survival, relations, civilization, and even sexuality. The contact with Marxism, and at the same time the influence of the French structuralist left, make his thinking ambiguous. In essence, I see in him the tendency of denial of historical materialism and a steady entry into the world of ideology. In this respect, whether it is politics, sexuality, or aesthetics—on any subject, when it comes to a conclusion, Godard hints at or shows a tendency in his films toward extreme simplification. That possibly comes from his ambiguous political thinking.

with our anarchist writing. I reject bourgeois capitalism like poison, but how far is it possible to support the kind of socialism that completely takes away the rights to free speech and criticism? I could never remain passive about the people's condition—sometimes I wonder whether it is enough to merely verbally express sympathy for the working class, who have been fighting on. But yes, I can't stand making a fuss about "people," which is largely found in the socialist camps.

I always remember that, whenever necessary, the reactionaries utilize this kind of semi-anarchist, semi-Marxist thinking in their own way.

He pierces the darkness from one corner, and has pressed his thin fingers, drawn together, down in the middle. Are these the fingers of the laboring class? Not at all. It doesn't look like that. Lazy. Yes, but he's human. And it's because humans live here that it's customarily dark. Viscous. Venous. Angular. Open drains. Fumes of burning gas. Through the hole, a bit of sky from the other shore, blue and dreamlike, broken and battered, arriving here in an old canister. It hangs. Licks it every once in a while, wanting to get the scent although his own corpse lies in the drain, the face, when it floats up, he comes running and, in fear, attaches himself above the neck, tries with all his might to move the stone, alone—entirely in his own fashion. No one notices, some make rotis on the fire, while some pull down the girl beside them to their own dustiness and run their hands over her breasts and buttocks. The doddering old octogenarian grandfather, cataract in the eyes, sits silently, while an eleven-year-old boy, Pipi, runs a spring-loaded fire engine in play.

No death is as heavy as stone All deaths are as light as a feather

Knotted plumes of smoke push their way up toward the sky. Below, slum-dwelling youths assist the fire brigade. Stumps of trees accumulated on four sides, a pile of motor oil tins and sacks of books. The walls of the warehouses and factories are collapsing. The burnt down walls collapse and bits of stone fly here and there. Houses and buildings are burning over an area of a few thousand square miles, a love named human. A fierce hot wind blows everywhere.

Ignited, burnt books, wood, and ash fly in the wind. Everywhere, the youths ignore the flames and, risking their lives, enter the fire and turn upside down the burning tree stumps that will keep burning. One hundred, two hundred, or even more, the operation being supervised by the concerned officer involved lots of people.

SASTA KHOON, MEHNGA PYAR

Matinee show. A cinema hall. A Hindi film currently ruling the market. The line for the front stalls snakes this way and that, and has now reached very far. Most of those in the line are young, moustaches have just sprouted on the upper lips of some. Books in hand, school skipped, now in line. Two youths—white shirts, white trousers, white zipped-up boots, and on the waist, above the belt, a garland of real hibiscus flowers—arrive singing in loud voices and stand in front of the line. Surveying all the sides well and raising his right arm as if performing a magic trick—while singing *"Hum Tum Ek Kamre Mein Band Ho"*—suddenly in a flash he clenches the fist of his left hand and punches the stomach of a simple-looking boy standing in the line. As if preplanned, the second person too, singing, *"Socho Kabhi Aisa Ho To Kya Ho,"* gives another tight punch to an accompanying boy in the line, who falls to the ground. In a trice, the two all-white friends occupy the vacant places in the line. Thereafter, in the usual fashion, the taunting of those pushed out of the line begins, with spontaneous laughter. The simpleton boy, now out of line, does not protest at all, but quietly mutters to himself: "I was standing in the line from morning . . . what bad luck, just after coming so close to the counter." The second youth is bolder. For the ears of the all-whites, he says: "Guru, I've seen wackos of A-class, B-class, C-class, and many other classes in my life, for that matter I've seen golden wackos, blue wackos, and orange wackos—but I've never seen such a Z-class pure-white wacko in my life." Yes, there are also pictures of dogs, plenty of them. They have collars on their necks, the looped leashes emerge in the fists of some people.

The people of the country ask in loud voices: "What's the main problem before us now?" The country's leader, the Big Boss, shouts: "Vanaspati mixed with the fat of cow and pig. Poverty, unemployment, illiteracy—all that's for later.
Save vanaspati first—save caste."

MAO TSE TUNG HAS NOT BEEN BORN YET, HERE, ON THIS BELOVED EARTH OF OURS

Monu said, "Listen, don't come and lecture us about conflict of values. There are pictures of Ramakrishna, Vivekananda, and Anukul Thakur in expensive wooden frames in Father's room. Incense is lit there every evening, and puja is performed, adhering to all the rules and rituals. And in the sitting room is a huge Lenin. Father works in the Calcutta Municipal Corporation. He reaches his office by noon, and after signing the attendance register, he places his bag carefully on his table, so that his name on the bag's nametag is clearly visible. After spending a couple of hours here, he goes to do his real job, in a private firm. He works there until four in the evening, and then he returns to his *legal* office. After doing a bit of this and that, and some talk with a couple of people, he picks up his bag and leaves for home. This is his daily work routine. Sometimes, there's a need for overtime. On some days, it's also Father's turn. Father says, the overtime at night is the most convenient of all. Because there's no work other than making the bed and going to sleep. There's no need then to do anything even for the sake of appearances."

Monu said all this very dispassionately. We were a bit uneasy. No one had ever shared their personal details with us openly like this. We waited to see where exactly Monu would finally go in his discussion of values. "And so, in this fashion, salaries from two places and quite a few hours of overtime. He received a fair bit of money every month. Besides, in that kind of job, the extra wasn't bad either. In fact, the under-the-table business was the real thing. Father built two houses in the names of Mother and my elder brother. He got my elder sister married, spending almost one hundred thousand rupees. Incense began to be ritually lit every evening before Ramakrishna and Vivekananda. And on May Day, et cetera, a garland on Lenin's neck. They used to go to Kalighat for puja every Saturday. Come rain, flood, lightning, or whatever, this rule was never flouted. Everything was going along just fine. But a problem arose. The political environment had changed over the last few years. New masters had arrived at the Writers' Building. There were some changes within the Corporation too. The new officers discovered the fact that Father worked in two places. It would not be correct to say that they discovered it, because everybody knew about it earlier but they never spoke about it. It wasn't just Father, many others did the same. The new masters plunged into trying to remove corruption. They issued a show-cause notice to Father, asking him to explain why he works in two places.

"But Father was a bit too clever in that respect. Nobody could provide any proof that he worked in two places. Besides, he was very close to the union bosses. He also occupied an important position in the union. When the officers went after Father, he went to the union straightaway to seek refuge. The union began to fight on behalf of Father. The day a notice of suspension was issued against Father, the union threatened to go on strike. The bosses' highhandedness would not be tolerated! . . . The suspension notice against Mr. Roy must be withdrawn!"

Monu lit a cigarette and let out a mouthful of smoke. He used to smoke one cigarette after three beedis. He said: "That was the situation from the outside. But the inside story is of a different kind. The problem was with me. The party whose union ruled in Father's office—fortunately or unfortunately, I had been associated with that party from my college days. I had fought on behalf of the student organization of the party. I had molded my own beliefs according to the party's beliefs. It had become a seamless part of my thinking that one day, under this party's leadership, revolution would be possible in our country.

"I had to halt in my tracks. I had to evaluate, once again, the leadership of my party. I established contact with the higher level. Needless to say, that was as a citizen, not as a party member. My conversation with them went as follows—

Question: Do you people keep tabs on the personal life of Mr. Roy, the person for whom you are fighting?

Answer: The party does not concern itself with anyone's personal life. There are huge responsibilities in front of the party now, a great duty.

Question: There's no trace of Marxism in Mr. Roy's personal life. He didn't get his daughters married without scrutinizing the horoscope and the caste status. Pujas, Kali temple, bribes, deceit—that's what his life consists of. How do you view such activities?

Answer: We have only one view—he is a sincere party worker. The only factor for us is how much he sacrificed for the party during the dark days.

Question: Okay, but you know that he works two jobs. He draws salary from two places. There's no reckoning how much he receives under the table. How can you accept an illegal affair like this?

Answer: As long as there isn't a fundamental change in the economic condition in our country, such things are bound to happen. If we worry about trivial matters like this, we'll deviate from our party's main objective.

"Consequently, I had to leave. Father was a slave to blind superstition, but as he had done some work for the union he was much needed by the party. That's how the party would value him."

Monu stopped now. All of us were watching him. Looking at us, he now lit a beedi. "You can understand that everything I've held dear for so long—has received a great jolt. Will this working-class party function only with people like Father? Will the value systems of such people really be transformed one day by close association with the party, as the leaders claim?"

Struggle gives direction
And song for me is oxygen

The famed revolutionary of Andhra Pradesh, Cherabanda Raju, died at the young age of forty-one. There was no report about his death in any newspaper, not a line was written anywhere. That's what our democracy-loving newspapers are like. And it's they who blatantly compete among themselves to publish minute details about the Prince of Wales, with a travelogue accompanied by pictures of Prince Charles's visit occupying page after page. What urgency in presenting the news and what public delight! The real psychological profile and colonial mentality of those who had cried hoarse about freedom and democracy during the Emergency blooms forth from their conduct. In 1979, after two operations for a brain tumor, Cherabanda Raju began losing sight in his right eye. He was admitted to hospital for a third operation. After remaining in a coma for six months, he died on July 3, 1983, at ten minutes past three in the morning.

I am the enemy of both classes
The rulers and their obedient opposition
I do not aim for the opposition seat
But I want state power.
Beloved motherland of mine, you alone are my mother
You are my God

Your nature is to have fun by
Climbing on the bed of the destroyed
Your allure is such that every part of you is mortgaged
To the marketplaces of the world
In all your youthfulness you sleep in the embrace
Of moneyed-folk
Your sleep is such as to not be disturbed
By the spit and dirt thrown at you.

A PERSONAL NOTE ABOUT VILLAGES

A story about a village could not be written even after much effort. Living in the city, I don't have any urban illusion about the village. That's my limitation. I somehow feel like a customary pimp. A superficial view? Perhaps so. I was born in a village. I've known its people for the last thirty years. In joy and sorrow, happiness and pain. I somehow feel like a thief if I write a story. A cerebral explanation has arisen. Yes, I'm a common city-babu, I have no shame in admitting that. I have only brought together whatever scattered bits and pieces were written in the diary.

a) Village life revolves around agriculture. Joys and sorrows, festivals and happiness, mutual relationships all emerge from agriculture. The context of life, and for that matter, mental makeup too, is created from this agricultural background.

b) It is farming that determines how village folk will fare the entire year. Farm work is not merely a means of livelihood, it is also a way of life.

c) Many times, while traveling in villages, I feel that a city-babu like me is a parasite. The big houses in the city, wide roads, schools and colleges, courts of law, my Writers' Building, or even the very governor's residence—everything is the direct or indirect fruit of farmers' labor.

d) The city is very often the place where innocent, simple village folk become corrupted—the villagers themselves think so. Associated with the city are court cases and litigation, and courts of law—which are a civilized means to make the rural people landless. Where a fourteen- or fifteen-year-old boy becomes a full-fledged agricultural worker in a world where reality is land-centric, becoming landless means getting completely destroyed. Because of the link with land and farming, water, cows, and trees are an inseparable part of this society, rain is not just about the monsoon, the cow is not just a means for milk production or a means to plow the field, it is also a god. This mentality assumes an entirely different meaning in the village, which is completely incomprehensible to city-babus.

The writer offered a cigarette and lit it for him carefully. The boy held it like a chillum pipe between his two hands, took a deep puff and began to cough. The boy's still coughing.

Thirty-six-year-old Dora Pezilli stood for elections in the Trieste region of Italy, with the support of the communists. She took up her electoral battle in a new way. When she delivered her campaign speeches in different venues, she was completely naked. This was a nude struggle.

One learns that Miss Pezilli has been fighting for the social recognition of prostitutes. For a long time. Was this her latest method, an inspiration? What if prostitutes demand the right to public nudity? And if they do, what then? No, they can never do that. They have an adequate sense of shame. It was reported in a newspaper in Rome that this nude campaign of Miss Pezilli's was not in support of prostitutes, but against the curbs on the freedom of nudists. They also used the term "burning protest." In Italy, swimming naked is illegal at all the beaches where people can swim and at all swimming pools. An electoral weapon to repeal this law? Miss Pezelli stood for elections with the communists' support. They did not protest against her. The Italian communist party is a very old one. It is quite influential in Europe. The theory of Eurocommunism and

No south Indian film by the name of *Sexy Dreams* was ever made. The real name was *Ratinirvedam*. The names were such that the audience would easily get attracted— *Her Nights, A Passionate Lover, Love Story*, and so on. Such names were also given as would immediately make one think it was a Bengali film. Like *Stree-Purush*. Tents are put up for film screenings in villages and all these films are shown. They're extremely popular. Father and son, mother and daughter, all watch together, they enjoy them. Not just that, the real stuff is better planned. These films received certificates from the censor board in Madras. Quite a few parts of all these films had been cut and removed for having objectionable and obscene scenes. But when the film was screened with a different name in Calcutta, the film's deleted objectionable parts were skillfully reattached. And that apparently was most alluring. The allure drew people in hordes to come running for such films. Sex-hungry masses. And who are the distributors of these films? It is worth noting that those whose names appear as distributors were foreign to the film sector.

the source of the theory. These communists did not protest. Miss Pezelli was going around naked, making her speeches of revolution. She is in the news. She blends nudity with communism. In a wonderful way. Most appropriately.

A few young businessmen from Burrabazar got together and started the business, a few lakh rupees had already been invested in the venture. Many were hopeful that a business catering to the sex-starved masses would be extremely successful. Another new horizon opened up in the world of business.

Then, when a massage-wallah passed by, amazingly making a ringing sound by holding two oil bottles in his left palm by their caps and rattling them lightly against one another, the man wishes to indulge. He has for long wanted to try out the massage thing. He calls out. In the darkness of the Maidan, the massage-wallah makes him take off his clothes and lie down flat on his stomach. Asking, mustard or coconut, the massage-wallah begins kneading the middle-class shoulders with both hands. Practiced hands massage the back, neck, waist, and ankles, making them glisten with oil. The man's eyes shut in relief and pleasure. Now, the massage-wallah has placed his fat, rough fingers on the man's temples, which throb while he thinks. Massaging with every finger, down to the scalp. Nearby, someone laughs loudly, accompanied by the clanging of a sugarcane crusher. As the man feels his forehead with one hand, and then as he lowers the same hand to his chest, he is surprised, with just one massage his ribs have . . . a lot. His chest has expanded, right where the thick black patch of hair is, which rises and falls with his breathing—it has expanded. Blood rushes to his chest, leaping. The folds of flesh on the palms of his hands seem to have come to life. The skinny, middle-class intellectual appearance has disappeared. Truly, the massage-wallah is a magician. The man opens and spreads out the palms of his hands and holds them up against the neon lights. Rapt, he swings his arms, this way and that. Suddenly, he becomes conscious of his surroundings. Looking around, he realizes it is very late at night now. People had been sitting here and there all over the Maidan. Now they are all gone. The area around Shaheed Minar is empty. Wind blows gustily over the desolate Maidan. A torn piece of yellow paper comes fluttering with the southern breeze. As the yellow paper comes flying, he casts his eyes toward the void and looks into it. The vast Maidan. Darkness. Grass. A tram goes by, snaking along. Hard earth beneath the feet. Nobody anywhere. In front or behind, near or far. Nobody anywhere. Only yellow. The piece of paper. Fluttering in the breeze. It trembles. Advances. Becomes still. It trembles again. Advances. Hands in trouser pockets. He remains standing. He. Like someone without any purpose. Looks. The same yellow. The piece of paper.

FIDEL CASTRO'S HISTORIC SPEECH	CASTRO'S CONDOLENCE ON BIRLA'S DEATH
"Those who think that they'll win the election against the imperialists are extremely childish, and those who think that the day will come when they will come to power through elections are even more childish . . . That socialism can come without a fight . . . through peaceful means, through the medium of elections . . . that's a lie."	Fidel Castro was grieved at industrialist G. D. Birla's death. In a telex message, he said, "G. D.'s sudden demise has saddened me. We had been counting the days to G. D.'s visit. His tour schedule had already been arranged. Kindly convey my personal condolences to G. D.'s family members and the members of the industrial group under his leadership."

In Bertolt Brecht's study there hung
A small framed piece of cardboard
On it was written: Truth is concrete

The wind blew gustily. Suddenly, it began to rain and three
middle-aged men with long sideburns came running and
stood under the portico overhanging the pavement. Right
after them came a girl wearing a frock. Unsure of what to
do, she too slipped into a spot near a dark corner under
the portico and stood with her neck slanted in a slightly
aloof manner, as if she were oblivious to the existence of
the three men. An adolescent girl. The way she stood, the
bright yellow frock, and below that her pretty, slender
legs too, the hem of her frock blowing in the wind—it
looked very beautiful. Heavy rain descended all over the
scene. The streets began flooding. From somewhere, a
bull came through the rain and forced its way to the spot
under the portico and the four men there were displaced,
especially the girl. Being pushed into an even darker spot,
closer to the corner, she looked at the bull with frightened eyes. The bull was black with white patches. It stood
still after having found a place for itself. The powerfully
built one among the three middle-aged men, the one who
wore a green punjabi over black trousers, and whose thick
black sideburns came down to the very bottom of his
jaw, moved up toward the bull's head and, holding the
two horns, pushed it hard. The bull moved back a few
steps, shook its head and tail, and did not do anything
else. The girl lifted up her head, looked, and then tried to

slip even closer to the corner. The fat, dark-skinned man again advanced toward the bull, and again held its horns and pushed it back. The bull moved a little bit. The girl did not have any more place to move. The bull's tail was now touching her yellow frock. A whitish wall behind her and in front, the legs, buttocks, and gray-colored tail of the bull. Circles of black and white. The rain outside grew heavier. A man rushed past in front of the space, umbrella in hand. A maroon-colored car went by, splashing fountains of water. A brown school bus came and stood beside the pavement. Through the rain, the loud chatter of children came wafting. Red belts shone over white school uniforms. The girl, the one wearing a yellow frock, pressed a book to her chest and looked outside. The rain continued to pour down. The bull was silent, almost touching her leg, only the gentle swishes of its wet tail wet her yellow frock, the man with the green punjabi over black trousers put his hand in his pocket and took out a pack of cigarettes and matches. Lighting the cigarette with a flash, he blew out a mouthful of smoke. He held out the pack to his two companions. Smoke filled the place. The girl lifted up her head and looked alternately at the rain and the bull. She pressed a book lightly to her breast with her left hand. Going by noisily on the road in front now was a double-decker bus. A wave of water spilled over on to the pavement. The swirling water flowed into the space beneath the portico and advanced bit by bit, it touched the bull's hooves, the feet of the three hefty men, and the girl's shoes. It accumulated. Water.

Here every word has an independent identity
And also punishment, for carrying that identity.

In a recent survey conducted in the United States of America, it has been found that thirty-one percent of women in major cities feels unsafe, even during the daytime, going five minutes' distance from home, fearing rape and similar physical assaults. The women of that country are tending toward giving up jogging and learning karate instead. In the minds of the people at large, a continued lack of a sense of safety. . . and because of this fear, as many as eleven percent of the American population of two hundred thirty-two million carry arms when they step out of the home, for self-defense. In another survey it was found that twenty to twenty-five percent of families possess revolvers or pistols and the like, and forty percent of families keep guns at home. In the opinion of the surveyors, this rate is rapidly rising.

Gaze at the image
Of Kali, venerated by robbers,
Together with family

What is it that is used most often in the writing of James Hadley Chase or Harold Robbins? What's the percentage of use of the word "murder" in their writing? How many words are used to create a murder scene? How many murders have direct descriptions from murder witnesses and how many are described indirectly? In all those descriptions, does the writer take the stance of enjoyment? Similarly, in the description of a rape case, some words tend to be used. Is the rule of enjoyment applied in such cases too, or is it not? How many such incidents are there in an ordinary novel, film or play? How many are direct and how many are implied? What is the percentage of books in which immoral or unsocial relations are described or are given importance? In plays and films as well. Nowhere are smoking cigarettes or drinking alcohol presented as reproachable matters. If they are, there's the fear of being labeled old-fashioned. But obscene conversation, hints, or acts of sexual perversion, animal-like behavior, or inhuman practices, are now being used as if they are accepted facts in society. The funny thing is, even if an ordinary reader raises questions about this, serious readers, the intellectual readers, don't really raise any objection to speak of.

MAO TSE TUNG HAS NOT YET BEEN BORN HERE— ON THIS BELOVED EARTH OF OURS

After that comes a time when Jhuma-di too has to leave home and go. She leaves home with a three-year-old child in her arms. She says, "Hey Bachhu, I've left home too!" She loosens the cloth on her back and shows it, saying: "See what they've done to me." One couldn't stand to look at Jhuma-di's back. I deliberately turn my face the other way. Jhuma-di continues: "Not just this—there's more, want to see?" I don't look. It makes your jaw clench.

"Do you blame Ramen-da for this?" . . . I think: "Am I able to do that . . ." Jhuma-di continues talking: "I went myself and saw everything."

I'm very eager to know what Jhuma-di saw. Looking at my face, she understands this and asks, "Would you like to know what I've seen? I've seen a really funny thing. Sheocharan-ji has built a wonderful factory. He's made the factory and a country-liquor shop next to one another.

He's fenced off the adda-site on one side for a gambling wheel. The workers go directly to the country-liquor shop after receiving their wages from the factory. Then they stand before the gambling wheel in a drunken state. The reverse also happens sometimes. They enter the country-liquor shop after losing or winning at gambling. Who's to restrain the greed to spin the wheel when there are crisp currency notes in the pocket? It does not take more than a few hours for the principal plus interest to return to the one who dealt it out in the first place. I get what remains. The entire force of a young man's mental anguish lands on my back."

I spring up in joy. So Jhuma-di too has come with us. Only one question about her description keeps striking my mind.

"Tell me, does Ramen-da understand all this . . . ?"

"Your Ramen-da? He returns home at twelve or one and then beats me. Every night. And every morning, he touches my feet and apologizes." I hug Jhuma-di in joy. I no longer feel any anger toward Ramen-da. He is merely a victim of society.

I say happily: "How happy we are to get you, Jhuma-di."

"Now is not the time for happiness. Didn't you all say the other day that there's a lot of work ahead of you—a lot of responsibilities. I have to get involved in that work now."

"Will you be able to do it, Jhuma-di . . . it's very difficult work . . . and shameful."

"It's because I can that I've come out of the house. I'll have to coax or entice a man and get information out of him, won't I? If necessary. I may also have to spend a couple of nights with him and get the job done. I'll definitely be able to do that. Didn't I marry your Ramen-da after falling in love with him? And are you thinking about me losing my dignity? Wasn't it you who said the other day that we've reached such a situation that there's nothing left to lose? So where does the question of dignity arise, dear boy?"

Saying so, Jhuma-di puts the child into my arms and ties the anchal of her sari around her waist. Laughing, she says: "Look at me and tell me, is there anything left in me now to entice a man, really, anything . . ."

In Tamil Nadu's
Match factories
Many child workers are aged four
After working the whole day
They earn about one rupee

The largest number of child workers in the world work in Tamil Nadu's match factories. In the Raghunathapuram district alone, of the one hundred thousand workers in match factories, forty-five thousand are aged below fifteen. Some child workers live in villages thirty kilometers away from the factories. Every morning, at dawn, all these children come by truck and bus and get off at the factories. For this, they have to wake up between 3 and 5 A.M. in the morning. They are taken back home between 7 and 9 P.M. at night. A survey was conducted in sixteen match factories in Raghunathapuram and it was found that three-fourths of the child workers in these factories are illiterate. They have to work for daily wages. Those who are aged between four and ten earn about a rupee a day.

If they are a bit older, the wages are higher, between six and nine rupees. All these children have to work in a terribly unhealthy environment. They use potassium chloride and other lethal chemical raw materials for over eighteen hours a day.

> Where did that silvery objectivity of yours go?
> You and your characters—as your characters
> increase in number, they become blurred and,
> equally, your views take dangerous turns.
> So you understand that if a person who thinks
> is honest, he cannot remain passive in the
> so-called silvery objectivity. He has to clearly
> communicate not just the side of the exploited,
> but also which particular method of the struggle
> of the exploited he has accepted . . . Am I close
> to the exploited? For that matter, even our Indira is.

"I WAS BORN IN THIS COUNTRY"

Trains continuously pass by the wall of the Corporation school inside the basti in Belgachia. The locality is notorious because of the great rail line, which runs opposite the holy Pareshnath temple. The school is a mark on the map of the maze of lanes under the bridge. The work on the construction of the metro rail is taking place on the main road now. That's why there's always the sound of machines. I couldn't get any clue about the school's whereabouts even after asking three or four people. Then a paan-seller under the bridge played the role of guide. His son is a student of this school. He's reading a book with pictures of peacocks. Going down lane after lane, feeling utterly harried by now, he finally noted down a bettor's number and then again explained the directions. At that point, a girl of about five asked me: "You want to go to the school, right? Come, I'll show you." The girl's name was Hasina. She had gone to the shop to buy jaggery. They eat jaggery and rotis for lunch. Hasina does not go to school. Why doesn't she go? Simply because her father can't afford it. We come to a two- or three-foot-wide courtyard-like space, with walls on three sides. On the fourth side, skirting an open drain, in a dark room with damp walls was the Rajrajeshwari Free Primary school. You can see feces floating in the drain . . . Just staying in such an environment from 11 A.M. to 4 P.M. makes you sick, never mind the matter of education. In response, the head teacher, Osman Ghani, said: "Fifteen years ago, there was an attempt to move the school. The effort continues. But it's not proving easy." I've heard there's a lot of trouble here, bombs are often thrown even during the day, aren't they? . . . "There were bombs this morning. Such things happen frequently." Isn't there a rail line adjacent to the school? "What about it?"—Didn't it occur to them that this was a matter to think about? "From time to time, a few children get injured, that's all. Last year, an eleven-year-old boy was killed by a bomb. Died on the spot. But that's normal, very normal. You can't have bomb-throwing without anyone ever getting killed, that just can't happen." The head teacher openly admitted that in his spare time, he took down odds in the satta numbers game. "Otherwise I can't survive. What can I do? Some boys in the higher classes are also in the profession. In the evenings, they too light a candle and sit down to pencil. The families do benefit a bit. What can they do? In times like these?"

When the head teacher of a primary school
Is a part-time satta-penciler
In order to survive, then
Just cast your eyes for one minute on this
calculation—

1982-83: Expenditures

Spent on Asiad	only Rupees 15,000 million
Spent on the Non-Aligned meet	only Rupees 4,000 million
Spent on the Commonwealth meet	only Rupees 2,000 million
TOTAL	only Rupees 21,000 million

Only 21,000 million rupees were spent

In the normal course of events, an invitation
letter reached him one day, requesting him to
write for a popular weekly. Holding the letter
in his hand, he thought, the right to express a
different view, the right to protest, has now to
be bartered away. So they have recognized very
well a writer's most vulnerable spot . . . And in
a society in which individual earning is the only
road to becoming established, where poverty
and deprivation bring disregard and non-recog-
nition, an artist's freedom is bound to be pushed
in a perverted direction.

About Indira in a Chinese periodical

Beijing, August 27, 1983
Anandabazar Patrika

The Chinese government has stopped the publication of the second part of a satirical article that severely criticizes the politics and personal lives of India's prime minister, Indira Gandhi and her father, Jawaharlal Nehru. This was to be published in a government periodical, *World Knowledge*. The second part of the article was to be published in Volume 16 of the periodical. But it was not published. No explanation was provided for the non-publication. However, the cover of the issue has a picture of two Indian women. They are bedecked in saris and jewelry. On first sight, perhaps an expression of China's goodwill.

This foreign affairs-centered periodical has a limited circulation. Its readership comprises only intellectuals and policymakers. The periodical is published with the financial support of the Chinese foreign ministry.

According to foreign policy specialists, the first part of the article about Indira and Jawaharlal had appeared in August. The article was a cause for unhappiness on the part of

The mighty are respected— Sanjay, in his final interview

New Delhi, June 28, 1980

A few days before his death, Sanjay Gandhi said in an interview: "Respect for India will grow only if there is a strong economy. In 1976, we exported cement, sugar, coal, and steel. But now we import everything. With the coming of the Janata government in between, the country is in the doldrums. Only the Nehru family can take the country to the Everest of progress."

Immersion of Sanjay's mortal remains

The mortal remains of the prematurely killed Sanjay Gandhi were today immersed in Allahabad's holy prayag-sangam and in various holy rivers and lakes. The mortal remains of Sanjay were brought to Allahabad in a special train by Rajiv Gandhi. He immersed the mortal remains in the deep waters of the triveni-sangam of the Ganga, Yamuna, and the almost-extinct Saraswati. During the immersion, V. C. Shukla slipped and fell into the water.

Ashes strewn in different parts of India by helicopter

India and an objection had been made in this regard.

On many occasions, critical articles had appeared concerning India (e.g. on wife-burning) in journals and periodicals controlled by the Chinese government. The stated article is the latest addition to these. In the first part, it was written that, in regard to tackling the India-China border problem, and in regard to Pakistan and Sikkim, former Prime Minister Nehru and current Prime Minister Indira simply continued the British colonial tradition.

The article also dwelt at length on their personal lives. It was written that there had been an unusually intimate friendship and exchange of personal letters between Lady Edwina Mountbatten and Nehru. Pictures of Edwina and Padmaja Naidu had been put up by Nehru in his bedroom. In the same first part, it was written about Indira Gandhi: Her marriage wasn't a happy one and her husband wanted to leave her. Even after seeing the dead body of her son, Sanjay, in pieces, killed in a plane crash, Indira had not shed a single tear. Apparently, she calmly put a key inside a cupboard after she received the news. After writing all this, with an eye toward Chinese readers, it was asked: What is your opinion about such a mother?

The author of the article is anonymous. The source for the Maneka Gandhi, together with her mother and brother, left with Sanjay's ashes for Haridwar. Sanjay's ashes were immersed today with due solemnity at Varanasi's Harishchandra riverbank, in the Ganga in Patna, the Godavari in Nasik, the Kaveri in Coorg, the Shatadru in Punjab, Pushkar, Matrikund, and Galata in Rajasthan, Narmada in Madhya Pradesh, and also in four rivers of Andhra Pradesh.

Aggrieved Vyjayanthimala's dance-plan

New Delhi: The famed danseuse and film actress, Vyjayanthimala, today informed the prime minister in a condolence message that she has made a plan for an appropriate dance toward expressing reverence for Sanjay's immortal memory, and that she herself would perform.

Immersion festival in Calcutta

Sanjay Gandhi's ashes were immersed in the Ganga in Calcutta on Saturday afternoon. Two union ministers brought the ashes in a special plane from Delhi. Their eyes were unslept. Wrapped in white cloth, the ashes were taken in a procession of Congress Party leaders and workers to the Chandpal riverbank. The minister's family had instructed that the ashes be immersed in the bosom of details about the Nehru family has been stated to be the book by his former secretary, Mathai. In the author's view, Indian society is very feudal. Of course, Nehru and Indira did not lose their respectability as a result of rumors about their personal lives. Perhaps everything was purely rumor. We do not know about their veracity. Nehru was brisk, eloquent, and given to excitement as well as indecision. Indira was always mute, one could not communicate with her; she was peaceful, proud, independent of mind. Nehru could not face political realities. But both father and daughter were one in regard to keeping the British colonial tradition intact.

In 1967, Indira devalued the rupee by fifty-eight percent and created a dangerous economic situation. She coined the slogan "*Garibi Hatao*" in order to finish her enemies and won the election by a huge margin. But now, after fourteen years, the rich have become richer and the poor have become poorer.

India's protest

India communicated its strong protest over an extremely objectionable article about Prime Minister Indira Gandhi and her late father, former Prime Minister Jawaharlal Nehru, in a Chinese periodical. A spokesperson of the Indian external the river before the onset of the inauspicious time. The two ministers and some Congress (I) leaders took the ashes by motor launch to the middle of the Ganga. They returned after the immersion. There was a little bit of rain then.

Boat with journalists capsizes in Bombay during the ceremony for immersion of ashes

A boat carrying journalists capsized in the Arabian Sea near Chowpatty in south Bombay. The journalists had gone there to cover the ceremony for the immersion of Sanjay's ashes. Fortunately, the incident occurred close to shore and the water was very shallow. All the journalists reached the shore safely. However, all their notes were drenched in the water.

Excesses in the name of Sanjay

The way in which democratic ideals have been disregarded in order to whip up public sentiment around Sanjay, has been severely criticized by the Lok Dal party. The declaration of national mourning and the flying of the national flag at half-mast were objected to by them. The way in which the site constructed to commemorate freedom fighters has been converted into a family crematorium was akin to throttling affairs ministry has stated that India has raised the subject at the diplomatic level with Beijing and with New Delhi's Chinese embassy.

Several discussions regarding foreign policy and international relations are published in the periodical, *World Knowledge*. The first part of the article in question was published at the beginning of this month. In response to India's protest, the Chinese government has stated that the country's media is not state-controlled. But this response did not satisfy India, which requested that China not encourage the publication of such articles. The second part of the article in the next issue of the periodical was therefore not published. There has been no further discussion after that. There is no news regarding this. We are waiting eagerly. If we get any news, we shall inform you.

democracy. The presence of the service chiefs at the last rites as well as the flying of a military helicopter have also been criticized by them. The country will not easily forget the way in which the difference between people, state, party, and family was erased.

Want Rajiv in place of Sanjay

"Let Rajiv be made the All India Youth Congress (I) leader!" Twenty Congress (I) leaders from various states sent a memorandum with this appeal to Indira Gandhi on the very day of Sanjay's death. Delhi's Congress (I) leaders have informed Indira Gandhi that only Rajiv could fill Sanjay Gandhi's place. They relayed that some Congress (I) workers would stage a silent and peaceful demonstration at the prime minister's residence demanding that Rajiv Gandhi be brought into active politics as soon as possible.

MAO TSE TUNG HAS NOT YET BEEN BORN IN THIS COUNTRY, ON THIS BELOVED EARTH OF OURS

In China, a strong campaign is underway at present to catch criminal offenders. The number of criminals has been rising continuously since the year 1956. China's public security authority has found seven kinds of criminals over the past three years. They are: murderers, rapists, burglars, thieves, vandals, users of explosives, and destroyers of state property. Officials are worried about the rate at which the number of criminals is growing. It poses a grave danger to communism. It is a matter of disgrace. They are of the view that, ever since the third session of the eleventh congress, the security system has not improved at all. Five years have passed in this way. Consequently, the number of reported and unreported crimes among China's civilians has risen manifold. They are worried about this. They are unable to sleep at night.

Basti-dwellers gaze greedily at the house above in which electrical inverters provide light during a power outage.

TO THE MAJORITY OF PEOPLE, EVERYWHERE IN THE WORLD / I

In an exploitative society, the state apparatus is created so as to perpetuate exploitation. When the survival struggles of ordinary people cannot be accommodated within the façade of democracy, they resort to bullets.

ALLENDE'S STORY

When Allende was elected President of Chile, workers across the country declared full support for him. But Allende wanted to work within the laws and constitution of the exploitative state apparatus. These laws, as well as the constitution—created under the bourgeois framework—were essentially against the public interest. In December 1971, a few days after Allende was elected, under the leadership of the MIR, the sharecroppers in southern Chile began a campaign of occupying land in the large estates. The centrist Allende and his communist ministers did not approve of this. "We are aware of the problems of peasants but we are against occupation of land in this manner." Allende wanted to please everybody. It's correct that he did not go against the common people, but he did not anger the exploiting class either. In this double-bind situation, just as Chile's elite class was unhappy, similarly American imperialism too kept searching for a pretext to intervene. They were frightened on seeing the efforts of the people to organize. They began to conspire to overthrow the government because they were not able to make Allende work entirely for them. As a first means, they tried to covertly bring about a military coup. That attempt failed. Even in such a situation, Allende did not want to leave his so-called legal route. The people wanted to organize themselves and build up armed resistance. Allende's democratic route came to be its biggest impediment. In an exploitative society, the state apparatus is created so as to perpetuate exploitation. Allende wanted to eradicate exploitation from the state apparatus. That's why the exploiter class adopted direct means of removing him. Thus far, they had been able to carry out exploitation under the banner of the democratic system, but now, by killing Allende they flagrantly followed fascist methods. Another version of whatever had once happened in Hitler's Germany and in Indonesia found full expression in Chile. When the survival struggles of ordinary people cannot be accommodated within the façade of democracy, they resort to bullets. Allende's widow, in an interview to *Excelsior* newspaper on September 29, 1973, said: "Now we can understand how correct the people were. Attaining power through elections is not all. There was a great need to arm the people and build a revolutionary army. It's because we were unarmed . . . we could not fight against the bombing."

When the survival struggles of ordinary people cannot be accommodated within the façade of democracy, they resort to bullets

---

TO THE MAJORITY OF PEOPLE,

EVERYWHERE IN THE WORLD / 2

A recent report from China: In the city of Shanghai, a person by the name of Si En Fushing used about ten young women as models, took obscene pictures of them, and made pornographic films. The Shanghai administration sentenced the man to death. Before that, the leader of the obscene racket had to, of course, present himself before the people's court. An ever-vigilant watch has been instituted so that this incident is not repeated. A leading newspaper in China said men like Fushing were akin to garbage dumps. In this regard, a question has arisen in the minds of some Sinologists about how such an incident was possible in that country, especially in the period after the Cultural Revolution. Was this an isolated incident, or were there more instances like this that are not always easily detected? Last year, there was a report from Japan that, although it was illegal in an ordinary sense, apparently the unhindered entry of hard-core pornography into homes had begun there, through videos and so on. Such materials were so easy to obtain that no one really worried too much about it; there was no curiosity either among the people at large. Father, mother, son, and daughter, all apparently sit together on any day of the week and enjoy such things, in a spirit of joviality. But the question in the minds of many is how such things were possible in a socialist country like China. In the opinion of some, it is the flip side of the repression of sex that had emerged in this incident. It was simply a reaction to the extremely puritanical attitude with regard to sex in socialist countries. But many were unable to grasp how it was possible for a space for the blue film business to be created within China's socialist economy—not just blue films, but the space for the business. But the fact of the incident cannot be denied either.

ARE YOU A MARXIST—A FEW MORE THOUGHTS I HAD EVEN AFTER WHAT I HAD WRITTEN IN REPLY, NOW, AT THIS MOMENT

I always keep in mind that, whenever necessary, reactionaries utilize all these half-anarchist, half-Marxist thoughts in their own way. If there's the slightest laxity, the entire process of thinking can be used by a certain class as an opportunistic scheme, could be so used—I'm aware of that . . . *Thinking is the greatest pleasure known to mankind*—how could I forget that Brecht sahib had Galileo utter these words. Unless a very *desperate drive* is undertaken, nothing is possible in this country. And the establishment will indulge this *desperateness* so long as it can be utilized for its class interest. Associated with that is the entire viewpoint on such matters—which angle it is being shown from. I believe in carrying out a kind of *"planned violence"* in my writing, in exactly the same sense in which Truffaut used the term.

The writer carefully lit a cigarette. The reader held it like a chillum in his hands, took a deep puff, and began coughing. And he would also write a letter about the text's impotence.

OUR MILKY WAY AND CROSSING ITS LIMITS

Having had a bit to drink the previous night, I woke up late. It was about six o'clock then. Even before I could have my tea, I got the news that someone was waiting in the sitting room to meet me. I felt annoyed that I couldn't even sip my tea in peace. I went and saw an extremely skinny-looking youth, wearing rather shabby clothes. We sat staring at each other for a few seconds. I realized he was finding it difficult to succinctly frame what he wanted to say. He had never been in such a situation before. After some time, he did open his mouth, but as if in a stupor. Need a job. A mother and several younger brothers and sisters at home, et cetera, can't survive without a job. I became thoughtful and was about to give a suitably non-committal reply—but I was not at all prepared for what happened next. Like a spring, the boy left his chair and shot toward my legs, he fell on his knees and threw himself at my feet. "Please do something . . . anything whatsoever . . . or else . . . or else I shall do something terrible . . . I'll become bad . . ." Many days have passed. I could not, or rather did not do anything about getting the boy a job. I didn't even remember him. I don't know whether he found a job or not. Nor have I tried to find out if he's turned bad.

Not finding out is the safest. Because if I learn that he has enlisted in the satta gang or become a wagon-breaker, then, at that very moment, I would feel the jab of a thorn within me—a thorn that wouldn't be easy to pluck out. It wasn't possible to worry about such things in the midst of one's own myriad responsibilities and problems.

THE FAST EXPRESS

In the view of modern war strategists, chemical warfare is much more effective than nuclear bombs and suchlike. If one could secretly release a few grams of the bacteria that causes infectious diseases like cholera, small pox, and plague into the enemy nation, the country would be reduced to a wasteland before anyone knew about it. Humans would drop like flies, but all property would remain undestroyed. Everything could be taken possession of, intact, later. And the most convenient aspect is that these could be easily and secretly taken and disseminated in the enemy nation in the name of medical research. Also being invented are things that once released on crops, would ensure that an entire people would remain mentally handicapped for decades to come—they would carry on with their normal lives and procreate, but would never raise the slightest objection to exploitation or authority. Such a time has indeed come.

Illi-da keeps running over the wobbly Chinese wall, which had at one time been securely built by Franz Kafka, that gray-checked man. The readers of this story would have recognized Illi-da as Number One.

Joydev Sadhu was a student of Class 4. His father soldered broken utensils. Father, mother, five siblings, and a goat lived in one room—a tin-roofed hut, rented at sixty rupees a month. A lamp had to be lit night and day. Joydev does not know about the Asian Games. Nor about the satellite Rohini. Bhajan Lal is nine years old. His father makes the soles of shoes. Adjacent to his house, skirting the railway line, is a cheap liquor outlet. He knows the name of Amitabh Bachchan. He knows about knives and pipe-guns very well. He knows that everyone's courage evaporates in front of such things. When he grows up, he wants to become like Illi-da. Illi-da was a notorious wagon-breaker of this region. That's how he had built a three-storied house on the corner of the road. Even the officer-in-charge of the police station minds his ways when it comes to Illi-da. He doesn't trouble him. Illi-da's nom de guerre is Number One. When he works for a party, then he's Number One, when he breaks wagons he's Illi-da. Ayesha Khatun is a student of Class 3. Her father makes leather boxes. Her brother's work is burning pen refills. He gets fifty paise for a thousand. What will she do after completing primary school? . . . Does she know the name of India's No. 1 woman? When asked, she merely stares back. She has one lipstick. Her father bought it for her last Eid.

Casuarina Avenue. Under the immense trees were cars with their windows up, and there was only a mysterious darkness everywhere. Everything was enveloped in mist. Every now and then, suddenly, a tittering laughter erupted from the groundglass windows when they were momentarily opened. Only—a few boys, bare-bodied even on this winter night, ran around collecting beer bottles thrown from cars. One boy's wore only a jute sack, like a coat. Every now and then, they rubbed their hands together to keep themselves warm. They had collected seventy or eighty beer bottles so far. As the night advanced, there would be more. "Look . . . look! That fatty has made the girl lie down on the back seat . . ." It was long past eleven at night. I would like to examine once again the well-known quote attributed to Darwin. Tonight itself if possible. Yes, the monkey—it was sitting on the German sahib's bookshelf, and in its hand was a human skull. The monkey was gazing at it very thoughtfully. Reader, do you think I'm very jealous—the jealousy of nonfulfillment—what do you think, sir? I forgot to mention, some Bihari folk had even made a fire with twigs on the Victoria Memorial grounds. They sat around the fire warming themselves in the winter night.

WHEN COLOR IS A WARNING SIGN

The question now arises about the realism of symbols. A hand with clenched fist, a red flag, or a grain of rice are all, in a simple sense, real and visible to our senses. Their identity as symbols is linked to their presence. But the meaning of the red flag—observing only its sensory aspect—is not confined to color, size, or luster. The meaning can be found only when it is seen as a symbol, in relation to other symbols. The difference between a red flag and a saffron or green flag is not confined merely to the distinction of color, it has to do with the recognized distinction of social meaning. That's why the second identity, of social relation, keeps getting privileged over and above the primary identity. In this system, the red color sometimes becomes a revolutionary party's symbol, sometimes a warning sign, and sometimes Hanuman's banner. And once again the ambiguities keep arising here, in the context of this elucidation, from the writer's class situation itself. What role does the writer play here, in this elucidation—is it one of self-defense or attack?

DOUSE WITH KEROSENE
AND LIGHT THE MATCH

A writer's rivalry is with his successful predecessors but also with his *ego*, together with arrogance, laziness, bits of cunning, and an apparently brave fearfulness. He does not leave out anything, *truth is concrete* to him, greatly so. Every writer has his own way, if he is a *conscious* writer, and possibly there's no fixed formula for this. It is dangerous to ask someone to write in a specific way because one doesn't learn to write in this way, rather one is taught to imitate. And perhaps he does not have any powerful capability to alter the stream of life, but this sincere admission of his own limitations makes him different.

On this earth of ours
In this most civilized world

Even in this year, 1983,
Every minute, thirty children die
Slowly, suffering,
Merely from lack of food

And
To manufacture weapons to kill people
To manufacture the most advanced nuclear bombs
We spend
$1.6 million
Every minute

And we
Civilization's shit-piss intellectuals
Read such facts in newspapers, read
And with great delight
Each of us, dash-ing the other
Do kultur, indulge in literature/culture
We piss and piss and spread
The stench of ammonia around
And through mutual dash-ery
Bring our sense of responsibility
To its highest expression

Now here's
The song of the culture of mutual dash-ery
Come, all of you   let's fuck ass
Swaying our buttocks and swelling our cocks
Let's indulge in some humanity
Humanity is somnolence
I've come to know the real thing
The pigeon flies over the roof

And under the roof's crookery
[Magnanimous reader!
The specific word denoting the region of your backside,
In the middle-region of your body,
From where shit emerges,
Imagine that in place of the "dash"
The press can't print such vulgar
Words, there's fierce fighting regarding the word.
The song couldn't be completed either.
The censor would block it, you see.
Just keep in mind that it's only in our country
That the word is called *"shabdabrahma"*
Reader babus, what do you all say?]

What have you done with your science?
What have you done with your humanism?
Where is your dignity as a thinking reader?

The two boats joined together keep trying to come apart
and move away. The tempo of the drum and cymbals
changes. Those who had been sitting down so far, holding the images, undo the bamboo frames and ropes with
nimble hands. The immersion, it's the immersion now, and
after that, after some time, the two boats move off to the
two sides and keep moving, a gap in the middle emerges,
which is only a gap, yes a gaping one. The image falls into
the water with a loud splash, for the last time the victory chant is uttered, *Durga Mai Ki Jai, Om Shanti, Om
Shanti*, there's a frenzy of sprinkling the water of blessing,
boys and girls begin to gasp and cry, the drummers play
their final beats with all their life. Who knows if anyone

intended to get you wet then, by sprinkling puddle water instead of the holy water.

BEGGAR FOR LOVE

Four marbles of four different colors are given to a child. He learns about numbers with these: one, two, three, four. He learns about colors: red, blue, white, green. He learns grouping: red and blue, white and green. In this way, the boy advances toward fullness. Thereafter, four color pencils of the same colors are also given to him. Now he learns addition and subtraction. There are eight things in all. Four marbles and four pencils. If they keep diminishing, finally there'll be one marble and one pencil. In that case, the grouping will now be according to color. Red color. That red color. Confusion. Once again, the burp of heartburn rises up—a sour taste inside his whole mouth. Pain on two fronts, one below the navel, from dysentery, and the other, below the ribs, from acidity. He has eaten a jilipi, a sourish red jilipi—which was as good as a grand rossogolla for a person like him. The acidic burp rises— the same sour taste all over his mouth. And in this way, in just this way . . . Confused? The film *Jukti, Takko Goppo* concludes. The police attack. A bullet hits Neelkanth, Ritwik. It strikes. Neelkanth is dying. The police bring out the dead body from the forest. They bring it. A single-file procession—Satya, Durga, Nachiketa, Bangabala. From a narrow path to a wide background. Only the old man, Ritwik Kumar Ghatak, staring with unblinking eyes within a square frame. Confused? Just then, Pupu, unseen: "Uncle, I'm not there. I'm not."

This man is dangerous for us
Why do you say that
Why do you forget, the man thinks

NITYAKALI RICE MILL FUNCTIONS, WILL KEEP
FUNCTIONING

"I leave my office by three or three thirty. I get a seat on the minibus. Yes, dada, a government office. After reaching home, and after eating hot luchis with fried potatoes made by my wife—oh, what comfort—I lie down on the easy chair with *Desh* magazine on my chest. The plot of land in Salt Lake had come about by the grace of God, now it would be good if a sizeable loan were sanctioned. Who knows what the price of a bag of cement is nowadays. After all, nothing can happen in a straightforward fashion, the way the country's going day by day . . . Oh God."

MAO TSE TUNG HAS NOT BEEN BORN YET ON THIS
EARTH—ON THIS BELOVED EARTH OF OURS

In this way, attaching newspaper clippings, he, the writer, carries on writing, continues writing. From the manner in which the newspaper clippings are arranged, it can be discerned that he, the one who didn't want to take any side, had at some point, unknown to himself, actually taken a side. Not the three meanings of the red sign, but at some point the position is firmly tied to one particular social belief. Hands, the color goes behind some helpless hands, which he draws as a clenched fist, in conviction. So then, nothing's objective—by custom, silvery? The political entrepreneur commits to memory the speech delivered following Caesar's death. In that case, in the next scene, that very speech shall erupt Hitler-style on the assembled masses. Not a speech, but a conviction. Yet, when they don't vote, then, openly, with kerosene cans in hand, Arturo Ui's disciples go to set fire to the Reichstag. Wherever violence rules, violence is the only means. Now he can distinguish brilliantly between class hatred and individual hatred. And only man can say, I am confused. Wherever there is man, only man can save him there. Mao Tse Tung has not yet been born on this earth, on this beloved earth of ours. We have to make even more preparations, and wait some more. Perhaps for some ages. Perhaps for many ages.

WHAT HAVE YOU DONE WITH YOUR SCIENCE?

WHAT HAVE YOU DONE WITH YOUR HUMANISM?

WHERE IS YOUR DIGNITY AS A THINKING READER?

ADDENDUM

In response, the writer held out a test tube. Look at this dust. This is cinnabar. A brilliant red is made from this. But in the light, the color takes on a blackish hue. I'm trying to make a kind of red that won't turn black even when brought to light. I don't know whether it can be done, nevertheless I'm trying. And what's the harm in hanging on to the belief that it can be done? As soon as I stand facing the sea, the color becomes very distant. Waves rise. The color of the waves is half cobalt blue and half ultramarine.

But

WHAT HAVE YOU DONE WITH YOUR SCIENCE? WHAT HAVE YOU DONE WITH YOUR HUMANISM? WHERE IS YOUR DIGNITY AS A THINKING READER?

But

HAT HAVE YO[
]NE WITH YOU
SCIENCE?
HAT HAVE YO[
]NE WITH YOU
HUMANISM?
/HERE IS YOU[
DIGNITY AS A
THINKING
READER?

HAV]
YOU
ON]

SUBIMAL MISRA is a Bengali novelist, short story writer, and essayist. He's considered by many to be one of most important, and experimental, Bengali writers of all time. Heavily influenced by Jean-Luc Godard and William S. Burroughs, Subimal Misra uses various cinematic techniques, like montage, jump-cut etc., in his literary works. The author of more than a dozen books, this is the first collection of his to appear in the United States.

V. RAMASWAMY is a nonfiction writer and translator based in Kolkata, India. As an activist working for the rights of the laboring poor, Ramaswamy has written about workers, squatters, slums, poverty, housing, and resettlement, and has been at the forefront of efforts to envision and initiate the rebuilding of his city from the grassroots. Since 2005, he has been translating the short fiction of the Bengali anti-establishment experimental writer, Subimal Misra, whose critical eye examines the society, politics, and culture of his time.

OPEN LETTER

WWW.OPENLETTERBOOKS.ORG

**OPEN
LETTER**